Virus Bomb

VIRUS
BOMB

a novel

D. GREG SCOTT

NEW YORK

LONDON • NASHVILLE • MELBOURNE • VANCOUVER

VIRUS BOMB

A Novel

Published in New York, New York, by Morgan James Publishing. Morgan James is a trademark of Morgan James, LLC. www.MorganJamesPublishing.com

ISBN 9781642791648 paperback
ISBN 9781642791655 eBook
Library of Congress Control Number: 2018907756

Cover Design by:
Megan Dillon
megan@creativeninjadesigns.com

Interior Design by:
Chris Treccani
www.3dogcreative.net

Morgan James is a proud partner of Habitat for Humanity Peninsula and Greater Williamsburg. Partners in building since 2006.

Get involved today! Visit
MorganJamesPublishing.com/giving-back

To the unsung heroes on the IT front lines who work day and

night to keep us safe. May we heed their advice.

An IT professional's job is like stocking toilet paper.

Nobody cares until there's an outage.

CONTENTS

EXPLOSION
Rare Earth Metals open pit mine, near Ely, Minnesota, 4:07 p.m.

He tapped the send button and watched through binoculars from a safe distance. Nobody heard the cell phone at the top of the load in the explosives delivery truck vibrate. Nobody noticed the two wires attached to the vibrator, connected to a smaller wire to create a short circuit with each vibration cycle. And nobody within three hundred yards survived the detonation. The blast wave washed over him as he terminated the call. It was glorious.

CUTTHROAT
Near Minneapolis, Minnesota, three months earlier:

Jerry Barkley pounded the conference room table. A few people in the row of office cubicles outside looked up. "I brought you guys into this deal for help-desk support. You wouldn't even be part of this if I hadn't called."

John Watson, POM Solutions sales manager, leaned back in his chair. "But now that we're involved, it was decided we'd be a better fit to take on the prime contractor role." He shifted forward. "But we need a technical resource, and you could fill that role."

Jerry leaned back. "And how would that work?"

"We'll sell the equipment and handle setup and day-to-day management. When we get into a situation we're unable to resolve, our escalation team will engage you."

"So, I'd be a subcontractor to you guys."

"Yes, but a valued one."

"And they'd buy all the equipment from you, not from me?"

"We can get better pricing. And you don't want the warranty hassles."

Jerry shifted forward and smacked his hands on the table. "That's a load of crap, and you know it."

John leaned back and interlocked his fingers behind his head. "Jerry, think about it. You're one guy who works out of his basement. You don't know anything about proposals and contracts. You can't take on a project this big. Nobody cares about your better mousetrap; they only want peace of mind. Which we offer."

Jerry rolled his eyes.

John put his hands in his lap. "They have truck terminals in, what, thirty-some states? And some in Canada? How would you deal with warranty issues? We have offices across the country, and we're a platinum reseller partner for everyone who's anyone in the IT industry."

"I architected it all out. Warranty issues and local presence isn't a big deal."

John shook his head. "Yes, it is. What happens when, say, Denver can't dispatch trucks because this box of yours is dead or their internet connection drops? What's your plan to get them back up and running? They want an SLA with a one-hour recovery."

"I covered all that. All I need is a help desk."

"You didn't cover any of it. Our techs laughed at your proposal draft." John looked at his watch.

"Got a hot date?"

John chuckled. "We recognize you worked hard bringing it this far. That's why we're offering to keep you on. Who knows, maybe our guys can teach you a few things. You know how many people would kill to be in your shoes?"

"You know how many outfits I could have brought in for help-desk support? I picked you guys, and you stab me in the back."

"Bottom line, we're bidding on this project. You can join our team or not. It's up to you." John interlocked his fingers behind his head again.

Jerry looked down and snickered. "Huh." He pushed himself out of his chair and walked away.

John swiveled. "Think about it, Jerry. As smart as you are, you're only one guy. How will you feed your family?"

Jerry stopped in the main office area and turned. "Same as always."

"You'll change your mind."

Jerry opened his mouth, and then grinned and shook his head. He turned and walked out of the office.

●——————●

"How did your meeting go?" The tone in Lynn's voice said it all. Always the worrier. Jerry would cure her one day. But not tonight at dinner.

"They stabbed me in the back."

"How?" asked Lynn and Jerry's daughter, Anne. Anne and her two sons, Alex and Aaron, lived with Lynn and Jerry. Three generations under one roof.

"They want to cut me out of the deal and bid on it themselves."

"That sucks. Can't you sue 'em?"

"Even if I could, we'd be dead after all the time and legal fees. Oh. And here's the best part. They offered to use me for second-level support. They said I'm a good technical resource."

"You mean, like a real job?" Lynn asked.

"No, as a subcontractor. They dangled that carrot to smooth everything over. They'll call me to handle the tough issues. Which means they'll never call because they'd have to pay for my time."

Lynn put her fork down. "What are you gonna do?"

"I'm gonna kick their butts."

"How?"

"They'll do a conventional bid. Name-brand routers, dedicated telecom circuits, the whole works. They want to sell a bunch of expensive equipment. I'll use redundant Barkley firewalls and encrypted tunnels over the public internet. And automated monitoring and failover if anything breaks."

"Nice geek-speak, Dad. What's it mean in English?"

"It means my initial project cost will be about half everyone else's because it's all open source. I have redundancy everywhere and automation watching all of it. And my ongoing cost will be about twenty percent less than anyone else's. I'll cost a lot less than everyone else and do a better job."

"But you're just one person," Lynn said. "How do you compete with a company that big?"

"Same as always. By offering something better."

"Wouldn't it be easier to just get a real job?"

"I have a real job."

"You know what I mean. Alex and Aaron depend on us."

Alex poked his tongue through the new gap in his smile and handed a tooth to his grandpa. "It finally came out today."

"And Aaron tried to put it in his mouth," Anne said. "We're with you, Dad."

"Thanks. I might need your help."

"Put me on the help desk. How does this sound?" She put her hand to her ear, imitating a telephone conversation. "Reboot it. That should fix your problem."

Jerry laughed. Lynn looked down and scowled.

SIOUX FALLS BULLIES

Brian Cox hurried past the sea of lockers lining the hallway at Sioux Falls, South Dakota, Jefferson High School on his way to first-hour math, enduring daily taunts from jocks and farm boys in this forsaken wasteland. Every day, he endured a vulgar play on words relating his name to a forbidden act of perversion. And more torment.

"Yo, Muzzie, loosen up that dress shirt."

He clenched his fists.

"Hey, Cox, polish your shoes."

A few students laughed. Why did these beer-drinking jocks keep doing this, day after day? A few students entered the math classroom ahead.

Cheryl Samuels met him at the door, wearing her usual tight blue jeans and skimpy blouse. "Hey, Brian, that skull cap is a turn-on."

Brian stopped to let her through first. She started and then turned to face him, blocking his way.

More students gathered in the hall behind them.

Brian stared at her, unsure what to do, unsure where to focus his gaze. He couldn't talk to her like this. Why wouldn't she move? Father had told him to blend in and honor the Prophet. How was he supposed to do that with temptation like this?

After a few seconds, she ran her finger along Brian's ear and down to his chin. Brian's heart raced. Her perfume filled his mind and triggered thoughts he was not supposed to think. These feelings were forbidden. Several boys wearing JHS letter jackets laughed.

Brian turned away.

"Your loss," Cheryl said. She sashayed to her seat.

Hands shaking, heart pounding, Brian entered the classroom behind her. Other students followed.

"Hey, Muzzie," one of the letter jackets said, "she's talking to you."

Mr. Pedersen entered the classroom. "Take your seats, ladies and gentlemen. We have a lot to cover today."

"I have my eye on you," letter jacket said.

Brian tried to concentrate on today's calculus lesson and put Cheryl Samuels out of his mind.

"Work on chapter eleven, problems eight through ten," Mr. Pedersen said at the end of class. "And I'll see you tomorrow."

Brian stayed in his seat as the rest of the class filed through the door.

"Brian, you looked distracted this morning," Mr. Pedersen said after the last student left. "Everything okay?"

"I hate it here."

"I keep telling you, give it a chance. It might grow on you."

"It won't. Everyone in this school hates me. And I hate them."

"They don't hate you. You just look different than they do."

"Is that why they jeer at me in the hallway every day? Is that why they steal my books and write Muzzie on my locker?"

"No, they do that because they're stupid. You can be bigger than they are."

"And look what Cheryl Samuels does to me. My religion forbids me to talk to girls that way. I hate her most of all because of the way she flaunts herself at me."

"Can I let you in in a secret?"

"What?"

"She puts a spell on every boy in here. It's not just you."

"How do you know?"

"I used to be eighteen."

"I wish my father never got that job out here. New York had everything."

"Didn't you say your dad got a promotion to move here?"

"He uprooted our whole family. Am I the only Muslim in this entire state? Back in New York, I had friends, and we could hang out at the mosque. Here—I don't have anybody."

"You've got me."

"You're not Muslim."

"No, I'm not. You and I are different. Doesn't matter to me. I told you last year after I met your parents that I'd help you get used to life in the Midwest."

"Why do you care?"

"You have a gift for math. That's why you're in my class. You could go a long way in this world. I like watching my students succeed."

Brian looked down.

"How's your email server coming along?"

"I found somebody online named Jerry who's helping me set it up. We've had a few chat sessions."

"You're the only student I ever met who took on building his own email server. You've got talent."

"It helps me stay in touch with my friends back in New York. I don't know what I'd do without them."

"There, see, you have friends everywhere."

"I guess so."

"This is your study hall period, right?"

"Yeah."

"Okay. Here's a problem to help tame your hormones. It's trigonometry, not calculus, but you'll enjoy it."

"Okay . . ."

"Reproduce how President Garfield proved the Pythagorean Theorem. Play around with that, and I'll give you extra credit for it."

It worked. After searching for "Garfield Pythagorean Theorem" with his cell phone, Brian spent the rest of his study hall period filling several sheets with trapezoids, equations, and right triangles connected point to point. As he marveled at the creativity behind this clever proof, Cheryl Samuels and her temptations faded away.

At least until the next class period.

"Hey, Cox, I heard Cheryl Samuels wants you," somebody in the school hallway said.

Another said, "Leave her alone, Muzzie, or I'll knock that cap right off your head."

On the way to his fourth period class, somebody knocked Brian's books out of his arms. A few students laughed while Brian picked up his books and papers from the floor.

Just look straight ahead. Ignore them. That's what Father told him every day. But how could he continue ignoring this daily torment? He would finish working on that Garfield proof during lunch.

Sitting alone at lunch, he took out his papers and worked on reproducing the proof. He drew the perpendicular triangles again, connected the vertices to form a trapezoid, and began writing the equations. It was marvelous.

Until somebody walked by and upturned Brian's milk container all over his papers. The jerk laughed and high fived his buddy.

Brian stood and shouted at their backs. "What's wrong with you?"

The boy turned.

"Put your butt back in that chair, Muzzie, or I'll do it for ya."

"Just leave me alone."

"Last warning, Cox."

Brian sat. He fought back tears. Father said crying was a sign of weakness. He mouthed a silent prayer: "Allah, please protect me from these, these, infidels." Yes, that's what they were. They were infidels. They needed help. That was their problem. "Thank you, Allah."

The rest of the day was a blur as Garfield and history and English competed with Cheryl Samuels and hallway taunting. She didn't really want him. But maybe she did. But what about her letter-jacket boyfriends? What would they do if he responded to her? But no—those feelings were forbidden. Responding to her would violate too many teachings from the holy Quran. But she was teasing, trying to torture him by igniting these feelings. No. It was real. No. She was teasing. Even if it was real, such displays of affection are prohibited. She was a slut. She wasn't worth his time. But such a girl's body! The things he would do with her body. No. These thoughts, these feelings are forbidden.

The closing bell rang. Brian gathered his homework from his locker and walked outside toward the line of waiting buses. The spring air smelled sweet. Winter snowbanks were a fading memory and grass and trees were turning green again. He would only have to endure a few minutes sitting alone on the school bus and then freedom for the weekend.

"Hey, Muzzie!" shouted one of the letter jackets. "Is it time to kneel down on your magic carpet yet? Tell yer buddy Mohammed Ali I said to kiss off!"

Brian stopped and squeezed his eyes shut. Maybe if he squeezed his eyes hard enough, it would all go away. No. They went too far. They insulted the Prophet.

Somebody laughed, behind and to his left. He opened his eyes and turned. The whole world narrowed to letter-jacket's laughing face. Brian's heart raced. He closed his fists and swung wildly. Again. And again. And again. He swung his fists as fast as he could, lashing out at anything and everything. He made contact with something. It was soft.

A sharp pain exploded in his right ear. Something smashed his nose. He tasted blood. Now his right eye. And another blow landed on his chin. He stumbled backward. Arms grabbed him and pushed him forward. More blows to the face. Laughter, delirious laughter. Stumbling backward. More arms pushing him forward.

Brian mouthed a silent prayer: "Allah, help me win this battle for your honor!"

A blow to the stomach. He doubled over. Something sharp in the face. He stumbled backward. Now a blow to the back of his head. He pitched forward. The world turned vertical. The ground rushed up to meet him.

He floated in a black tunnel. Something felt cool and soft on his face. "What's going on here?" Sounds were muffled, far away. Grass, in his eyes, his mouth, and up his nose. He needed to breathe. He rolled onto his right side.

Vision came back. The world came into focus. Sounds were sharp again. He was alone. Kids ran in every direction, away from Mr. Pedersen who was walking toward him. Brian's right eye was tender and swollen. Blood streamed from his nose and pooled on the ground under his face. A wave of nausea swept through his guts.

"Let me help you up."

Brian staggered to his feet, shaking off the assistance. "I don't need help!" The world spun as he turned and threw up. The ground rushed to his head again and sticky school lunch remains pressed into his face. The smell was overpowering. He lifted his head and heaved again, this time soaking his pants.

"At least let's get you to the nurse's office and cleaned up," Mr. Pedersen said. "I'll get you a ride home."

"No!" shouted Brian.

"Who did this?"

"Kuffar!"

"Kuffar, who is that?"

"They are all kuffar!"

"What does kuffar mean?" Mr. Pedersen asked.

"I'm not done with you, Muzzie!" shouted letter jacket from the student parking lot.

"You and I have an appointment with the principal tomorrow," Mr. Pedersen said to the bully. "What's wrong with you?"

Letter jacket climbed in his car and started the motor. "Up yours!" Tires screeched as his car rounded a corner, out of the parking lot, and down the school driveway. As he passed the bus area, he extended his arm and raised his middle finger. "You're mine, Muzzie!" The car roared down the school driveway.

"Brian, I am so sorry for what those jerks do to you," Mr. Pedersen said. "Not everyone here is like that. I'm going to make sure they feel consequences for this."

"They're all kuffar!" shouted Brian. He staggered to his feet and lurched toward his bus, blood still dripping from his nose. Tears mixed with the mud, blood, and vomit on his face. His white shirt was grass and mud and vomit stained. His pants were torn.

More than five hundred faces watched from school bus windows as Brian found his bus and climbed aboard. He rode home in silence.

"America calls itself the land of the free and the home of the brave," wrote Brian in a blog post later that night. "But it is really the land of the sluts and home of the bullies. Why do these farm boys always attack me? I only wish to live cleanly and worship Allah. America claims everyone has freedom of religion, but they persecute me at every turn."

Brian stopped writing and looked at himself in a mirror. After studying his thin arms, swollen and tender right eye, and torn clothes, he realized his mistake. He should never have taken that first swing. That was stupid. Farm boys who threw hay bales and letter jackets who threw tackles would always be physically stronger. He would beat them with his mind.

"I will have my revenge," he wrote. "My mind is stronger than their muscles. They will pay a thousand-fold for this day."

One day, Allah would have his revenge on all this rabble. And maybe, just maybe, Allah might see fit to allow Brian to help in this noble purpose. After all, does not Surah 5:45 of the holy book say: "And We ordained therein for them: 'Life for life, eye for eye, nose for nose, ear for ear, tooth for tooth, and wounds equal for equal'"?

This would be sweet indeed. These kuffar would pay. All of them.

RECONNAISSANCE

You give away the information I'll use to kill you. You always do. The person behind the Elaine Devereux persona smiled and stared at a computer monitor, connected over the internet to a virtual machine inside a server farm in a windowless data center operated by a shell company in Paris, thinking. And plotting.

And I'll find it with reconnaissance, starting with the basics, as always. A Google search found the website for the American Centers for Disease Control, www.cdc.gov. An impressive website. It even included a helpful Ebola update.

Browsing the website, the Elaine persona found a few helpful documents. The CDC IT Strategic Plan offered interesting facts: "CDC reports more than 600 information systems supporting functional areas throughout the agency."

And a nugget from a bulleted list of business goals: "Reduce CDC existing software licensing costs by 20 percent through competition, conversion to software as a service, and open-source products."

Ah—no wonder reducing software licensing costs is a business goal: "Between 2004 and 2011, CDC experienced a steadily widening gap between costs for sustaining an adequate level of IT services and the actual budget to deliver the services. The current gap between budget and the projected need based on normal inflation since 2004 now stands at a 42 percent deficit."

No doubt security bore the brunt of this gap. Possibilities . . . Attack the website, perhaps?

A DNS lookup resolved the name www.cdc.gov to several IP addresses. Most looked like cached copies and not good attack vectors.

What about email? An email header from a sender inside CDC would provide helpful information. An mx dig query returned only spam filters and nothing valuable for reconnaissance. So, how to retrieve an email header with information about the email server at the CDC internet boundary?

The jobs page looked promising. CDC needed medical officers in several US cities. And here was a convenient email address, hrcs@cdc.gov, for questions and correspondence with the Human Resources Office. Could it really be that simple?

EDeveraux115@gmail.com composed and sent a test email to hrcs@cdc.gov. Five minutes later, an automated reply arrived. The email header came from a Microsoft SMTP Server, which meant this was probably an internal Microsoft Exchange infrastructure, which meant CDC employees probably used Outlook calendars. Yes, this could be exploited. A team of specialists would see to it.

ZERO-DAY

The candlelight gave Turlach Flanagan's room above a pub in Belfast, Northern Ireland, a rustic feel, even though it was crammed with computer equipment. "You're knackered," he shouted and pounded his desk. He leaned back in his chair and rubbed his eyes. But what else besides Irish whiskey could numb the pain after losing his family during the troubles after the Irish Troubles?

He rose from his desk and staggered to his bathroom. The image in the mirror, with deep bags under his bloodshot eyes and greasy, grey hair, mostly pulled back and tied off into a ponytail with a rubber band, looked more like a homeless refugee than a former college professor.

How does your mind still function?

But maybe his mind wasn't functioning so well after all.

He lurched back to his desk and stared at his work in progress. The laptop screen, Microsoft Exchange reference books, hand-drawn flow diagrams, code listings, and empty shot glasses all mocked him. He swept his arm across the desk, sending it all crashing to the floor. A lit candle also went flying, landing on the floor in the middle of all that paper. It smoldered and then ignited.

"You nappy arwshe, maybe it's time to get it over with."

Like a scientist monitoring an experiment, he watched the flames consume a few papers and then a notebook and now some newspapers. The carpet smoldered and plastic jewel cases around a few CDs started to melt, filling the room with acrid smoke. Would one hundred proof Irish whiskey put it out or make it worse?

He grabbed his last remaining unopened bottle, twisted off the cap, downed a swig, and then poured it over the growing flames. "Ow!" The flames jumped and singed his hand.

"You're a flaming eejit, but it's not time to die in a ball o' fire yet!"

He ran back to his bathroom and filled a bucket with water. He ran back and poured it on the flames.

The flames hissed and smoked and then subsided as the water spread across the black spot on the carpeted floor, leaving a pile of wet paper and ashes and a smoky distillery aroma in the air.

He tipped the bottle back to finish it off and then dropped it in the middle of the wet mess and teetered to his bed.

"You're a manky neddy!" he mumbled as he drifted into a fitful sleep.

Five hours later, the room still smelled like smoke, which didn't help his growing headache. He swung his feet to the floor, rubbed his eyes, stood, and opened a window. A few birds chirped outside, announcing predawn of another miserable day on this miserable little planet. He staggered to his now-empty work desk and surveyed the damage from last night. "Serves ya right, ya mongo sap."

He picked up his laptop from the edge of the booze-soaked pile of papers on the floor and dried the bottom with his body-odor-stained shirt. He pressed the power button and waited. After a few seconds, it showed the familiar, "Press CTRL + ALT + DELETE to logon."

"A rake of good luck," he mumbled. "Now, stop arsing around, and let's find what we're looking for."

A few hours later, Turlach leaned back in his chair, ran a hand through his greasy hair, wiped it on his shirt, and smiled. The "Hello World" window on his laptop screen wasn't important. What was important was the method he came up with to generate that little picture. The sunlight made his head hurt. And he needed to use the bathroom. He didn't care. Not yet.

Document what we have first. He launched Notepad and composed a first draft of an ad he would post on an underground internet forum. The ad read:

```
A new zero-day XSS exploit with Microsoft Ex-
change. Launch OWA, log on, and compose a new
message. Put a specially crafted string in
the 'bcc' field to run a local script of your
choice. Requires phishing to intercept the ini-
tial logon to deploy your payload script. $30K
in bitcoin, including consulting to implement.
I will provide a sample script to grab the
user's cookie and upload to Dropbox. You can
modify as appropriate. Serious buyers only.
```

Turlach stared at the ad text for a few minutes before clicking the "Submit" button to post it. He smiled. Which made the hammer inside his head pound even harder. But no matter. If successful, this exploit would pay for all new computer equipment and more.

Now he could pee. He returned a few minutes later with a glass of orange juice. Responses were already coming in.

One response, from somebody named John, was typical: "Give me more information. How would this work?"

Turlach shook his head. "Idiots!" But if he wanted the money for the exploit he discovered, it was obvious he'd have to spell it out to these neddies. Thirty minutes later, his next post summed it up:

> For all you newbies, a zero-day exploit is one that hasn't been discovered yet by the software vendor. OWA, or Outlook Web App, is the Microsoft webmail function that comes with Microsoft Exchange Server. The exploit I discovered allows you to use OWA to run an arbitrary script on your computer if you place a specially formatted string in the bcc field. This script could upload a cookie with authentication information, or it could access your email and calendars, or it could upload documents from your profile. Or it could do anything else you want, limited only by your primitive imaginations. I provided a sample script to upload a cookie. You can use my sample to build something more elaborate if you want. Or pay me to do it. The object, of course, is not to run the script on your computer. The object is to entice somebody else to run it on his computer and send every important piece of information about his pitiful life to you. To take advantage of my exploit, you need to convince your targeted user to run the program I wrote to deploy your script. That's why it requires phishing. And I'll also answer your next obvious question. No, your targeted users will not see the string my program injects into the bcc field because the string contains nonprintable characters.

In Tehran, 6,200 kilometers away, the mastermind behind the Elaine Devereux persona spotted the ad while scouring the usual forums. He stroked his chin. Yes, this could be useful.

MINISTER MEETING

Iranian Intelligence Minister Hassan Saidi dipped his napkin and wiped an invisible food particle from his neatly trimmed beard. Eating at this five-star hotel in Beijing was almost decadent. But this meeting could be the key to the whole project.

The overweight man sitting across the table and his translator both wore Western business suits. With a tie. But, of course, nobody from the West ever installed a Chinese leader who plundered his people, so the Chinese did not share the same aversion to all things Western. Saidi wouldn't hold it against them.

He pushed his plate aside. "Excellent meal," he said through his own translator.

Chinese minister of state security, Geng Yun, smiled. "I will make sure we pass along your compliments to the chef. I eat here often. But now, business. Why did you travel all this way to meet me privately?"

"We congratulate you on your recent cyberattack against the American Office of Personnel Management. We understand from media reports that you have dossiers on every American government employee. Is this true?"

Geng leaned back in his chair. "Sometimes media reports are inaccurate. But as you are surely aware, no intelligence gathering service would disclose its secrets without good reason."

Saidi smiled and stroked his beard. "Perhaps we can provide that good reason."

"I'm listening."

"After the Americans and Israelis launched the Stuxnet cyberattack against our nuclear centrifuges, we spent considerable effort refining and repurposing the software weapons they left in our computer systems. Our minister of science, research, and technology says we now have the capability to launch a similar attack against the Americans."

"I see. Since you now possess this capability, why do you need us?"

"Perhaps you have information about certain American government employees in the Centers for Disease Control we can use to our mutual advantage."

"Excellent," Geng said. He took a sip of wine. "Assuming we have what you want, how do you plan to use it?"

Saidi leaned forward. "Our team has also done considerable research into the Ebola II virus currently plaguing West Africa. Information about the Americans who work in the agency with the mission to manage this virus would be valuable to us."

"How valuable?" Geng now leaned forward in his chair.

"Extremely valuable. Oil Minister Radan sends greetings and asked me to thank China for its investments in our oil fields."

"I'll pass that along," Geng said. "And I'm sure Iran and China will work out something mutually beneficial around oil. But my craft is information. Assuming I have what you want, what are you prepared to offer in return?"

Saidi reached into a briefcase and pulled out an Iranian visa. "We have a cabinet-level meeting coming up soon to discuss our project. Why don't you visit Tehran and attend as my guest? I'll personally select cuisine you'll find enjoyable."

BIDDERS' CONFERENCE

The gathering crowd of people wearing suits and ties and handing out business cards reminded Jerry Barkley of a flock of Minnesota turkeys preening for a female.

Jerry, wearing his usual khakis, white socks, tennis shoes, and a sweater—he always tried to wear nice sweaters to these things—found an empty seat in a middle row. That backstabber, John Watson, made eye contact from a few seats away. Jerry met his gaze. Jerry reached to scratch his nose with his middle finger but, at the last instant, changed his mind and rubbed his chin instead. Sorry, God. I know I'm supposed to be better than that. John didn't seem to notice.

Watson looked away and started a conversation with one of the few women in the room. Smiling and preening. Like always.

Bidders' conferences were always theater and rarely generated useful information. Jerry showed up for the same reason everyone else did—to see and be seen. And, maybe he could ask a few thought-provoking questions. I'm David, and I'm in a room full of Goliaths. I could use a slingshot. He put on his most confident smile. He'd put those acting skills from years on his church drama team to good use. Time to hand out a few business cards. Never let 'em see you sweat.

A few VIPs took seats behind a table on the stage. Tent cards showed their names and companies. Dan Standish, from the local company New Brighton Transport, scratched his neck behind his tie knot. He was wiry, with grey hair and a thin mustache. Jerry smiled. I could get along with this guy. They probably made him wear that suit.

Conversations around the room tapered off as one of the bigwigs approached a standing mic on stage in front of the tables.

"Good morning. I'm Dalbot Hawthorne, and I want to welcome all of you to our NAECN bidder's conference this morning. First things first. I want to thank POM Solutions for the coffee and snacks in the back." He gestured toward John Watson. "John, now I have peace of mind knowing our bidders are well-fed."

John half-stood, looking embarrassed. "Help yourselves, everyone. I'm afraid I went overboard on the doughnuts."

Polite laughter. Jerry shook his head.

Hawthorne continued. "Now, I know most of you are IT and telecom people, and you all have your own language and acronyms. Sometimes I feel like I need a translator to talk to you guys."

More polite laughter from the audience. Jerry rolled his eyes.

"Well, freight carriers have a language, too. NAECN stands for North American Extended Carrier Network, and LTL means "less than a load." Our member companies spend a lot of money to move LTL freight, and we can grow a competitive edge by joining forces to combine LTL shipments on long-haul routes. Any time we can combine partial loads onto one full truck, everyone saves money. We have an army of programmers testing the software to make all this work, and now we need a state-of-the-art communication network to pull it off. And that's why you guys are here. But you know that already. Let's get to some questions."

A few people around the room raised their hands. With two weeks left before the proposal deadline, somebody asked about extending it. The answer was no. Another question was about refurbished equipment vs. new. And some others. All typical bidders' conference questions, none about anything interesting.

Jerry raised his hand.

"Yes—the gentleman in the middle row in the, um, sweater?"

Jerry stood. "I didn't see any references to this in your RFP, and I was wondering what provisions you wanted in the proposal about defending against possible cyberattacks."

"We're just looking for a communication network. Member companies provide their own defenses." The chairman looked for other questions.

"Okay, but if you receive a proposal that includes a cost-effective means for cyber-defense, would that factor into your decision?"

"We won't rule anything out, but again, we're an association of trucking companies, not technology experts. All our members have IT departments to deal with cybersecurity."

"But what happens if malicious traffic makes its way onto this network? Wouldn't you want a plan to defend against it?"

"We're really getting into a level of detail best left for the techies. Thank you for your concern, but we need to move on to other questioners."

The guy from New Brighton Transport looked curious.

Hawthorne called on John Watson. By first name.

"What's the most important attribute you're looking for in proposals for this network?"

Hawthorne smiled. "Peace of mind."

"But, what if somebody offers you a better mousetrap?"

"We don't want a science experiment; we just want it to work."

Watson looked at Jerry and winked.

After the conference, Watson ambled over. "Listen, Jerry, I asked my questions to try to show everyone we have this bid locked up. Think of it as a public service to save everyone from wasting more time. I'm not trying to beat you up here, but I don't know why they even let you in the room today."

"Maybe for the same reason they let you in."

"I'm not the bad guy here."

Jerry rolled his eyes.

"You're a good technical resource. You always were."

"Digital Systems was a long time ago."

"You had a daughter. She was what, maybe three? How old is she now? Late twenties? I heard she has two kids, and she's still living with you."

"You had ethics back then. What happened to you?"

"You know who asks about ethics? Losers. Like you."

"Well, you taught me a lesson about trusting old friends."

"Jerry, I'm trying to help you out here. I got to where I am by being a student of what makes people tick. You're a good technical resource. Maybe one of the better ones I've worked with. But that's all you'll ever be. Try to play in the big leagues like this, and you'll get beaned every time you step up to the plate."

"Yeah, whatever."

The guy from New Brighton Transport kept looking this way. Jerry made eye contact and moved down the aisle toward the stage. They met in the middle.

"I'm Jerry Barkley."

"I'm Dan Standish." They shook hands. "Were you the guy harping about cybersecurity?"

"Yeah, that was me."

"You brought up some interesting points."

"Thanks. Will anyone care?"

"Probably not."

●——————●

Jerry delivered his proposal ahead of the deadline. One week later, the email arrived: "Dear Bidder, Thank you for your interest in our project." Bla bla bla.

EVIN PRISON

Bahir Mustafa shuddered at the screams and wails echoing through the concrete-block walls deep in the bowels of Evin Prison in Tehran, Iran. How long had he been in this nightmare? A day? A week? Months? Day and night became meaningless in this dingy cell, alone with his thoughts. He tried to block the agony surrounding him by reading messages past residents had somehow scrawled on his cell walls. But the constant shrieks and moans never stopped.

He touched the welts on his face. They were still fresh. Was the last beating only a few hours ago? Did other prisoners cringe when they heard his cries the way he cringed when he heard theirs? His wrists still showed marks from the plastic tie wraps that made his fingers numb. Did the guard who finally freed his wrists nick his skin on purpose?

Bahir was a respected computer system administrator at a prestigious university in Tehran, not some political dissident. He had cooperated with everything the university sponsors asked of him and even pretended to be enthusiastic about their insane political schemes and fanatical religion. Yet a group of Basij thugs had rousted him from his sleep in the middle of the night and dumped him in this hell hole. Why?

Yes, he was also a businessman, but that was private and no threat to their precious revolution. They could not have known about that. He took too many precautions. And besides, those ministers of idiocy didn't know an ftp site from an email server. Surely this was all a misunderstanding.

Footsteps echoed down the corridor. Waves of nausea rippled through his stomach as the footsteps grew louder. Another beating? Maybe the guards were coming for somebody else? Maybe bringing another prisoner back to his cell? Yes, surely that was it.

The footsteps stopped in front of Bahir's cell. He cowered as two guards looked in. They looked like Olympic weightlifters.

"Bahir Mustafa?" said one.

"Yes," he whispered. "Please! Why am I in this place?"

"You will stand away from the door as we open it and face the back of your cell. You will leave your arms at your sides."

"Why am I in this place?" Bahir asked, louder.

"If you continue to resist, we will punish you."

"Why am I in this place?"

One guard raised a baton. Bahir stepped back from the cell door, turned and faced the wall in the back of his cell.

His shoulders shook. "Why am I in this place?"

The cell door slid open. Footsteps reverberated behind him. A baton whistled and found its mark on his back-right side.

"The prisoner will be silent."

Bahir collapsed onto the floor. "Why am I here? I've done nothing wrong!"

Another blow, then another to the back of his head as the guards pulled him to his feet and put a dark hood over his head.

"You will accompany us. Any resistance will be met with force."

"Just try to be quiet," the other guard said. "Learn to accept your new life."

"I've done nothing wrong!"

More blows to the head and body. Bahir collapsed again. The guards pulled him up under each arm and yanked him out the door.

More guards now, surrounding him. More footsteps. His arms hurt as the guards dragged him down the corridor. He tried to bring his feet under his body, but the pace was too fast. More blows every time he stumbled.

He entered a different room. The air was fresher. And cool. An air conditioner hummed. And this room was bright. He could sense it even with the hood. The guards pushed him into a chair and zip tied his hands to the chair behind his back. His knees hit a table as they pulled the hood from his head.

Bright fluorescent light illuminated the room. He squinted while the unpainted concrete-block walls slowly came into focus. The concrete floor under his feet was clean. His body ached all over as he scanned his surroundings. His hands, tied behind his back, were uncomfortable.

Somebody sat across the table. Tall, dark hair, neatly trimmed beard, blue suit jacket. It was Atesh Zare of the Basij. Atesh, with the Ministry of Science, Research, and Technology.

"Atesh, thank Allah! Help me explain that I've done nothing wrong!"

"That's a problem, Bahir. You have done something wrong."

"In the name of Allah, I beg you. What?"

"You're an arrogant fool, Bahir. You think we're technological illiterates. It is your fatal flaw."

Bahir's palms started to sweat. Every welt on his head and body throbbed.

Atesh rose from his chair and paced back and forth.

"We know all about your business, your global network of robot computers, your botnet, as you call it. We know the true purpose of your Zagros Mountains website. Breathtaking images, by the way. We know how you used those images to lure people around the world into downloading embedded malware onto their computers. We know about your command and control servers, and we know how you abused university resources to enrich yourself."

Atesh stopped pacing. He put his hands on the table and leaned over Bahir's head.

"We've watched you grow more sophisticated as your network has grown. We watched you rent your botnet to those pornography lovers in Qatar. We even watched you help your Russian friend attack that American retailer, Bullseye Stores."

Bahir put his face in his hands. He would be dead before this day was out. How could he have been so foolish? They monitored the traffic in and out of the university. Of course. That was the only way they could have known. But it was all encrypted. How would they know about the content?

"Yes, you're figuring it out. We watched all your network traffic. And we broke your encryption. You should have at least used TLS 1.2 and made it a challenge for us. Your master control server using an obsolete SSL version? Bahir, you of all people should know better. Do you think we are fools? We watch everything. Look around you, Bahir. Do you see the video camera above my head and to your right? We watch everything. You have no secrets from us. We know everything you know. Everything."

But wait—if they knew all this for so long, why did they allow it? There was hope. He might yet live to see tomorrow.

"We know all this—we've known about all of it since you started fifteen years ago," Atesh said. He paused.

Bahir looked up at Atesh's unblinking eyes.

"We know all about your little operation." Atesh paused for a breath. "And we don't care."

Bahir's shoulders slumped. "But why . . ."

"Because you committed an unpardonable sin! You planted your malware in *my* computer. And for that, I have found you guilty and sentenced you to spend the rest of your days in a dark, putrid cell, surrounded by screams of agony from the dying and the smell of death. You are guilty!"

Atesh strode around the table past Bahir and toward the door.

Bahir turned his head to follow Atesh with his eyes. "Wait! There must be something I can do to redeem myself!"

Atesh disappeared from Bahir's view.

"Wait! Please! I will do anything you ask, just please don't let me die! I am sorry!" Bahir sobbed.

Atesh's footsteps stopped.

Bahir waited, heart pounding. His sobs reverberated between the hard, concrete walls.

"Atesh, please!"

The footsteps echoed again, and when Atesh appeared in Bahir's field of vision, Bahir sagged forward and wept.

Atesh moved to his chair across the table and sat. He leaned back and stared at Bahir. Tears flowed down Bahir's cheeks. Atesh watched for a few minutes until Bahir composed himself.

"Lean closer and turn your ear toward me."

Bahir leaned in.

"There may be something you can do to redeem yourself."

"Name it! I am your servant!"

"Excellent," Atesh lifted his left hand and gestured to the video camera.

A few seconds later, the door creaked open. Footsteps echoed behind Bahir and stopped at his back. He turned to see a guard with a knife in the corner of his eye. He cowered.

"No!"

The guard raised the knife.

"Please, no!" sobbed Bahir. "I do not wish to die!"

"You will never plant malicious software on any of our Ministry computers again." The guard cut the restraints from Bahir's wrists, sheathed his knife, and stepped back toward the door.

"I swear by Allah. I will never tamper with your computers."

"Good. We have two projects we would like you to work on. First is ensuring our Ministry computers are protected from malware. If we ever find evidence of anyone tampering with our computers again, that knife will stop at your heart. Your life depends on our computers staying clean."

"The second project is more in your area of expertise. You've heard of Stuxnet?"

"The virus the Americans and Israelis unleashed to attack our nuclear centrifuges in 2009?"

"Yes. They set our nuclear program back by several years. It was only due to chance that we learned of their treachery. We've adapted some of their techniques for our own purposes. We will use their own weapon against them. You will use your contacts in the West to expand your botnet and help us gather intelligence about the targets we select. We will compensate you for your work by sparing your life."

MAKING CONNECTIONS

"Thanks, Mr. Urbino."

The valet pocketed Frank Urbino's generous tip and hopped out of Frank's red Lamborghini, leaving the door open and engine running.

"Thanks for taking good care of her."

Another valet opened the passenger door.

"See, Janelle, I told you it's mine."

"Jerilyn. I'm Jerilyn."

A couple valets standing around the car chuckled.

"Ohh." Frank took a deep breath of the warm Miami night air and gave a wink to the lead valet. "My apologies. Janelle's my cousin's name. She has hair almost as nice as yours, and you remind me of her."

Jerilyn smiled and slid into the passenger seat. "I like your chains." She ran her finger along one of the gold chains around Frank's neck.

"I like your sequins." Frank closed the door. "Watch and learn, boys. Someday, you might be me."

———•———

Frank unlocked his fifty-eighth-floor condo and followed Jerilyn inside. "Let me just check my messages, and I'll pour us that nightcap."

He opened his laptop and logged on.

Jerilyn watched over his shoulder. "Why not just play them back on the machine?"

"These are different kinds of messages."

"You mean, like email?"

"No, these are private messages from an international group I work with."

"And what is it you do again?"

"I told you, I'm the king of email marketing."

Jerilyn removed her shoes and dug into the plush carpet with her toes. She swept her arm and twirled in a complete circle. Frank smiled as she took in the leather couch, glass tables, and state-of- the-art electronics everywhere. She picked up a remote control and pressed it to open and close the blinds.

"And it pays for all this?"

"And more."

"So, are you one of those computer hackers?"

Frank laughed. "No. I just send emails. Lots of 'em."

He opened an underground internet discussion forum. A private message was waiting from Alma.

"Who's Alma?"

"He's a friend of mine from, um, overseas."

```
Would like to use your services for a special
bulk email project. Looking for people with
jobs at American trucking companies to probe
their computers at work. My associates and I
realize the difficulty of this project, so we
offer 10x our usual payment.
```

"And they call you Duceml?"

"Yeah."

"Ten times their usual payment? That sounds good. Why do you look worried?"

Frank closed his eyes and nibbled his upper lip. He opened his eyes and smiled. "Me? Nah, I never worry. But I need to get back to him. This will only take a second."

```
No prob, Alma. I'll handle it. Send me what
you want to deliver when you're ready. I'll
round up your contacts and get you a count in
a few days.
```

"Wait a minute. You're one of those government agents, aren't you? This is some kind of sting operation, isn't it? Why are you showing this stuff to me?"

Frank laughed again. "No, really, I don't work for the government. But I know a few governments who pay me a lot of money."

"Well, you do know how to impress a girl."

Frank smiled. "What did you want in that nightcap again?"

Jerilyn wrapped her arms around his neck. "Why don't we skip the drink?"

After an enjoyable evening and even more enjoyable night and morning and after driving Jerilyn home, it was time for business. Wongladee was in the usual online hangout.

```
Duceml: Hey, Wongladee. How's my favorite
email relay service? I have another project
for you.
Wongladee: Hey, Duceml. I like you projects.
Come visit China. I show you good time.
Duceml: Forget China. Why don't you set up
shop over here in the land of the free? Miami
is warm this time of year.
Wongladee: I like it right here.
```

Duceml: Your loss. Tell ya what. I'm feeling generous. I'll pay you a little bit extra on this one because it's special.
Wongladee: Thanks, Duceml. Maybe you gonads not so small after all.
Duceml: LOL

Now, the hard part: find the target audience. He'd work on it this afternoon and then take a nap and sample another taste of the Miami nightlife overnight. He had a streak to maintain. And a reputation to protect. But something didn't feel right about this deal. Why was Alma offering ten times the usual payment? And how was he supposed to find people who work at trucking companies?

He would come up with something. Hey—it's a living.

RUSSIAN ROULETTE

A white mountain of clothes on Jerry and Lynn Barkley's bed had shrunk while stacks of neatly folded underwear grew. Lynn folded another undershirt. "When do you decide enough is enough and start looking for a job?"

"We've been over this before."

"And you've never given me a straight answer. Put your underwear away."

"What about the undershirts?"

"I'm not done folding those yet. I want a straight answer. John Watson offered you a position, and you turned him down. When do you decide to say yes?"

"Those guys stabbed me in the back. I can't believe you want me to go to work for them."

"We might lose our home, Jerry. You need to swallow your pride."

"We're not gonna lose our home. We've done it more than twenty years this way."

"You need a regular paycheck and benefits."

Jerry shook his head. His cell phone rang. "I gotta take this."

Jerry finished his call. The mountain of unfolded white clothes was down to a few odds and ends.

"Who was it?"

Jerry grabbed a stack of socks. "It was Sally Brock with Maverick Marketing."

"And, she's important because?"

"I told you about her. I met her at that Burnsville Chamber meeting a couple weeks ago. She said she was looking for better IT service."

Lynn finished folding. "And she's offering you a contract?"

"Well, no, not yet. Nobody can get to their documents, and the whole company is shut down. After I get her company back up and running again, she will."

"After, huh. What if you can't?" Lynn brought a stack of towels to the bathroom.

"It's probably a messed-up server. I'll fix it."

"But what if you can't?"

Jerry put his stack of socks away. "There's no such thing as can't."

"What if you fix it and she doesn't pay?"

Jerry rolled his eyes. "And what if an earthquake swallows the car? I gotta get over there."

"I'll pick your clothes out for you."

"I know how to dress myself."

"No, you don't."

One hour later, Jerry sat across from Maverick Marketing General Manager Sally Brock in her office in Burnsville, Minnesota.

Sally's grey hair, pulled back in a bun and barely visible over the top of her computer monitor, made her look like a disembodied voice. Jerry scooted his chair sideways to make eye contact.

Behind Jerry, outside the front glass wall of Sally's office, writers, producers, and designers in rows of cubicles normally churned out PR campaigns for

Fortune 500 companies and movie stars. But nobody was churning out anything this morning.

"Tell me what's going on," Jerry said.

"Our business depends on the internet to operate," Sally said. "But we can't get to the internet, our email doesn't work, and we can't access our proposal library. We can't even print. If we don't get this fixed right away, we're out of business."

"Hmm. Well, let's see. Show me how you access your proposal library and what happens." Jerry moved to Sally's side of the desk.

"When I click on my "Proposals" icon here," Sally clicked on the screen icon, "this error pops up."

"Well, isn't that special? May I?" Jerry gestured at Sally's computer mouse. "Let's see what you can talk to."

Jerry's fingers flew across the keyboard as he expertly manipulated Sally's computer mouse.

"You're not getting any DHCP service."

"What is DHCP?"

"You need a DHCP server to help your workstations figure out where they are."

"It worked fine yesterday."

"Which suggests something broke last night."

"You found that pretty fast. How long have you been a geek?"

Jerry grimaced. He needed Sally's business. Best not to provoke her. On the other hand . . . "I never liked that word, geek. I like to think I'm a professional."

"I thought you guys liked to be called geeks."

"Not me."

Sally shook her head. "What's next? I assume if you can get this DHCP—whatever that is—working again, we'll be back in business?"

"Maybe," replied Jerry. "But it might be part of something bigger. Show me your server."

Sally led Jerry down a hallway and opened the door to a utility closet. A heat wave blasted Jerry's face. He scanned the tiny room and cringed.

The company server was a dusty minitower with an ancient CRT monitor. It sat on a table against the left wall, plugged into a yellowed power strip on the concrete floor, about three feet away from an upside-down mop bucket over a drain. Boxes of cleaning supplies partially obscured a faucet on the right wall. A rat's nest of telephone and network cable, punch-down blocks, and a patch panel were mounted on a piece of plywood on the back wall. Dozens of network cables ran from the patch panel to a stack of devices with blinking LEDs mounted on a wire shelf above the server table. Dusty manuals and papers sat on top of the stack.

"This room is part of your problem." Jerry walked inside. He lifted papers and manuals from the top of the stack of devices and blew the dust off. That was a mistake. Jerry sneezed, and his eyes watered. He touched the top of the stack.

"Ouch!" Shaking his hand, he said, "You have to feel this. Just put your hand on top of that switch for a second."

Sally slowly extended her finger and touched the top of the switch. She quickly pulled it away, leaving a dust print. "It's hot!"

"Yup," Jerry said. "And that's not good. What are you running on your server?"

"We do lots of proposals. Do we have to stay in here?"

"Only for another minute. I meant, what operating system is on your server?"

"I don't know; Windows, I guess."

Jerry shook his head. "Is it okay if I log on and look at some things?"

"Go right ahead."

Jerry leaned over the table to see the monitor screen. "Oh, wow. Here's your problem." He gestured for Sally to look and stepped back.

Sally moved in front of him. "What does 'NTLDR is Missing' mean?"

"It means your server boot loader disappeared. With no boot loader, your system won't boot. Your server is dead. That's your problem."

"How did that happen? Did somebody do something?"

Jerry rolled his eyes. What did she think had happened? "Usually, it's more mundane," he said out loud.

Jerry squatted for a closer look at the floor drain.

"See how the floor is damp around this drain? Tell me you don't fill your mop buckets and drain them in here."

"I assume that's what the cleaning people do. That's why these are called utility closets."

Jerry closed his eyes and silently counted to three. "Sally, the heat in this room feels like Death Valley. There's dust everywhere, and you have water splashing against the power strip that feeds your company server. Water probably interrupted your power strip last night, which killed the power to your server, which is why we found it trying to boot itself this morning. That power event most likely corrupted its boot drive, so it's dead."

"What does all that mean in English?"

"It means the set-up in this closet should be in a TV torture test ad. You've gotta get this equipment outta here."

"Out of the question. We bring clients through our office, and we don't need noisy, ugly equipment cluttering it up."

Jerry shook his head.

"Can you fix this, or do I call somebody else?"

"If it's recoverable, I can recover it."

"That doesn't give me much confidence."

"Maybe you can call somebody who will lie to you."

Sally stared at Jerry. He met her gaze.

Something reflected off Sally's glasses. Jerry turned to the server and noticed a flashing amber LED. "Oh—look at this. You have a bad hard drive, which means you probably have others getting ready to go bad."

Sally folded her arms. "How much time do you need?"

"No way to tell. Do you know what version of Windows is on this system?"

"Windows 2010 or something like that? I don't know."

"That's not a Windows version. Do you have any paperwork that might give me a clue?"

"Can't you just look it up?"

"It's easier with a working server, but there are ways to find out. We might need to restore this from bare metal. What do your backups look like?"

"I change a tape every Friday," Sally said.

"Why do you still use tapes?"

"We don't need the latest gadgets here. We're a marketing company."

An ejected cartridge protruded from the front of the tape drive. Jerry removed the cartridge, exposing a red LED error indicator light immediately below the cartridge slot.

"What does that mean?" Sally asked.

"It means your backups are no good and your server is dead. You might be in a world of hurt."

Sally sighed. "What's next?"

"I have some tools in the car. I'll bring them in."

"You need tools?"

"Plumbers have pipe wrenches. I have software tools."

Jerry returned a few minutes later carrying a cardboard box stuffed with CD and DVD jewel cases, screwdrivers, cables, and a portable DVD reader. "First things first; let's find out what we've got here." He connected his portable DVD reader to a USB slot on the server.

"I thought you said you're a professional. But you keep your equipment in a cardboard box?"

"Minimal overhead. I'm a tech company, not a marketing company."

"You mentioned plumbers before you ran out to your car," Sally said. "If I'd called a plumber, he could've told me what I needed and priced it out over the phone. Our whole business is shut down, and we're losing money every minute. What is it with IT people that you can never tell me what's wrong and give me a simple answer to fix it?"

"Some questions don't have simple answers."

"I don't buy that."

Jerry took a deep breath and turned to face Sally. "I know you're stressed. But before I can tell you anything worth the air to carry the soundwaves, I need to assess what's here. That's step one, figuring out what you have and exactly what's broken. Maybe you'll get lucky and I'll find an easy fix."

"Fine. Do your thing." Sally turned and walked out of the room.

Jerry watched her leave. His armpits were already sweaty.

Nothing like a good crisis to get the adrenaline flowing. First things first. He pressed the Ctrl/Alt/Delete keys on the keyboard and watched the system go through its power on self-test. At the appropriate time, he pressed a key to launch the RAID configuration utility. He studied the screen. The failed hard drive was part of a RAID 5 set, which meant the system should still operate in a degraded mode without it.

Jerry removed the hot plug drive and noted its make and model number. "I wonder . . ."

He reseated the drive, and the amber error light went out. He tapped a few keyboard keys to instruct the RAID firmware program to rebuild the array. The amber LED error light flashed again a few seconds later.

"Bad for sure."

He inspected the tape drive and recorded its model number. Next, he called a parts broker. Somebody answered after a few rings.

"Hi. I need pricing on a few things."

Jerry negotiated over the phone for pricing and availability for the parts he wanted.

"Okay, sounds good. Send me an email with the quote, and I'll get back to you in a few minutes if this is a go. How fast can you get it here?"

Walking back to Sally's office, the hallway air felt nice after enduring Death Valley. Jerry lifted his shirt and blew on his chest.

Sally was on the phone.

"Yes, we're working on your press release right now. We should have it out to the media in a couple of hours . . . Yes, of course . . . We'll send you a review copy before we release it . . . Yes, it's an exciting announcement . . . Thank you for letting us handle the publicity."

Sally ended her call. Jerry knocked on her office doorframe.

"I have an update for you." He shook his shirt, fanning his sweaty stomach.

"I just told one of our biggest customers we'd have their press release ready for review in a couple of hours. But the draft we've been working on all week is inside that system you're playing with."

"I can't promise you'll be up and running in two hours."

"We need that draft."

"I'm not a miracle worker. Meanwhile, I have an estimate for replacement hardware and some spare parts to have here next time that system breaks. And there will be a next time. New motherboard, RAID controller, power supplies, extra RAM, and five spare hot plug hard drives. It's an older system, so these parts are getting scarce. Your tape drive went end-of-life five years ago. I can find used ones, but they come with thirty-day warranties. We'll use a rotation of USB backup drives instead. Replacement cost is $7,999. I can have all that here later today."

"No."

"No?"

"I'm not spending eight thousand dollars on computer toys. What do we need to just get back on our feet?"

"That hard drive was part of a RAID—"

"I don't want to hear geek-speak. What hardware do we need right now to get back on our feet?"

"None. But you'll be naked."

"Then, why did you just tell me I need to spend eight thousand dollars on hardware?"

"Because I don't like Russian roulette. I can cut that cost by about one third and improve the way you do backups."

"What's the bare minimum hardware I need?"

Jerry did some mental calculations. Naked was bad, so the replacement hard drive was a must. It was a small server. USB backup drives, four terabytes each; three of them should do the trick for backups. Put in one more spare hot plug hard drive, just in case. Jerry figured his cost would be around $1,100. "Eighteen hundred dollars. Bare bones minimum. Oh—add seven hundred to that for a decent UPS so you're feeding it clean power."

"Fine."

"Do you want the UPS, too?"

"I don't know what a UPS is. I'll spend the eighteen hundred you talked about."

"You need that uninterruptable power supply for clean power."

"No."

Jerry shook his head.

"How soon will we be back in business?"

"No way to tell. Can I bring a chair back to that room?"

•———•

Now sitting in front of the server again, Jerry inserted a DVD labeled "Fedora Live" into his portable DVD reader. He typed a few keyboard commands and waited for the server to boot from the DVD. After it finished booting, he peered closely. He typed a few commands and smiled. "Windows 2003. Figures."

He shut the system down and inserted another CD, this one labeled "password recovery tool." He booted it and typed a few more commands. When he finished, the new administrator password was "Barkleyrulez!"

He shut down again and rummaged through his box of CDs and DVDs. He found a Windows 2003 installation and booted it. He pressed R to run the recovery console, selected the installation and entered the password he had just reset, and ran the fixboot program. It ran cleanly. So far, so good. He shut down.

Now, the rubber meets the road. He disconnected his portable DVD reader and powered back on again. The system started another power on self-test. Jerry held his breath and watched the output on the screen.

Booting . . .

He smiled when the video went to graphics mode and eventually painted the familiar Windows 2003 "Press Ctrl/Alt/Delete to login" screen. The system was running degraded, with a naked RAID set and no backups, but at least it was running and they could access their work in progress. He packed his equipment.

He logged in to see how much storage space it used. About five hundred gigabytes. Which meant a four terabyte USB backup disk could hold six save sets with room to grow.

Jerry walked back to Sally's office and poked his head in. "Try it now." He moved next to Sally's desk so he could see her computer monitor.

Sally clicked her "Proposals" icon. This time, the normal window with a list of files on the server proposals directory appeared. Sally smiled. "You are too a miracle worker."

"No, I'm not. You got away with a Russian roulette round. Next time might not be so easy. I have a replacement hard drive coming to make your RAID set whole again. And we're going to use your computer for backups so you don't have to run back to that room every Friday. I'll show you how to manage your backups after I set it up."

"While I'm waiting for parts, is it okay if I look at some things on your server and document what you have here?"

"Be my guest."

Jerry trudged back into that hot room and started investigating. Using the Notepad program, he documented what he found. After a few minutes, he launched a web browser and visited a popular website to generate a free internet port scan back to the requestor. His eyes widened as he scanned the report.

"Oh, no." He looked closer. "Unbelievable."

He found a reference to a printer and sent his Notepad notes and port scan report to print. He also saved copies on the server desktop and launched OWA, the Microsoft web email program, and emailed copies to himself.

Somebody poked their head in the door. "Man, it's hot in here!"

"Tell me about it," Jerry replied.

"A courier just dropped off the stuff you ordered."

"Thanks."

Jerry opened the package and swapped the failed hard drive. He noticed green LED lights begin to blink a few seconds later. "Good, it's rebuilding."

Now, the fun part: putting together a server backup script. He had done many of these before and had a prototype ready after a few minutes. He collected the USB drives and walked out to Sally's office again. The office was quiet, except for the sound of keyboards and mouse clicks.

"No more tapes. We're going to backup over the network to one of these USB drives connected to your computer. You'll label these A, B, and C with a piece of masking tape and change them every Tuesday and Friday at the end of the day. If you follow the schedule, you'll have three weeks' worth of Monday through Saturday full backups. If one of these fails, you won't lose an entire week; you'll lose six days interspersed over two weeks. I'll be back tomorrow to check up on tonight's backups. I also need to show you some security issues I uncovered. I know you're catching up today, so we'll combine the backup training with the security stuff tomorrow."

Sally looked up from her typing. "Thanks, Jerry, and I'll see you tomorrow."

"I bought you a couple new shirts today," Lynn said in their bedroom that night. Grey had replaced some of her dark hair around the edges, but she still had that same feisty streak Jerry loved about her. And she had that look in her eye. Probably because of the shirts. "How did it go this morning?"

Jerry flipped the TV channel to a *Star Trek* rerun. "Another day, another heroic rescue. But they have more problems. I did a port scan, and every single port is closed." She knows it's coming. Let's get it over with. "Why did you buy more shirts?"

"That's good, right?" Lynn said.

"No. I don't need new shirts."

"They were on sale. And you know that's not what I meant."

"You mean the closed ports? No, that's as bad as it gets. I told you what that means."

"Do we have to watch another *Star Trek* tonight?"

"You don't remember, do you?"

"You know I don't know anything about computers."

"You never remember what I teach you." Jerry handed Lynn the remote.

"With everything that goes on in this house, I'm lucky to remember my own name some days." Lynn scrolled through the on-screen TV directory.

"It means they're in trouble and they don't know it."

Lynn turned the TV off, stood, and stretched.

"No TV tonight?"

She smiled. "I changed my mind."

"I like the sound of that."

"Shut up and turn the lights off."

Jerry laughed. "What will the children say?"

"Go lock the door if you're worried."

ALLAH ON THE PRAIRIE

Alone and in his basement bedroom, one week after the fight—another week filled with insults from jocks and farm boys at school—his eye was still swollen and his body ached. Brian retreated to his favorite project to take his mind away from it all.

His parents had protested the fight, and adults wearing business suits met with other adults in suits and held endless conversations filled with words like "diversity" and "tolerance." But it was all talk.

He had tried to make the best of his new life here in the cornfields. Bigshot jobs at a large bank must pay well for Father to afford a house like this, with a full basement, main floor, and upstairs bedrooms. And five acres, all fenced in. Instead of an apartment overlooking Central Park in New York City, it was almost as if they now lived in an entire apartment building in the middle of their own private Central Park. But surrounded by cornfields instead of civilization.

The internet extended civilization, even to the cornfields. While locals played football, fed pigs, and got pregnant, Brian spent most nights and weekends setting up the surplus server equipment Father brought home. He explored tech support forums around the world, and before long, he had a website, an email server, and a library of downloaded knowledge in hundreds of electronic documents.

And he enjoyed the dialog with Jerry, his online friend.

> **Bcoxsf:** How do I run my blog website and email server here at home so my friends in New York can see it, but keep it behind my firewall?
>
> **Jerrybarkley:** You need a public IP address, and then put your servers behind a NAT gateway.
>
> **Bcoxsf:** What is a NAT gateway?
>
> **Jerrybarkley:** There's lots of info on all this. Google is your friend.
>
> **Bcoxsf:** May I ask you a personal question?
>
> **Jerrybarkley:** Sure.
>
> **Bcoxsf:** How long have you been doing this kind of work?
>
> **Jerrybarkley:** A long time.
>
> **Bcoxsf:** Did you work on computers when you were in high school?
>
> **Jerrybarkley:** Yes, but it wasn't like today.

Real computers looked like refrigerators with front panel lights when I was in high school.

Bcoxsf: What did you do?

Jerrybarkley: Lots of stuff. One of my favorites was playing golf.

Bcoxsf: They had computer games that long ago?

Jerrybarkley: Not like today. I used a golf program to teach myself about programming.

Bcoxsf: How?

Jerrybarkley: I printed out the listing and spread it out on my bed. Then I followed the program, line by line, by hand. I used a pencil to mark where I was in the program and a notebook to track all the variables. I spent an entire weekend following this program to play two holes of golf. I only came upstairs to eat. My mom and stepdad thought something was wrong with me.

Bcoxsf: What did your friends think?

Jerrybarkley: Didn't have many of those.

Bcoxsf: Why not?

Jerrybarkley: I didn't fit in. My parents were alcoholics, and too many people tried to pick fights with me. I'm not much of a fighter, so I decided I liked computers better than people.

Bcoxsf: Kids pick on me, too. Because I'm Muslim.

Jerrybarkley: Maybe. It could also be you're too short or too tall, too fat or too thin, or maybe you have acne or wear glasses. Anything that's different. But it's most probably because they're stupid.

Bcoxsf: It's my taquiyah.

Jerrybarkley: What's that?
Bcoxsf: You might call it a skullcap.
Jerrybarkley: Yeah, that'll do it.
Bcoxsf: They are stupid. But they call me Muzzie, and every day since we moved here two years ago, they steal my books or push me down in the hallway or ridicule me or pick fights. I hate it here.
Jerrybarkley: I'm sorry you have to put up with that crap.
Bcoxsf: I don't know what to do.
Jerrybarkley: You win by being smarter than them.
Bcoxsf: How?
Jerrybarkley: Come up with something that knocks the world's socks off.
Bcoxsf: How?
Jerrybarkley: Think about something you want and then find a way to make it happen. Reach out online for ideas. I'll be your manager for ten percent of your first $billion.
Bcoxsf: Thanks.

Jerry was right about finding things online. Brian could not take his eyes off the images in *Dabiq*, the online Islamic State magazine. Picture after picture showed what happened to Western crusaders who dared defy Allah. He chuckled at an image of a bearded freedom fighter holding the severed head of a crusader. "Aww, don't lose your head over it." Unlike his parents, who could only talk and talk, these guys were the real deal. Talk was cheap. He imagined himself holding a severed head of one of the letter jackets who made his life at school a living hell. And Cheryl Samuels, who forced all those forbidden feelings—he would find a special place for her, too.

But how to contact these guys? Twitter maybe? He searched for "#ISIS" and found several tweets criticizing ISIS. One showed a clipart drawing of a man pointing a finger and dressed in a robe with Christian symbols. The tweet had the tag "#DestroyJihad." ISIS must still be a powerful force if so many are tweeting against it. But nothing useful for contacting them turned up.

Maybe "#Jihad" would be more helpful. He tried it and found several tweets denouncing Jihad. But one looked interesting. "Make #paradise on earth. #Jihad will rid the world of #kuffar." It had a picture of a young man with tangled black hair and a long beard. He wore dirty clothes and boots and had a rifle slung over his shoulder. He stood on a mountain path, looking down at a village. He had a cell phone to his ear. The post came from somebody named @yazidkal. Brian's heart pounded. He clicked the heart-shaped button indicating he liked what he saw.

His palms were sweaty. He wiped them on his shirt and searched for other posts from @yazidkal: "Unhappy with your life? Join with us in #jihad and create #paradise." And, "Bullies will rue the day they met you after we teach you what happens to #kuffar."

It was as if Allah himself was calling. He clicked the "Follow" button on yazidkal's profile.

It was late. His phone needed a charge. Brian went to bed and fell into a fitful sleep. Cheryl Samuels offered herself to him, and he eagerly accepted. But she pulled away and laughed at his skinny arms, at his clothing, at his faith. She ridiculed him for succumbing to her temptation. And then offered herself again, only to pull away once more and walk down the school hallway, arm in arm with one of the letter jackets. The other letter jackets looked at Brian and laughed. The picture of @yazidkal came to life and stood beside Brian.

"Use it," @yazidkal said and handed Brian a rocket-propelled grenade launcher.

Brian mounted the weapon on his shoulder, aimed at Cheryl Samuels and her letter-jacket friend. The other letter jackets stopped laughing. They were afraid. Brian fired.

He was at peace.

Seven hours later on Saturday morning, the swollen eye still didn't feel better. Looking in the mirror, he noticed it had turned even more shades of purple, green, and black. His whole body ached even more. He would ask Allah to use him to avenge these kuffar and do everything in his power to be worthy when Allah called. Forget his parents' ideas about peace.

His phone chirped at noon. It was a new Twitter follower who left a private message.

```
@bcoxsf, Thank you for the like and for fol-
lowing me. Tell me about yourself.
```

Brian's heart raced. He immediately composed a private reply.

```
My name is Brian. I enjoyed your tweet about
#paradise. I want to find out more about #ji-
had. I want the bullies who hurt me every day
to suffer.
```

The reply from @yazidkal came back a few seconds later.

```
How do I contact you outside of twitter?
```

Brian sent his email address. An hour later, Brian found an email in his inbox:

```
Subject: Your tweets
Brother, in the name of Allah, I greet you
and wish to know more about your plight.
You are right to seek revenge. But now I
caution you. Many say they want to walk
this path. Only a few actually do so. May
you choose wisely. Inshalla! For now, know
that your voice has been heard. Tell me
about yourself. Privately. Do not tweet
any of our discussions or share any of it
on social media.
```

Brian composed his reply immediately.

Subject: RE: Your tweets
Yazid, thank you for writing. And I also
greet you. I'm afraid Allah did not bless
me with the strength of these farm boys. I
am small and devout, and I love math.
I study the holy Quran as much as possible, but it is difficult to do here, and I
do not know Arabic. Allah will reveal this
to you anyway, so I will tell you—I can
barely pronounce my Muslim name, only my
American name. For this I am ashamed.
I wish to learn Arabic and learn of my
heritage. I want to join the holy cause
of ISIS. I may not be able to defeat my
enemies with my fists but perhaps with my
brains. I long for the day I am part of a
holy group doing the work of the Prophet.

•——————•

Atesh Zare smiled when he read the latest email from this American youth, Brian Cox. His enthusiasm could be extremely useful. Brian Cox would strike a blow against the Great Satan in the name of those Sunni ISIS dogs, leaving Iran to exploit the situation for the benefit of all true Shia Islam believers. But for now, he would cultivate the relationship and prepare this teenager for the coming war.

YET ANOTHER REJECTION

"Jerry, don't wear tennis shoes and white socks," Lynn said the morning after Jerry recovered the Maverick Marketing server.

"Nobody cares what color socks I wear."

"That shirt has holes in it."

"No, it doesn't."

"When I get done tearing it off of you, it will."

Jerry laughed. "I like it when you want to tear my clothes off."

"Just put on the new shirt. You need to look professional."

Like Klingon General Martok in *Star Trek: Deep Space Nine*, Jerry knew he would not win this battle with his wife. Best to order a tactical retreat and focus on the overall war. He pulled off his old shirt and reached for a new one. "Just don't buy any more new clothes. We have better ways to spend money."

An hour later, Jerry Barkley sat in Sally Brock's office again.

"Here's where you're vulnerable. While I was waiting for parts yesterday, I generated a port scan . . ."

"Port what?" Sally peered past him across the office, as if looking for an escape.

"A port is . . ." Sally's eyes wandered. "A port scan report . . ." She glanced at her watch. "Um, well, it shows how vulnerable you are to internet attacks," concluded Jerry. He leaned back in his chair and drew a hand down his face.

"Let me explain it this way. You're connected to the internet, and people you don't want in here are probing all the time. Think of it like somebody knocking on your front door where you live. You have three choices. You can open it, ignore it, or tell them to go away. But when you tell them to go away, you're really telling a potential attacker you're home. That's the last thing you want to do. That's what this port scan report is telling you about your internet connection."

"I'm not a techie, and I have no idea what you just told me," Sally said.

Jerry bit his lip. "There's a whole criminal industry that wants to get inside here. Why do you want to advertise to them?"

"I don't know what you're talking about."

"You're telling attackers around the world that you're here. It's like pinning a "kick me" sign on your back."

"Did some hacker break our server the other day?"

"I doubt it."

"Then, why are we wasting time on this?"

"We're not wasting time. First of all, you're never up against just some hacker. You're up against a whole underground industry of specialists, and they all collaborate in real time."

"More geek-speak."

"Do you use email?"

"Of course."

"So do bad guys. And they use other collaboration tools. I worked an issue a while ago where somebody in Ukraine came up with an exploit and sold it to some Russians. The Russians probably used a Chinese email relay service to spread phishing attacks across the country. And there are probably other pieces to that puzzle I never found out about."

"We don't keep national security secrets here," Sally said. "Thank you for fixing our server yesterday, but I have a meeting in a few minutes, so I don't have a lot of time."

Jerry had one shot left to get her attention.

"Okay. Swap those USB drives every Tuesday and Friday afternoon and check them every day like I showed you," Jerry said, "But you need to replace your server and network equipment and get everything out of that hot room. It's all going to fail again, and you could lose everything. I just told you about the security threat at your internet boundary, and we haven't even looked at your antivirus yet. You're sitting on a disaster that hasn't happened yet."

"We just want all this to run smoothly," Sally said. "We're a marketing company, not a tech company."

"To make this all run smoothly, you need to make some changes."

"What will that cost?"

"It won't be cheap. But if your business shuts down again, it will cost even more. If I put a detailed proposal together, would you consider it?"

"Of course."

Jerry delivered his proposal a week later. He met Sally in the front lobby. "I want you to know, I put lots of effort into this. You told me access to your proposal library is critical for your business. Without it, your whole company is shut down, which is how you were when we met last week. I used quality on a budget as my guideline, and I can't wait to show you what I cooked up."

"I have about fifteen minutes, and then I have to run to a meeting. We'll have to do the abbreviated version." She took her copy of Jerry's proposal and skimmed with her thumb to the "total cost" line on the last page.

Jerry rushed through his plan of attack. "What questions can I answer?"

"You've done a thorough job. Thanks for coming in, but we've decided to go a different direction. We're bringing in a cloud provider and planning to put all our documents in the cloud."

"What happens if your internet connection hiccups?" Jerry asked. "How do you get to your stuff if it's off in the cloud somewhere? How do you guard against viruses?"

"The vendor we chose has a system to address all those issues."

"Did they tell you how . . .?"

Jerry never finished the question as Sally turned her back and walked away, leaving him standing in the lobby. Alone.

"May I help you?" asked the receptionist.

"Huh?" Jerry shook his head. "No. You guys need to help yourselves first."

PHISHING

Frank Urbino slipped out of the nightclub and into the warm Miami evening.

"Leaving early tonight, Mr. Urbino? Want me to get the Lambo?"

"Yeah, I'm afraid so. Duty calls."

"And alone? Doesn't that end the streak?"

"Yeah. But I'll start another one this weekend." The valets laughed.

Back in his condo, Frank paced back and forth. How would he find those contacts? Same as always, start with the basics. He did a Google search for "wildcard search whois records" and found a website with this claim: "enables you to find every registered domain name in the com, net, org, edu, biz, us, info, and name zones that contains all of the search terms you enter, anywhere within the domain name itself. Our database is updated nightly to reflect the most recent changes to the Domain Names registry."

This looked like as good a place to start as any. He entered "truck" in the search box, and the website returned fifty sample results, with the promise of thousands more for $29.99. He bought the list. It had more than sixty thousand domain names. But some were truck dealerships; others were for sites to teach drivers or otherwise unrelated to moving freight. He also bought lists containing "logistics," "freight," "transport," and other similar words in their domain names.

Next, he found a marketing list service, complete with SIC code searches. He filled out the appropriate web forms and found seventy-eight thousand leads. He also bought that list.

He spent all night combining the domain name lists, eliminating irrelevant records, harvesting email addresses from any available "contact us" website links, and merging all that with the marketing list. By noon the next day, he had contacts from trucking companies across the United States. It wasn't perfect but would do on short notice. He started a chat session with Alma.

> **Ducem1:** Hey, Alma, I have the count you wanted. I found 161k email addresses for you.
> **Alma:** Excellent. I'll have the package I want delivered ready in a few days.

●————●

After fixing a discrepancy in a bill of lading, adjusting not one but two mistaken invoices, and hunting down a driver in Peoria to pick up a trailer in Moline for an emergency delivery to Beloit, Leah Anderson's mind was ready to explode. Just another day in the life of a truck dispatcher, but she needed a few seconds to clear her head. She took off her headset and reached for the picture of her husband and new baby. She smiled at the image of her family smiling for the camera. She loved living only five minutes away from the New Brighton Transport office in suburban New Brighton, Minnesota.

Her phone light blinked. That had to be Izy, checking in. Next week was Leah and her husband's turn to babysit Izy and Farah's kids for their husband and wife date night. Leah put her headset back on. "Hey, Izy, you wearing your lucky hat today?"

"Yeah, why?"

"I have a bonus load for you. The GPS shows you about twenty miles out of Ely."

"Sounds about right," Izy said. "And thanks."

"Call me after your drop-off, and I'll get you details."

Leah's computer chirped, signaling a new email. The subject said, "Please see the attached bill of lading and reconcile." Leah opened the email and then opened the attached document. A yellow bar appeared in the window above the document, saying, "Security warning. Macros have been disabled." A button next to the warning said, "Enable content." She clicked the button—how was she supposed to look at any document without enabling content?

The document looked like a bill of lading but didn't make sense. It was for a different trucking company, and she'd never heard of that customer. Maybe somebody sent this to the wrong Leah. She had never heard of the sender, but that was not unusual since most of the shipping paperwork flowed through her inbox. She deleted it and forgot about it.

Thousands of people from freight companies across the United States opened similar emails that day. Some contained instructions and attachments around bogus invoices. Others were similar to the fake bill of lading Leah Anderson opened. Still others had inquiries about non-existent shipments. Had anyone looked at the email headers, they would have found they originated from somewhere in Florida and were routed through a Chinese email relay service to their destinations.

In Tehran, Atesh Zare smiled as systems across the Great Satan began checking in once per hour with his confiscated command and control server, formerly under the exclusive control of that weasel Bahir Mustafa. Atesh still chuckled over the image of Bahir, cowering in Evin Prison like a dog. If there were pictures, perhaps Atesh would make one his screen saver.

Within a few days, the Iranian Ministry of Science, Research, and Technology had detailed schedules for freight shipments across the Great Satan.

Now for the next phase: use the Chinese data to go after the American CDC, the real prize.

Bahir Mustafa sat in his university office, watching dots light up across the United States as new drones in his botnet came online. The welts were healing, but his head ached after staring at a computer monitor too long.

Normally, dots lighting up would be good news. The more drones, the more powerful his botnet, the better for business. But that was before he had underestimated those ministers of, no, not idiocy, but madness.

He put his head in his hands. Atesh was right; he had been an arrogant fool. Somebody was watching and listening and recording his every interaction with the internet. And now, his days were numbered. As soon as the Ministry got what it wanted and didn't need him anymore, he would be an accident victim. Or worse—rousted from his home again in the middle of the night and tossed back into that hell hole, this time to rot forever. He was doomed.

Unless . . .

What about an alternate path to the internet? One that Atesh and his monsters would not find? He could use it to set up new command and control servers, perhaps at a collocation site in the West, out of their reach. Yes, that could work.

Who knows, maybe he could even ask for asylum in the West and search for his long-lost American father, the oil executive snake who left his pregnant mother during the 1979 revolution. Allah willing. Well, forget Allah—Bahir could learn the Western Christian words the same way he had learned Muslim words if it helped him get away from these thugs.

But first, how to get to the internet privately, away from prying eyes?

Satellites. Plenty of commercial satellite internet providers operated in Tehran and hopefully nobody would notice one more satellite dish on the roof of his data center building. Bahir would pay for it himself to keep it away from prying eyes snooping through university financial records. And then he could use it to relocate somewhere in the West. First, virtually, then, perhaps, physically before Atesh and his thugs made him disappear forever.

WEST AFRICA

Heather Magnussen peered through the face shield of her yellow protective suit and surveyed the makeshift hospital ward, filled with children's bodies devastated by war against an enemy too small to see with a normal microscope. A new Ebola virus strain was back with a vengeance across Sierra Leone in West Africa, frustrating researchers who had spent years developing and testing a vaccine against the original strains.

"Hi, Heather, how are you feeling today?" Five-year-old Lahai Taylor smiled as Heather approached her cot. It was the greeting Lahai gave every day and the reason Heather could not detach. Not this time. This girl was a fighter.

"And good afternoon to you too, bright-eyes."

"I like your blue eyes." She reached toward Heather's face shield but could not raise her arm high enough. Heather took her hand and held it.

Heather gently stroked Lahai's hair with her other hand. "Thanks." She squeezed Lahai's wrist to check her pulse.

"Heather, how long will I live?"

Heather blinked away tears. "Only God knows how to answer that question. But we have the best team in the world right here, and I promise we'll do everything we can to beat this thing together."

"Thank you," Lahai said, coughing.

As a blonde-haired, blue-eyed emergency room trauma nurse from St. Paul, Minnesota, Heather could not have come from anywhere more different than the Port Loko hospital north of Freetown where she was assigned. Although Minnesota was muggy in the summer, the rainy season in Sierra Leone made

Minnesota feel desert-like by comparison. Hospitals back home had modern equipment, sanitary conditions, and plenty of medicine in stock. The Port Loko hospital had donated IV fluid bags for patients, and tanks filled with bleachy water and outfitted with garden spray hoses for sanitation.

A seven-foot fence behind the main hospital surrounded the Ebola isolation area. The temporary buildings reminded Heather of a Midwestern pole barn city. Each building was long and narrow with a concrete floor and white plastic walls stretched over a wood frame. Plastic sheets also formed roofs over the top of a few prefabricated trusses. Five cots lined the inside long walls, leaving an aisle in the middle for yellow-suited caregivers to move among the patients. Volunteers in protective gear stocked supply shelves near the front.

The young patients looked up from their cots at yellow-suited caregivers with eyes begging for help. Many would never see the next day. Most who survived would never see their parents again. Their fragile, thin hands reached out for human contact any time a volunteer passed by.

Some late-stage patients, who, less than a week ago, were able to function, now bled from all their body openings and even through their skin. Most were unconscious, and none were able to move or communicate anymore. Others bled internally, frequently vomiting up blood and liquified pieces of organs.

But even surrounded by death and with her own potential death one mistake away, Heather could not imagine serving anywhere else. Despite the primitive conditions, her Médecins Sans Frontières team was filled with top professionals.

Little Lahai Taylor came in last week. She connected with Heather immediately, as did so many other younger patients. Heather watched Lahai's condition deteriorate every day and knew she was powerless to stop it. The professional approach would be detachment. It's not cruel; it's how we're able to function in less-than-ideal conditions. Triage, stabilize, move on. But sometimes . . .

Lahai turned and heaved onto the floor. Heather's training took over. The discharge was full of red and brown mucous. Not good. Please, Lord, heal this little girl. Or end her suffering and take her into your arms to a better place. Heather retrieved a disposable washcloth from the supply shelf, wiped Lahai's face, and dropped it on the floor. Somebody would come by later to hose everything on the floor with bleach water into a makeshift drain dug into the mud behind the temporary building. The smell of chlorine bleach was strong, but not strong enough to overcome the smell of death all across the ward.

"Heather, would you read me a happy story?"

"Uh, sure, let me see what I can find." While packing for her mission, something told Heather to bring along a few children's books. She brought enough to stock all the wards, and the books quickly became popular with the younger patients. She picked one up from the supply shelf.

"Here's a Dr. Seuss book."

"Who is Dr. Seuss?"

"He wasn't a medical doctor. He wrote children's books."

"I think I would like to be a doctor after I get well."

"Come visit me in Minnesota, and I'll introduce you to lots of doctors. But bring a coat. It snows in Minnesota. Sometimes the snow is this deep," Heather said, motioning with her hand about hip level.

"Does it all melt in the summer?"

"Sure. It's almost as hot as here. Almost."

Lahai's eyes drifted shut. She pushed them open. "I think I would like to visit in summer then."

Heather laughed as she opened the book. "Let's see . . . Here we are. The title of this book is *Green Eggs and Ham*. It's a funny story." She read the first page and paused to turn to the next page.

"Green eggs. That is funny," Lahai said. "But can we finish later? I should like to sleep a while."

"Sure, sweetie. I'll check back on you later."

Heather missed Lahai's greeting the next day. She looked down at Lahai's unconscious body and stroked her hair. She found a chair and sat, holding her hand. She sang softly.

"Amazing grace, how sweet the sound."

Lahai's lips turned up as in a smile. The color drained from her face. Her breathing stopped. Heather felt for a pulse. It was gone.

"That saved a wretch like me!"

A tear fell from Heather's eye and hit the bottom of her face shield. She watched life slip away from another innocent child, knowing she was powerless to stop it but grateful to God who brought the little girl home.

"I once was lost, but now am found. Was blind, but now I see."

"Lord, please accept this little girl named Lahai Taylor into your kingdom. Give her a life in heaven better than she had here on earth."

Heather tried to control her crying. She was a professional. As an ER nurse, she had seen many patients die. She knew she would see death on this mission. She knew the statistics. So, why was she here? What good was she doing? This was an innocent child, sentenced to die in this hell on earth. Her tears turned into sobs. A few nurses and orderlies touched her elbows and gently escorted her outside.

"Heather, your two hours in the suit were up more than thirty minutes ago," Clemence, her supervisor, a doctor from France, said. "Go decompress. And hydrate. I'll join you shortly."

"I couldn't help her," Heather said.

"Oui, there are many we will not help, despite our best efforts," Clemence said, looking across the ward filled with the sick and dying. "But you comforted her in her last minutes here on earth. And that is a help."

"Thank you, Clemence."

"De rien."

Heather made her way to the staging area separating the isolation area from the rest of the compound, where a volunteer trained observer followed CDC guidelines and helped her remove her apron, face shield, hood, shoe covers, and outer gloves, disinfecting her outer gloves before each step. Next, she carefully removed her respirator and coveralls, disinfecting her now-exposed inner gloves before each step. Finally, she sprayed down her shoes with a bleachy mix, disinfected her inner gloves one more time, and carefully removed them.

She washed her hands and then rubbed her eyes. She should have soaked her hands in another bleachy mix first.

Inside the ward, a doctor extracted a fluid sample from Lahai's now lifeless body before other volunteers lifted her remains into a bag and zipped it. They carried it outside to a waiting truck, already loaded with dozens of zipped bags. The truck's grim mission: deliver what used to be people to an incinerator built with money donated from a UN fund, where the bodies would be incinerated to kill the multiplying Ebola viruses.

After removing her suit, Heather paced past the tent city volunteer living quarters to a group of portable showers to start her rehydration routine. The shower buildings looked like outhouses with fifty-five-gallon drums on top, filled with water and warmed by the sun. After her shower, she drank a bottle of water in the tent she shared with seven other nurses. A generator provided electricity, which, in turn, allowed her to keep the battery charged on her most-prized possession—her cell phone, her lifeline to home. One more week left in her volunteer assignment.

The living area had a wi-fi connection, which somehow worked with a satellite to connect them to the internet. She wasn't sure how it worked or who paid for it, but each volunteer had a timeslot reserved for video calls home, and Heather's time was coming up. She launched the video app on her phone, and a few seconds later, Mike's rugged face appeared on her screen. She smiled.

"Hi."

"Hi, Heather. Hold the phone close."

Heather brought her phone closer to her face. She knew what Mike was looking for.

"Why were you crying?"

"A five-year-old little girl died today. Lahai Taylor. I knew her name. She knew my name. She came in last week, and every day, she asked me how *I* was feeling. Until today." Heather set the phone down and rubbed her eyes. "This is the most horrible disease. It's the devil himself murdering these people."

"I'm so sorry," Mike said. "How many is that now?"

"Too many. And I wish I could help them."

"I wish I could be there with you and help make you feel better."

Heather started to tear up again. "I miss you, too. I'll miss this place and the work here, but I can't wait to see you again for real, instead of over the phone."

"Well, maybe this will help make the time go by faster." Mike's camera turned to show Heather a familiar video image.

"Mike, why are you at my parents' house?"

Heather watched as her sister, two brothers, mom, and dad walked into the video frame. The video shook for a few seconds. Mike backed away from his phone and posed with the rest of her family.

"Can you see us all okay?" Mike asked.

"Yeah. What's going on?"

Three of Heather's roommates walked in behind her.

Mike reached for his back pocket and pulled out a small jewelry box. He opened it and showed its contents to the camera. Then he got down on one knee and faced his camera.

One of Heather's roommates screamed. Another opened the tent flap and shouted to anyone nearby. "Come here! Quick!"

Heather wiped her tears and laughed. And then she cried again. "Is this really happening?" she asked.

"Heather, will you . . ."

"Yes, yes, yes, yes!" she said.

She wiped her tears and watched as her brother playfully punched Mike in the shoulder. "About time, you wuss," he said.

"Finish asking!" her other brother said. "And don't mess it up."

Heather laughed, wiping away her tears. Her parents smiled over the video link. Her mom's eyes glistened.

"Marry me?" finished Mike.

"Yes, yes, yes!" Heather said. "I love you!"

By now, a dozen volunteers had gathered behind Heather. Somebody asked, "Did he just . . ."

Somebody else answered, "Yes, he did!"

"What did she say?"

"Yes!" cried Heather, turning to her impromptu audience. "Yes, a thousand times, yes!"

"I love you, too," Mike said over the video. "The ring isn't much, but it'll do until we can afford a better one." He picked up the ring and put it close to his camera so Heather could see it.

"It's a beautiful ring!" Heather said.

"Wait," one of Heather's roommates said. Let me take a picture of this for you. She took out her cell phone and snapped several pictures of Heather talking over the video link to her family and future husband, half a world away but connected for the next few minutes via the miracle of the internet.

Somebody asked, "Are we invited to your wedding?"

"Of course!"

●———●

One week later, Heather looked out the window on her long flight home and watched the West Coast of Africa recede. Lahai Taylor and the others would stay with her the rest of her life, and she vowed that someday she would return to Sierra Leone and try to find the families of all the patients she cared for. She knew she would be profoundly and forever changed by her experience in the makeshift Ebola isolation ward.

But, for now, she was tired. Maybe too tired. Probably adrenaline and letdown. Three months in tropical conditions in a hot isolation suit would make anyone tired. She drifted to sleep. The Atlantic Ocean rushed by below.

SPEAR PHISHING

Dr. Benjamin Alfred Donovan IV took a break from email and looked up at his favorite possession hanging on his office wall at the United States Centers for Disease Control in Atlanta—an 1860s-era black and white photo of the original Ben Donovan, taken after three years as a free man. "You'd be proud of me, Pops. We're this close. I can feel it. We're going to lick Ebola again. Thank you for enduring."

But this email he just opened didn't make sense. It was from a colleague and the subject said, "Results from the latest tests." The body of the message said, "Tentative positive results. See attached." That was it. But when he opened the attached zip file, nothing in the zip archive had anything even remotely resembling meaningful test results. The files looked more like random paragraphs of text strung together.

Even more peculiar, he checked his colleague's calendar and noticed she was presenting at a symposium. Ben would need to ask what that crazy email was all about the next time they were both in Atlanta at the same time.

For now, there were more important issues to deal with. An epidemiology conference was coming up at the University of Minnesota, and in the wake of the 2014 Ebola outbreak, Ben was on a panel to discuss the medical community's recommendations for future policy decisions in the event of an outbreak here in the United States. This matter took on added relevance because another Ebola outbreak raged in West Africa, and CDC would no doubt be asked to get involved.

Ben read the next several emails. They were field reports from Doctors Without Borders describing conditions in West Africa. Medical volunteers from around the world were mounting another heroic fight against the disease. He leaned back in his chair, pondering how CDC would respond if this latest strain was to show up in the United States.

Ben forgot all about that zip file as he composed new emails to other doctors about how best to respond this time and how to catalog specimens.

Half way around the world, Atesh's team also began cataloging specimens as newly installed malware buried in that zip file on Ben's and other doctors' computers began exercising their payloads. The spear phishing attack against Ben and other CDC doctors was a group effort, started by an anonymous crazy man from Ireland who wanted to make money, facilitated by the roster of CDC employees so generously contributed by the Chinese, and refined by a group of Iranian programmers who developed that zero-day vulnerability into a useful attack.

After a few days, Atesh and his team had detailed schedules for every CDC staff member. Sooner or later, one of the Great Satan volunteers in West Africa would come home sick. And Atesh would be ready. Yes, this was worth every *rial*. And more.

EBOLA IN THE HEARTLAND

Seven days into the government-mandated twenty-one-day quarantine, Heather Magnussen wanted to break protocol. After months of being on a different continent, she was now so close to Mike, she almost smelled his aftershave on the summer breeze. She craved his touch. His nose snuggled against her neck while his body spooned against hers in the swing bed. His hand on hers when he slipped the ring on her finger.

Heather flung herself on the sofa and covered her face with a pillow. Fourteen more days.

Suddenly it was too hot, even with the windows open. She sat up. A wave of dizziness hit. A jackhammer pounded behind her eyes. She reached for the digital thermometer. Her hand trembled.

Ninety-nine degrees at noon, passing one hundred thirty minutes later. After watching so much death in Sierra Leone, she might not live to kiss Mike again. She fought the urge to panic. She was a professional. And this was the United States, not Sierra Leone.

"911, what is your emergency?"

"Hi, my name is Heather Magnussen, and I'm pretty sure I have Ebola."

A few seconds passed. "Um, would you mind repeating that?"

"I was a nurse volunteer at an Ebola clinic in Sierra Leone in Africa. I've been home for a week, and now I'm showing Ebola symptoms. I'll need an ambulance."

"I'm, um, searching for the response protocol. We had a meeting about this possibility a few months ago."

"What's your name?" Heather asked."

"Denise. Here it is. The first triage question I'm supposed to ask is, why do you think you have Ebola? You covered that already. I'm sending an ambulance."

"Thanks, Denise. Make sure the driver and paramedics have isolation suits. I probably need to go to Unity Hospital in Fridley."

"Yes. That's on the checklist. I'll stay on the line with you."

"Thanks. Is it okay if I call my fiancé?"

"I'll patch him in. What's his phone number?"

Mike answered a few seconds later.

"Mike, it's me. I think I have Ebola."

"Oh, no."

"Say a prayer for me, please." Heather started crying.

"The ambulance is fifteen minutes out," Denise said.

"Thanks." Heather paced in front of the window but sat again when her legs felt wobbly. Her hands shook. Her training told her this was mostly an adrenaline response to fear, but she knew all too well what was coming. She fought to keep her composure. She knew she would need that adrenaline later, as this predator tried to consume her body. She didn't want to waste it now. "I'll take my temp again."

"We'll get through this together, Heather," Mike said.

After a few minutes, Heather heard sirens approaching. Her fever was now up to 101.

A FIFTY-FOUR-HOUR WORKDAY

Jerry Barkley's watch said ten o'clock. One of these days, he'd get a watch that said a.m. and p.m. The sun was up, so it had to be morning. Lynn had insisted today was Saturday and he needed sleep. But first, he wanted eggs, and that was why he was in his car on his way to Sam's Club. Since it apparently really was Saturday, he was going to pick up some eggs and fix a nice breakfast and then crash for a few hours. Anyone have a problem with that?

It was the finale to his private disaster recovery operation on a budget. Three, count 'em, three, server hard drives he'd bought from some clown on eBay failed simultaneously early Thursday morning, knocking the Barkley IT Services website offline and shutting down his company. It was embarrassing.

But all that was behind him now. After fifty-four hours and hundreds of dollars for replacement hard drives, he had fully recovered everything. Thank God for good backups. And thank archive.org for copies of every page from the company website he'd built and meant to backup but had never gotten around to it. He still wasn't sure how Friday had come and gone.

But now, it was time to celebrate. With an egg breakfast, since it was morning. He should get some bread, too. And maybe some bacon. And, may as well put gas in the car. The glamorous life of an independent IT consultant operating on a shoestring. He would have to remember this moment the next time somebody complained about his hourly billing rate.

Jerry was startled when his cell phone rang.

"Jerry, this is Sally Brock with Maverick Marketing. You worked on our server two months ago."

"Um, yes, I remember," Jerry said. The disappointment still stung. Next time he met someone with a server stuffed in a hot utility closet, he was walking away. But down deep, he knew better. He needed customers to pay bills.

"Hang on a second." Jerry finished filling his gas tank and drove to a parking spot. "So, what can I do for you this *Saturday* morning?"

"We're trying to get a proposal out before three o'clock so our potential client can evaluate it over the weekend on his flight overseas, but we can't access some of the material we need to put it together. You must have missed something when you worked on our server."

"I thought you were putting everything in the cloud."

"We haven't finished that project yet."

Jerry rubbed his eyes. "Okay, let's try a couple of diagnostics to help figure out what's going on. Do you still have the icon to look at your proposals?"

"Yes, I use it all the time."

"What happens when you click it?"

"It shows me all the proposals. That's not broken."

"Well, what is broken?"

"I just told you—I can't get to the other material I need."

Jerry pursed his lips. Something didn't add up.

"Jerry, are you still there?"

"Yeah. What's the material you can't get to?"

"We need a few testimonial quotes from our customer's customers in a publicity package, and we want a sample in our proposal. But we're not able to access them."

"Where are these quotes?"

"On different websites."

Jerry ran his hand over his head.

"Jerry?"

"Yeah, I'm still here."

"We need you to come in and finish fixing our server. Frankly, we're a little disappointed you didn't catch this the last time when we were down all day."

"Wait a minute—you're having trouble getting to websites?"

"Yes."

"Why do you think that's a server problem?"

"Because the server stores the information we gather from websites."

"Right, you store information on your server, but accessing websites isn't a server thing. It's an internet thing."

"But, you said yourself, if our server isn't running, we can't access the internet."

"That's true. But you just proved your server is working. Try another diagnostic test for me. Launch a web browser and go to www.google.com."

"Okay . . ." After nearly a minute, Sally said, "It's taking a long time." Another minute passed. "There it is."

"Okay," Jerry said, "now pick one of the proposals at random on your server and bring it up."

"We don't need to work on any of those."

"I know. Just humor me. Click on your icon and bring up one of those proposals. You can close it down without saving anything." Jerry pinched the bridge of his nose.

"It came up."

"Any delays or did it feel normal?"

"It felt normal."

"Your server is still a ticking time bomb, but it's not your problem. Your problem is at your internet boundary. Which was also a mess as I recall."

"You know I'm not a technician. We just need you to come in and fix it."

"What happened to your cloud vendor?"

"They aren't able to respond to us as quickly as we need this morning."

"If I fix your emergency this morning, do I have a shot at being your IT service vendor?"

"We'll consider you for future projects, but we've already made our selection."

"So, I'm good enough to fix your weekend emergency, but not good enough to be your regular partner?"

"I wouldn't characterize it that way, no."

"Well, how would you characterize it?"

"We need an immediate resource to help us through this situation. And we thought you might appreciate the work opportunity."

"Look, Sally, normally I'd jump at the chance to help you because I do need the work. But I've had about one hour of sleep in the past three days, and I'm about to eat some food and go to bed. What was wrong with the proposal I gave you anyway?"

"I'm sure your proposal was good, but we had to go with the other vendor."

"Your mind was made up before I ever delivered it."

"I spent time with you that day and evaluated it. We needed a more business-focused approach. Yours was too technical."

"Too technical. Meaning the part where I talked you through a couple of diagnostic tests to figure out your problem?"

"I'm not a techie. I just need somebody to help us gather what we need so we can deliver our proposal."

"How critical is this proposal?"

"It's for a major piece of business. But we have to deliver it before three o'clock today."

"How much money does this proposal represent?"

"Millions."

"What happens if I help you through this? Do you leave me standing in your lobby again after your emergency is over?"

"Of course not! I told you, we'll consider using you for additional IT projects."

"You can do better than that. If I come in, I'll bring in a piece of my equipment to find out what's going on with your traffic. If I solve your problem, you'll get rid of whatever my competitor put in at your boundary and replace it with my stuff."

"I can't make that commitment."

"And I'm having trouble staying awake. Why don't you call me Monday and we'll talk about it then?"

"We can't wait until Monday."

Maybe he could salvage a victory for a change. Which would be sweet after recovering from this disaster. But he'd been jerked around before. Too many times. But leaving a customer in a lurch?

"Let me see what I can do. I need something from you when I come in."

"What's that?"

"Several bottles of cold water to help me stay awake. I don't drink coffee."

"I can arrange for that."

"Groovy. I have to build a bridge. That will take an hour. And it will take some more time to drive to your site."

"What does that mean, to build a bridge?"

"It's a piece of equipment I'll use to tap into your internet connection to see what's flying in and out of your site. It'll take me about an hour to set it up. Oh—and one more thing."

"What else?"

"I'm not a resource; I'm a person. Don't ever call me a resource again."

He was home a few minutes later. Lynn looked tired. Anne's red hair swished in a ponytail as she loaded the dishwasher.

Seven-year-old Alex and three-year-old Aaron ran from their bedroom. "Grandpa!" They hugged Jerry's legs while their crazy black Labrador Retriever jumped in the air and head-butted Jerry's chin. As the dog landed, one paw smacked the top of Aaron's head. Aaron burst into tears and ran for his mom in the kitchen. But he tripped and hit his nose on the kitchen floor. The dog, sensing a play opportunity, pounced and barked at Aaron, who screamed as if a body part were being amputated. Anne scooped him up, and Aaron buried his head in her chest, sobbing. A few seconds later, he squirmed out of mom's arms and chased his big brother and the dog down the hallway, laughing and screaming.

"Where's the groceries?" Lynn asked.

"I never made it inside the store. I need to do a little work first. I'll be downstairs."

"That's it?" Lynn asked. "We only see you hunched over a computer for three days and you walk in and head for the basement?"

"Yeah, what's up with that, Dad?" Anne asked. "Your grandsons missed you. Spend some time with them."

"I will later," Jerry said. "But a customer called a minute ago, and I have to look into it. Gotta take the work when it comes. And then I need some sleep."

"Do what you have to do," Lynn said.

"This sucks," Anne said.

Jerry trudged downstairs. One hour later, he loaded a small computer in his car and left again.

He arrived at Maverick Marketing thirty minutes later.

"What is that?" Sally asked, looking at the computer under Jerry's arm.

"The bridge I told you about. It'll tell me what's going on in your network."

"We can't let you connect anything to the network without permission."

Jerry shook his head. "I'm tired, and I'm not in any mood to dink around. If you want to solve your problem, I need to connect my box."

"Our vendor told us not to connect anything without permission."

"Well, then, have a nice day. I'll send you my bill for driving across town." Jerry turned toward the door. The clicking from people typing on keyboards stopped. Heads popped up above cubicle walls, watching Jerry head toward the door. Some glanced at Sally. Others looked down and shook their heads. The office became silent.

"Stop!" Sally said. "Jerry, just wait a minute!"

Jerry turned. "If you want me to fix your problem, then get me what I need and let me do my job."

"Fine," Sally said. "Do your thing."

Jerry invited Sally to watch as he setup his appliance.

"I've tapped into your network just inside your firewall. From here, I'll see everything in and out. If you have something unusual going on, I'll find it." He logged into his appliance and started to work.

"Hey, Sally, what's the system at IP address 192.168.32.115?"

"What's an IP address?" Sally asked.

"Never mind. I'll find it on your server."

A few minutes later, Jerry found his culprit.

"Sally, who owns the computer named 'drew'?"

"That's probably Andrew's computer, our company owner's nephew. Why?"

"Because that computer is blasting traffic across the internet. I'm capturing and recording it. It's flying out of here like water out of a broken fire hydrant."

"What do we do?"

"For now, disconnect it."

"I don't think Andrew would like that."

"You want to call him?"

"Not on a Saturday."

"Well, what do you want to do?"

"What happens if disconnecting it doesn't work? Or if it breaks Andrew's computer?"

"It'll work. And it won't break Andrew's computer.

"How do we disconnect it?"

"Just show me where it is."

Sally brought Jerry to Andrew's cubicle in a corner of the office. The desk was strewn with papers and opened cardboard boxes. Glancing at the boxes, Jerry saw several computer game titles he recognized. Two twenty-seven-inch monitors filled the back of the desk, with a keyboard and trackball at the front. An unopened cardboard box sat in the office chair.

Jerry shook his head, crawled under the desk, and disconnected the network cable from this computer. Then he trudged back to his appliance and watched for a few more seconds.

"How does the internet feel now?" He already knew the answer.

"Snappy!" Sally said after browsing a few websites.

"Groovy," Jerry said. "You might want to have somebody look at that computer. I suggest you keep it off your network until somebody cleans it up."

Jerry was home an hour later. He walked into his bedroom, sat on his bed, and turned on the TV. "The Rifleman!" said an off-camera announcer. Chuck Connors looked into the camera and walked down the dusty main street of a western town on a 1959 Hollywood set. He fired twelve shots from his hip and twirled and reloaded his rifle. Jerry put his head on a pillow and stretched his legs. Just for a minute.

What felt like a few seconds later, Alex and Aaron jumped on his lap. Jerry woke up and grunted. It was late afternoon, and a John Wayne movie blared on the TV.

"Wanna smell my stinky armpit?" taunted Jerry.

"Oooohhh, yuck!" they both yelled in mock horror.

"Nice to see you join the family," Lynn said.

"Jet-lag is my friend."

"Are you done playing with all those servers in the basement?" Lynn asked.

"Yeah."

"Are you eating dinner with your family tonight?"

"Huh? Oh, yeah, that sounds good," Jerry said." Turning to Alex and Aaron, he said, "Okay, guys, want me to throw you down the stairs?"

Both boys ran screaming and squealing down the hallway, with Jerry stumbling after them, arms flailing like a swamp monster.

"I just spent three days chasing your grandsons while you holed up in the basement. You owe me."

Jerry stopped chasing the boys and hugged his wife. "It will all pay off."

Lynn shook her head and smiled. "I like it better when you're upstairs with us."

TRAFFIC

Jerry rubbed his eyes. At four o'clock in the morning, he should have been upstairs in bed next to his wife, not staring at patterns of hex numbers on a computer monitor in his basement. But those hex numbers in the packet traces he'd collected from Maverick Marketing told a story that made no sense. Why was that workstation interacting with *The Onion Router* (TOR) anonymizer service and a local company named New Brighton Transport? And why did he care?

Good questions. He cared because it was a mystery, and because something was wrong. Onion routing was a hassle, and people who took the trouble to use TOR either wanted to keep secrets from totalitarian governments, or they were crooks who didn't want to get caught. Which meant somebody had to be using Maverick Marketing as a pawn, because if they were doing something crooked, why call Jerry to diagnose it? So, what does a trucking company have in common with a marketing company interacting with a TOR anonymizer relay to who-knows-where? And why *this* marketing company, with less technology expertise than his second-grade grandson? He leaned back in his chair and closed his eyes. Just for a few seconds. He woke fifteen minutes later and his neck hurt. He stretched and trudged to bed.

●———————●

"Hey, Sally, I'm on my way over to your place. I was looking at the data I collected Saturday, and that workstation is part of something big and ugly." It was mid-morning Monday. Sally would never return his voicemail.

He hung up and dialed the main number.

"Maverick Marketing, how may I direct your call?" asked a perky receptionist.

"Hi, this is Jerry Barkley. We met on Saturday when I fixed your internet problem, and I'm coming over to do some follow-up."

"I'll transfer you to Sally."

"I already left her a voicemail. Just get me in front of that workstation we disconnected on Saturday."

"I don't know what you're talking about. I wasn't here Saturday."

"Just get me in front of that workstation. I'll be there in a few minutes."

Jerry put on his tennis shoes and grabbed a box of cereal and a cup of water and put them in his car. Breakfast of champions for active people on the go. He chuckled at his own private joke.

●———————●

"Jerry, why did Cindy pull me out of an important meeting to meet you here?" Sally Brock asked as Jerry walked into the receptionist area.

Jerry looked at the receptionist and mouthed, "Thank you." Turning to Sally, "Because somebody is messing with that workstation we disconnected on Saturday, and we need to see what's going on."

"Look," Sally said, "we appreciate you coming in on Saturday to get us through a difficult period. But we didn't ask for any follow-up, and now we need to run our business. If there's something wrong with Andrew's workstation, we'll have our IT support company address it. But thanks for your feedback." Sally turned to walk away.

Jerry watched her for a second. "Do you have any confidential material inside your computers? Maybe a major proposal you don't want the whole world to see? Because, there's a good chance somebody is looking at it right now."

Sally's back stiffened. She turned.

"Are you trying to blackmail me?"

"What? No! First of all, it's not blackmail; it's extortion. And second, I'm not the bad guy. I'm the guy who found your problem. And I'm trying to tell you some clown owns that computer."

Sally glared. She took a deep breath. "I will say this only once. If we find you've taken any of our confidential data, you will regret the day you were born. We've been threatened before by people much bigger than you."

Jerry laughed. It turned into guffaws. He coughed and his eyes started to water.

"Do you find this amusing?"

"Yeah." He wiped his eyes. "I don't know why I go to the trouble." He shook his head and wiped his eyes again. "And I'll only ask this question only once. Do you want to be another clueless victim, or do you want to know who's messing with you?"

Sally paused. She put her hands on her hips. "What do you want?"

"I need to look at that workstation more closely."

"Out of the question. It belongs to our company owner's nephew."

"And as I recall, he loaded it down with computer games. It has malicious software inside, and we need to find out what it is."

"What do you propose?"

"Let me clone its hard drive."

"What does that mean?"

"I can boot that workstation from a DVD and run a program that makes an image of its hard drive onto something else. Then I can analyze it at my place with my own tools."

Sally looked at Jerry for a few seconds. "If I say yes to this, what does that do to Andrew's computer?"

"Nothing. I use that copy to build another workstation and put it under a microscope."

"If anything breaks on Andrew's computer, it's on you to fix. And we're not paying for it."

"Andrew's computer is already broken. I won't make it any worse. You can you use your new IT support company for that."

Sally looked at Jerry, exposing just a hint of a smile. Jerry met her gaze. "Okay. You have fifteen minutes."

"I need more like two or three hours."

"Uggh," Sally said as she shook her head. "Follow me."

Four hours later, Jerry walked into Sally's office. "I have what I need. I'll let you know what I find. Do *not* connect that computer to your network until it's cleaned up. And if your IT support company can't handle it, you have my phone number."

Jerry spent the rest of the day setting up an isolated environment and building a virtual machine based on the disk image from that workstation. It was up and running by midnight and interacting with TOR a few minutes later. Having trouble keeping his eyes open, Jerry crashed for the night at 12:40 a.m.

•————•

Twenty-seven miles south of Salt Lake City, in the middle of a Utah moonscape on the west side of State Highway 68, sits one of the world's largest data center facilities. It cost more than 1.5 billion dollars to build and spans twenty buildings and more than one million square feet, including a one hundred thousand square foot Tier III data center.

The United States National Security Agency is vague about the purpose of its newest property but acknowledges it stores massive amounts of data. The United States National Security Agency is also vague about why it keeps thousands of 1U servers in the bowels of telecom companies and cloud facilities across the United States. As are other spy agencies in their own countries.

And somewhere inside NSA headquarters in Fort George G. Meade, Maryland, in a sea of anonymous cubicles, one anonymous data analyst responded to a yellow event. The algorithms from Utah called out a new actor in Minnesota interacting with the TOR anonymizer service, starting shortly after 1 a.m. eastern time. Which, by itself, would not be noteworthy. But a corresponding increase in traffic from a TOR exit relay in Germany made it very noteworthy.

The TOR Project and the NSA are sometimes friends, sometimes foes. When friendly organizations use the TOR anonymizer service, TOR is a friend. But when hostile entities use it, TOR is an enemy. This new actor in Minnesota? Hard to say, but probably hostile.

The system flagged that destination IP Address as the master command and control (C&C) node in Tehran for the Zagros botnet. Which put the probability at seventy-six percent that this new Minnesota actor was up to no good.

The Zagros botnet was a long-time NSA foe. It first appeared around 2003 and used screensavers packaged from stunning pictures from the Zagros Mountains in Iran as bait to ensnare anyone who downloaded them. NSA staffers had monitored this botnet as it grew to hundreds of thousands of computers around the world and watched it evolve into ever-more sophisticated malware. But hatching new C&C nodes in the United States was a new twist. This was the second to show up in Minnesota in just the past couple weeks.

A routine whois lookup on the domestic IP address for this latest Minnesota traffic showed it belonged to a contractor named Barkley IT Services. Why was this Barkley outfit suddenly showing all the footprints of a fully functional C&C node? Something was up. Time to file a report.

———•———

"Hi, this is Jerry Barkley." At half past seven in the morning, this must be another first-thing-in-the-morning trouble call. So much for checking email and easing into the day after another long night. The caller ID looked familiar.

"Good morning, Jerry, this is Special Agent Ronald Blackwell with the Minneapolis-area FBI office. We're working on an investigation and wondering if you could help us out."

Jerry started pacing. Dealing with the FBI was always an adventure. And it generally started with a phone call. "Well, good morning to you, too, Agent Blackwell. How's Connor Duncan these days? I haven't talked to him since we nailed those Russians at Bullseye Stores."

"I wouldn't know. Would you be able to come in this morning?"

"You want me to drop everything and drive downtown? What's up?"

"We'd like to talk to you, and the matter does have some urgency."

"I can be there in a couple hours. I need to make some phone calls and rearrange some things. You guys will give me a voucher to pay for my parking, right?"

"We're not in downtown Minneapolis anymore. We moved to a campus in Brooklyn Center, and the parking is free. So, we'll see you at ten?"

"Make it ten thirty, and you guys pay for my mileage. It's about a sixty-mile round trip."

"Fine. We'll see you then."

The new FBI campus looked like a mini-city behind a wrought-iron fence. Outbuildings with armed guards protected both entry gates. Jerry approached the nearest guard building.

"Show me an ID," one armed guard said.

Jerry dug out his wallet and showed the guard his driver's license. The guard waved a portable scanner over it and handed it back. "Be advised that starting next year, you'll need an enhanced driver's license to get in here. Or a passport."

"Why, is this a foreign country?"

"Minnesota driver's licenses don't meet federal standards."

"But I'm okay for now, right?"

"You can't bring that cell phone in here."

"Do you have a locker or somewhere I can put it while I'm here?"

"I suggest your car."

"Fine." Jerry trudged back to his car and returned.

"Please empty your pockets and step through the visitor scanner," the guard said.

Jerry emptied his pockets into a bowl and set it on an airport-style conveyer belt that disappeared into a scanner. He started toward a body scanner.

Another guard blocked his path. "You can't go in unless we scan your shoes."

"Why didn't anyone tell me that before?" Jerry asked.

"Sir, you need to comply."

Jerry took a breath and placed his shoes on the conveyer belt.

"You'll also need to take off your belt."

Jerry followed instructions. "Guys, this is getting weird."

The guard looked him up and down. "Please proceed through the body scanner."

Jerry passed through the body scanner and waited on the other side. The conveyer belt had stopped. It backed up, stopped again, and inched forward. Two other guards watched a video image on the conveyer belt scanner and huddled quietly. One gestured toward Jerry.

A third guard met Jerry after he passed through the body scanner.

"What are those guys looking at?" Jerry asked.

"Please follow me," the guard said. He led Jerry to an area near the inside end of the conveyer belt and passed a wand up and down Jerry's pants. Then he put on a pair of surgical gloves.

"What is going on?" Jerry asked.

"I need to pat you down. Please stand with your legs spread apart and lift your arms over your head."

"You're kidding, right?"

The guard stood, waiting.

Jerry assumed the position, and the guard went to work. The other two guards were still huddled around the video image on the conveyer belt scanner.

After his pat-down, Jerry waited for his property to come through.

The guard who frisked him said. "Sir, we have a problem with one of the items from your pockets. Is there anything you want to tell us about?"

Jerry rolled his eyes. "Maybe, I dunno. What's the problem?"

"You have disallowed items. What did you want to tell us about?"

"Oh. Well, um, okay. Um, if you're hungry and in a hurry, bring some cereal and water with you in the car. But you want cereal that doesn't make your hands sticky. If you wash your hands and the bathroom's out of paper towels, use your socks to dry your hands. And when a bureaucrat wants you to drive across town to help out, just say no. You want to show me what's disallowed?"

Jerry's guard motioned to the others. Jerry's property appeared on the inside of the conveyer belt.

"After you zapped my stuff with all that radiation, am I gonna glow all day?"

Another armed guard joined Jerry's guard, blocking the path to the conveyer belt. Jerry's guard, still wearing gloves, picked up the bowl and examined its contents.

"Here it is." He picked up a pair of fingernail clippers. "These are disallowed."

"You guys went to all that trouble for a pair of fingernail clippers?"

"They're disallowed. Trying to smuggle disallowed items into a federal jurisdiction is a felony."

"What? C'mon, guys, they're fingernail clippers. How am I supposed to know that fingernail clippers are on the bad list?"

"We do have a website where we spell that out. Weapons are not allowed in here."

Jerry shook his head. "Fine. How about you hang on to them, and I'll pick them up on the way out?"

"We can't accept liability for disallowed items," one of the guards said.

"Guys, they're fingernail clippers." Jerry stared at the guard. After a few seconds, Jerry grinned and nodded his head. "Why don't I take these back to the car?"

"That would be acceptable," the guard said.

Jerry put on his shoes and belt, put his items back in his pockets, and proceeded through the approved exit under the watchful eye of his armed escort.

He was back a few minutes later. "Do you guys have any hospital robes? If I strip down to my underwear and put on one of those robes while I'm here, will that make you happy?"

"Please empty your pockets and proceed through the scanner."

Jerry rolled his eyes. "You guys want my belt and shoes, too, right?"

After another security scan, one guard escorted Jerry into the main building where Blackwell was waiting. They shook hands, and Blackwell escorted him to a first-floor interview room where another agent was waiting.

Both agents wore blue suits. Blackwell had a red tie. The other agent had a yellow tie. Blackwell's hairline was receding, and Jerry predicted in another five years, most of the jet-black hair on his head would be gone. Jerry took a mental note in case he needed to break some tension with a bald-guy joke.

"Jerry, this is Special Agent Jake Channing, in charge of cyberterrorism," Blackwell said. The other agent had short, brown hair and blue eyes and looked like a Hollywood movie star.

"Nice to meet you," Jerry said, shaking Channing's hand. They directed Jerry to a chair on one side of an oval table in the middle of the room. Blackwell and Channing sat on the other side, facing him. Jerry looked up at the fluorescent light above him, recessed into a suspended ceiling. At least it doesn't have a swinging lightbulb. "Before we get started, can you guys get me some kind of voucher for my mileage getting here?"

"We can handle that later. But first, how long have you been an IT contractor?" Channing asked.

"Since 1994," Jerry said, leaning forward. "This sounds like déjà vu all over again. Do you guys know Connor Duncan?"

Channing and Blackwell exchanged glances.

"That's the second time you've asked about Agent Duncan," Blackwell said. "Why?"

"Well, we worked together. The breach at Bullseye Stores. We spent most of a night together sniffing out a Russian crook. It'd be nice to say hi. What's he up to?"

"We don't know him," Channing said.

"How many FBI guys work here?" Jerry asked.

"It's a medium-sized office. But Agent Duncan is no longer associated with the FBI," Blackwell said. "I looked him up after you mentioned him earlier. I'm afraid he left the FBI before our time in this office."

"Really? So, did he retire or what?" Jerry asked.

"And there's no record of a Jerry Barkley working on the Bullseye incident," Channing said.

"That figures," Jerry said, sitting back in his chair. "Well, guys, I was there." He probed the wall behind Blackwell and Channing with his eyes.

"What are you looking for?" Channing asked.

"I'm just curious. Where's the camera?"

"Why do you assume there's a camera?"

"Because you guys sat me in this chair. So, there must be a camera somewhere, facing me. And mics. I help out with an event on top of Medicine Lake every winter, and I have a terrible time with my built-in mics. What kind of sound quality do you guys get in here? Maybe you could play some of this back for me when we're done. Does it sound like we're in a tunnel?"

Blackwell and Channing exchanged glances.

"Of course, you guys don't face the same problems in here as I do on the ice. It's the background noise with all the generators and other stuff. When I try to get people's voices, the background noise overwhelms it. I'm not a sound engineer, and it drives me nuts. If you guys have any sound engineers, I'd love to pick their brain."

"We're not technicians," Channing said.

"I didn't figure you were. But since I drove across town and went through a strip-search to get in here, maybe you could free up somebody for a few minutes."

"Possibly later," Channing said.

"Okay, fair enough. So, what can I help you with today?"

"Have you ever been to Iran?" Channing asked.

"What?"

"It's a simple question. We want to know if you've ever visited Iran."

Why are they asking me about Iran? Oh, wow—I wonder if this about that workstation. I'm talking to Iran, huh. What made them notice it? And what else are these guys watching? Bureaucrats with power. Anything I say can and will be used against me . . .

"No. Why is that important?"

"Tell us about any dealings you've had with anyone from Iran."

"I don't know anyone in Iran." Jerry shifted in his chair. "Why don't you guys tell me why I'm here."

"What do you know about botnets?" Channing asked.

"You gotta be kidding me. If you've got a botnet problem, I can help. I'm working on a botnet problem right now. Connor Duncan and I went through this with Bullseye Stores when I sniffed out what was going on with their servers."

"That's not what our records indicate," Blackwell said.

"Really? Well, what do your records indicate?"

"Special Agent Duncan led the forensic team that uncovered the parameters of the cyberattack against Bullseye Stores and shut it down."

"Huh. Do your records say anything about the people who spent all night at the store on Lake Street figuring it out?"

Channing and Blackwell exchanged glances.

"Figures. Government CYA."

"Jerry, we checked. You were never an informant or a contractor to the FBI," Channing said.

"That's right. So, what?"

"So, how were you involved in the Bullseye Stores incident?"

"A couple ways. I was one of the forty million victims. I called Uncle Sam Bank, and we chased down every single transaction on my card. And then I called the FBI, and you guys blew me off."

"You said you spent all night at a Bullseye store?" Channing asked.

"That's right. Connor Duncan, some Bullseye people, and me."

"What did you do?"

"I bought a sandwich and did a bunch of analysis to find my credit card number where it shouldn't have been."

"How were you in a position to be in this store all night with our forensics team?" Channing asked.

Jerry laughed. "I *was* the forensics team that night. The FBI guys looked at lots of server logs and chased down the exfiltration vectors over the next few days. I chased down the core of the attack."

"How do you account for us having no record of your involvement?" Channing asked.

"There are lots of things about the United States Federal Government I don't know how to account for."

Channing stroked his chin and stared at Jerry.

"Guys, I was there. And I wasn't working for the FBI; I was working for Uncle Sam Bank. Maybe that's why your records are messed up."

"I thought you said you're an IT contractor," Blackwell said.

"That's right."

"Then, how is it you were working for Uncle Sam Bank?"

"The bank was my customer. Now, you guys want to tell me why I'm here?"

"We're investigating unusual internet traffic with Iran," Blackwell said.

"And how do I fit into this puzzle?"

"You tell us."

Jerry rolled his eyes. "I don't have ESP." He paused. "Are you guys watching my internet traffic?"

"No," Blackwell said.

Jerry leaned forward and put his hands on the table. "You know, the FBI has jerked me around for a long time. I called you guys back in 2000 with a compromised DNS server. You blew me off. I helped nail an embezzler back in 2002 after you guys took five years to work that case. You guys blew me off in 2013 with my credit card problem, and I helped you out with Bullseye Stores anyway. And now, you guys are sniffing my internet traffic and won't own up to it. And you expect me to answer a bunch of questions? You should apologize for invading my privacy."

"We know you're exchanging internet traffic with Iran," Channing said. "And we want to know why."

"If you're not sniffing my internet traffic, then what makes you so sure?"

"You tell us," Channing said.

"I don't like it when people are mysterious with me." Jerry leaned back and interlocked his fingers behind his head. "Tell ya what. Why don't you guys demonstrate some good faith here? Where's the camera?"

Blackwell and Channing exchanged glances again.

"It's in the ceiling," Channing finally said.

"Where?"

Channing pointed to a spot next to the light box where a tiny, silver-colored wire hung about an inch below the light.

Jerry stood to get a closer look. "Wow, I would have never noticed that. Where would I get one of those?"

"We wouldn't know," replied Blackwell.

"Huh. What's the audio quality like in here?"

"Let's get back to your internet traffic with Iran," Blackwell said.

"Fair enough. Like I said, I'm working on a botnet problem. From your questions, my guess is the C&C server must be in Iran. How do you guys know that?"

"C&C?" Blackwell asked.

"Command and control. The mothership controlling the drones all over the world."

"Are you aware Iran is an enemy of the United States?" Blackwell asked.

Jerry rolled his eyes. "Really? Really? And are you aware that wasting my time is a lousy way to win me as a friend and influence me? Let's cut the crap, or I'm walking out of here right now."

"That would be ill advised," Blackwell said. "Please answer our questions."

Jerry looked at both agents. They were serious. He leaned back in his chair.

"Okay, yes, guys, I'm aware that Iran is an enemy of the United States. I heard there was some trouble at the American Embassy before you guys were born. Next question."

"What business dealings do you have with anyone in Iran?" Channing asked.

"None."

"Are you connected on social media with anyone in Iran?"

"Not that I know of."

"Have you engaged in any electronic commerce or other internet activity with anyone in Iran?"

Jerry rolled his eyes and then looked up at the camera. "Get a nice, tight shot so when your experts evaluate what I say next, you'll have a good look. And for the record, I want to make sure your supervisor sees all this, too. Is your AV team ready? Make sure you record this. Here goes."

Now he focused on Channing. "I'm one of the good guys. If you ever infer again that I'm somehow collaborating with enemies of my country, then only one of us will walk away on his own power. Don't bother to ask me if that's a threat. It's not; it's a promise."

"Nobody is inferring you're collaborating with anyone," Channing said. "But interfering with a federal investigation may carry negative consequences."

"As far as I know, I'm not interfering with anything. What are you guys worried about?"

"Don't interfere with our investigation."

"What investigation? What are you guys investigating? Ya know what, why don't you just write me a check for my mileage and I'll head back home."

"We don't have a mechanism to pay for your mileage," Blackwell said. "But I'm sure you can deduct it as a business expense. We can provide documentation that you visited our office."

Jerry shook his head and rolled his eyes. "That figures. Guys, while this whole thing has been an experience, I really need to get some work done today. So, do you guys escort me out, or do I find my own way?" Jerry stood and walked toward the door.

Blackwell and Channing exchanged glances again. "Are you declining to cooperate with the FBI?" Blackwell asked.

Jerry stopped. He paused for a few seconds, took a deep breath, and then turned and faced both agents.

Calm. Stay calm. "Do you guys have a piece of paper? Maybe a legal pad or something like that?"

"We can get some," Blackwell said.

"Yeah, go grab a notepad with some lined paper."

Channing left and returned a few seconds later with a pad of yellow legal-sized paper.

"Thanks." Jerry started writing:

FBI Agents Jake Channing and Ronald Blackwell have just suggested I am refusing to cooperate with the FBI. I am answering that accusation in writing. When the FBI tells me what it's looking for and why, I will be happy to cooperate in any way I can. Until then, you can go pound sand. In Iran.
—Jerry Barkley

"You guys can file that paperwork as you see fit. Unless somebody out there plans to shoot me, I'm leaving."

DIGGING DEEPER

Jerry Barkley stared at packet traces all afternoon, hoping a pattern would emerge. Nothing like a good mystery to get the juices flowing.

By now, after several whois searches, he recognized the IP addresses. There was a constantly running conversation with that TOR relay, mixed with conversations with different trucking companies, mostly New Brighton Transport. The TOR connection with Maverick Marketing was easy to guess—sloppy security. But what linked New Brighton Transport and these other trucking companies with Maverick Marketing?

Why not find out? Two hours later, Jerry had a Windows virtual machine ready with the same public IP address as advertised by New Brighton Transport. He started up the Windows Resource Monitor on the simulator, put in a routing rule on his internet router to send all New Brighton Transport packets to his simulator, and watched the data conversation between his Maverick Marketing clone and the simulator. If any new programs were loaded onto the simulated workstation and from his Maverick Marketing clone, Jerry would capture them and send them to Saphas Antivirus for analysis.

Nothing happened. The Maverick Marketing clone sent packet after packet to the simulated New Brighton Transport system. Nothing came back.

Jerry stared at the data stream for a few minutes. Then he shook his head and smirked. Duh! This thing will be behind a firewall in the real world. Any activity would have to start from the New Brighton workstation going out, not from the outside coming in. He chuckled. And that, ladies and gentlemen, is why we test with simulations. I think I'll keep this little mistake to myself when the reporters ask how we cracked this case wide open.

He removed the special routing rule and shut down the New Brighton Transport simulator. The conversation with the real New Brighton Transport picked up again. Time for plan B. What was that guy's name at the bidder's conference?

"Good afternoon, New Brighton Transport," a pleasant voice said.
"Hi, um, my name is Jerry Barkley. Could I speak to Dan Standish please?"
"I'll transfer you."
"Thanks"
So far so good.

"Hi, this is Dan," a gruff voice said.

"Hi, um, Dan, my name is Jerry Barkley, and I, um, there's some stuff going on I was hoping you could help me figure out."

"Do I know you?"

"We met at the NAECN bidders' conference a few weeks ago. I think you have a computer virus. You're sending data to a marketing company in Burnsville and it's sending stuff through TOR to Iran."

"You were the guy who asked all the cybersecurity questions."

"Yeah, that was me.

"And now you're calling to tell me I have a cybersecurity problem?"

"Yeah, I am."

"You don't think that's a coincidence?"

"All I know is, I'm watching network packets fly between you and a company in Burnsville right now. That company is talking to a TOR relay, and the FBI says Iran is on the other end."

"So, now you're telling me we're talking to Iran?"

"You might be, yeah."

"Did you ever stop to think it might be normal for us to talk to a company in Burnsville? You have thirty seconds to tell me why I shouldn't hang up."

"Fair enough. That marketing company in Burnsville is another customer— well, not really a customer . . ."

"The clock is ticking."

"No way this is normal. I found that system blasting out to the internet. So, I cloned its hard drive and put it under a microscope here. It's sending traffic into TOR and exchanging traffic with you and some other trucking companies. But mostly you. I spent most of this morning getting jerked around by the FBI, and I think you have an infected workstation that has something to do with it. I want to find out what's going on, and I need your help."

Jerry waited. Finally, Dan said, "I'm trying to decide if you're a lunatic or if I should believe you."

"Well, a few people have called me a lunatic. But they usually apologize when they find out I'm right. Do you have a way to watch traffic in and out of your network?"

"We might."

Jerry thought about Dan's answer for a second. "No, you don't. If you did, you'd see the same stuff from your point of view that I see here and you'd shut it down."

"Our internet provider watches all that for us and hasn't said anything."

"What a surprise. Want me to send you the packet traces I'm collecting?"

"How do I know they're real?"

"Because you have users complaining about how their internet access is crawling and you don't know what to do about it."

"Is this a shakedown?"

"No, just a hunch."

"Why do you care?"

"I want your business for one thing. You guys need my stuff at your network boundary so you can see what's going on. But even if your association stays married to the other guys, if this leads to something important, it would be good for marketing."

Dan paused for a few seconds. "That might even make sense. What do you want to do?"

"I want to put one of my systems in front of your firewall."

"No."

"No?"

"No. You're not connecting anything into my network."

"Okay, so why don't I come over and build you a sniffer? Then you'll have your own. Got a box with two NICs?"

"I might."

"Groovy. How does tomorrow morning sound?"

"Did you really just say, 'Groovy'?"

"Yup."

"Were you even born in the 60s?"

"I'm afraid I was."

"Be here at seven thirty."

Even at 7:25 a.m., the sun was already beating down on the asphalt in front of the New Brighton Transport building. Jerry backed his car into a parking space with the nose facing outward. It was a trick he'd taught himself to help find his car in parking lots.

He surveyed the tan brick building he was about to enter. Five shallow, concrete steps led to a small landing in front of a glass entryway door. A red awning shielded the south-facing entrance from the sun.

The air conditioning offered relief as Jerry entered the building.

"May I help you?" asked the receptionist sitting at a desk, partially hidden behind a tall counter, offset to the left in an enclosed front lobby.

"Yes, I'm here to see Dan Standish."

"I'll see if he's in."

Jerry watched her pick up an outdated handset and dial an extension.

"I'm sorry, but Dan's not answering. Would you like to wait?"

"Sure, why not?"

Jerry sat in a hard, plastic chair across from the counter. Below the receptionist counter, he noticed an inset display case adorned with softball and bowling trophies and framed letters. He moved closer to the counter to read the letters. Apparently, a hardware store in rural North Dakota desperately needed shovels and other supplies one harsh winter. A letter from a company named Rare Metals Mining, thanking New Brighton Transport for a long and fruitful partnership, caught his eye.

"That's a nice letter from Rare Metals Mining. Who are they?" Jerry asked.

"We deliver loads for them," the receptionist said.

"What's in the loads?"

"I don't know much about it. They're a big customer."

"How big of a customer are they?"

"I don't know. But we haul a lot of stuff for them."

The phone rang.

"New Brighton Transport, this is Sheila. How may I help you?" she answered. "Yeah, I can look that up. Just give me a minute. My computer is slow today."

Still standing, Jerry watched as Sheila navigated to a website and waited for it to load.

"You need to be in Madison before five," she said. "That's a little more than nine hours from now. You'd best shake a leg." She paused. "You're welcome."

"What was that all about?" Jerry asked.

"One of our drivers dropped off a load."

"How many drivers and trucks do you have?"

"About a hundred, give or take."

Jerry craned his neck to look over Sheila's shoulder. "And this screen shows you where they all are?"

"Um, yeah. There are a few screens. Like, if I want to look at a summary of everyone's schedule, I just click here and fill in the dates. But lately, it's taken lots longer to look things up."

"I wonder what's going on," Jerry mused.

"Not sure."

"Maybe we can find out. Right-click on your task bar on the bottom of your screen and click 'Task Manager.'"

Sheila followed his direction.

"There you go. Now click that tab that says 'Processes' and then click the CPU column until the little arrow points downwards. That shows all your processes sorted inversely by CPU usage. Now, try your report."

Sheila launched her schedule summary report, selected some dates, and waited. And waited some more. And some more after that. After what seemed like several minutes, the screen finally displayed a table of dates, trucks, estimated pickups, and comments.

"The CPU was mostly idle and not much network traffic," Jerry said, showing her the relevant Task Manager displays. "Let's look at one other thing." Jerry directed Sheila through the mouse clicks to look at the Control Panel System applet. "Four gigs of RAM. But the Task Manager says you're only using two gigs. And you have sixteen gig of page file space. The bottleneck isn't here."

"Bottleneck?" Sheila asked.

"It's like being on the freeway and the lanes back up. Let's check out something else."

Jerry showed Sheila how to use the ping command to test the round-trip time to Google. Minimum round-trip time was thirty-four milliseconds. Maximum was 367 milliseconds.

"Look at that jitter," Jerry said.

"Jitter, what's that?"

"It's a measure of variability. This is my quick and dirty test to see how long it takes to go to Google and back. Looks to me like you're pounding the snot out of your internet connection. That's your bottleneck."

Sheila looked up at Jerry. "You can tell all that from that little bit?"

"It's strong evidence. This report used to run lots faster, right?"

"Yeah."

"And now it's slow. So, something changed. The bottleneck isn't in your computer, so it's gotta be somewhere else."

She stared at Jerry.

"So, we do a quick and dirty probe to a popular website, say Google," Jerry said, "and we see how long it takes. That jitter tells us you have a bunch of cars trying to get on the internet freeway. The on-ramp backs up because it has more cars than it can handle. The internet is probably slow for everyone here."

"Wow! Is that what you're here to see Dan about?"

"Sort of."

"Oh—you were the guy who called yesterday afternoon."

"Yeah and Dan told me to be here at seven thirty. What time is it now?"

"Almost eight. He's not exactly an early riser. He gets a lot of telemarketing calls, so he tells them to be here at seven thirty because he doesn't like sales people."

Jerry shook his head. "Unbelievable. I'm not selling anything."

"Well, then, why are you here?"

"Trying to figure out why your internet connection is so slow."

"Oh. Well, let's see if I can hook you up with somebody."

Sheila picked up her handset and dialed an extension.

"Hey, James, I have a gentleman up here waiting to see Dan, but Dan's not in yet. Can you come up here?" She paused for a second. "Thanks."

Jerry smiled. Never know where a little charm might lead.

A tall and athletic younger man with thinning hair and glasses approached the receptionist counter.

Jerry extended his hand. "Jerry Barkley. You're James?"

"Umm, yeah. What's goin' on?"

"I called Dan yesterday afternoon. It's a roundabout story, but I think you guys are trading a bunch of data with Iran, and Sheila just showed me some more evidence of it."

James smiled, eyeballed both Jerry and Sheila, and then chuckled.

"Look," Jerry said. "Take a look at the milliseconds here in Sheila's computer when we pinged Google."

James glanced at the Windows Command window on Sheila's computer.

"C'mon, James—three hundred milliseconds to get to Google and back? Who's your ISP, and how much bandwidth do you have?"

"Only two were three hundred milliseconds," James said. "The other two looked pretty good."

Jerry rolled his eyes. "Doesn't that jitter make you curious? Why is it thirty milliseconds sometimes and more than three hundred other times? When you browse websites, how does it feel?"

"A little slow sometimes," James said.

"Want to find out why?"

James paused. "What did you have in mind?"

Jerry picked up the small desktop computer he had carried in. "I built this bridge and put a bunch of bandwidth monitoring tools and packet capture stuff inside. Let's insert something like it right in front of your default gateway and see what it tells us."

"A bridge, huh?" James said. "What software?"

"Fedora, with Wireshark and tcpdump. Oh, and iptraf. Well, iptraf-ng since this is a newer version."

James studied Jerry for a few seconds. "Any iptables rules?"

Jerry smiled. James knew what he was talking about. "No. Wide open on this one. But I build firewalls, and I have some pretty slick iptables scripts if you're interested."

James nodded. His lips turned up into a barely perceptible grin. "Okay, why don't you bring it back. Boot it up and show me how it's set up. And then maybe we'll hook it up to our network."

"Dan said I couldn't hook anything into your network."

"Well, why'd you bring it then?"

"As a baseline to build one for you. I need to bring in a monitor."

"Don't worry about it."

Unlike Maverick Marketing, this server room, with its own air conditioning unit, a long work table, and several racks filled with servers, looked and felt more like a real data center. The masses of network and power cables were all neatly arranged. It was obvious somebody took pride in keeping this operation running smoothly.

"Set it up right here," James said, "and show me what you've got." James directed Jerry to a table with a disconnected keyboard, monitor, and mouse.

Jerry set up his system and showed James the software he had set up. "Looks good," James said. "I'll let everyone know we'll have a blip on the internet for a few seconds."

Five minutes later, Jerry and James watched as streams of letters and numbers flew across the screen.

Jerry's stomach tightened. "I recognize this pattern."

Jerry and James watched for a few more seconds.

"What's at IP address 10.169.3.117?" Jerry asked.

"I'll look it up," James disappeared into an office in the corner of the server room and came back a few seconds later. "It's Leah Anderson's workstation."

"What's Leah Anderson's workstation?" a voice asked from behind them.

"Oh, hi, Dan—check this out," James said. "This is Jerry Barkley."

"Oh, hey, Dan, how ya doin'? Nice to see you again," Jerry said. "You wanted me here at seven thirty. What time is it now?" He extended his hand for a handshake.

Dan looked more comfortable in casual clothes than he had at the bidders' conference in a suit.

"What's going on here?" he asked, absently shaking Jerry's hand.

"Something's up with Leah Anderson's workstation," James said. "I was just about to go over there."

James turned back to the display. "Look—there goes another one!"

"Yup. Looks like it sends a burst every thirty seconds or so. The bursts take about twenty seconds, and then the network goes quiet for ten; then it starts again," Jerry said. "These IP addresses look familiar," he said, pointing at the screen. "That's me. And that's Maverick Marketing where this all started."

"Somebody want to fill me in?" Dan asked.

"Why did you want me here at seven thirty when you don't come in until later?" Jerry asked.

"Because you called with that cockamamie story, and I figured you either wouldn't show up or wouldn't stick around."

Jerry shook his head and chuckled. "Story of my life."

"You told me on the phone yesterday, the FBI thinks you're a foreign spy. And now you have this contraption plugged into my network?" Dan asked.

Jerry smiled. "Something like that, yeah."

"After I told you not to hook anything into my network?"

"It's a bridge," James said. "And Jerry didn't connect it. I did. We just found something going on with Leah Anderson's workstation. I'll run a virus scan on it."

"Hang on a second," Jerry said. Now looking at Dan, he said, "I'd like to take it with me."

"I just met you," Dan said. "And now you want to walk out of here with one of my workstations?"

"Yup," Jerry said. "Pretty brazen, huh?"

"Well, I'll give you this. You've got cahonas."

Jerry smiled. "I'll bet we're looking at a zero-day here, and none of the signatures know about it yet. Which means virus scans won't find anything. That's why I want to bring that thing to my place, copy it, and put it under a microscope. But let's ask Leah if anything unusual happened in the past few days."

●━━━━━●

"Well, this looks important," a short, red-headed Leah Anderson said, looking up from her workstation at the three men surrounding her.

"Leah, this is Jerry," Dan said. "He's, um, showing us some stuff that came from your workstation."

"Hi, Leah, nice to meet you," Jerry said, extending his right hand. "Sorry about the intimidation factor here. But has anything unusual happened with your workstation the past few days?"

"No, nothing I can think of. What's going on?"

"It's a long story," Jerry said. "But I think your workstation and another workstation from one of my customers have something in common with Iran."

Leah laughed. "You mean, like Iran with the ayatollahs, that Iran?"

"Yeah, that's the one," Jerry said. "Data packets are flying out of your workstation right now to a virtual machine in my basement, and I'm sending them to a TOR relay. From there, I think they're going to Iran."

"I don't know what that means, but why not stop sending my stuff to Iran? Seems simple enough," Leah said.

"Right," Jerry said. "But I'm trying to figure out what's going on. Your workstation's the missing piece of the puzzle."

"Guys, I'd love to help, but I need to move some trucks today," Leah said.

"I know," James said. "But we need to rebuild your workstation anyway. I have a spare in my office, and I'll set it up for you so we can work on this one."

"Seriously? I'm doing some kind of international spy stuff with Iran?" Leah asked.

"I don't know," Jerry said. "But I think Iran might be doing some serious spy stuff with your computer."

"Oh—you know what? I did get a weird email last week. It was a bill of lading for somebody I'd never heard of."

"Still have the email?" Jerry asked.

"No, I don't keep that stuff."

"Bummer," Jerry said. "The header could have told us some things."

Back in his basement office that afternoon, Jerry cloned Leah's hard drive into another virtual disk image and set up a new virtual machine around it. This time, he would run his simulation with a copy of the actual New Brighton Transport offending workstation, instead of the freshly built Windows virtual machine he'd tried yesterday.

He booted the virtual machine and watched for packets to analyze. But nothing happened. Not one single packet addressed to Maverick Marketing or its clone came from this virtual workstation. Which didn't make sense. Jerry massaged the back of his neck. He turned his head toward Leah's physical workstation sitting in a corner of his lab, crammed with equipment, cables, and parts from long forgotten computers, and then back to his computer monitor, watching the virtual machine simulators stay silent.

What's different between you and your twin? Only one way to find out. He booted Leah's physical workstation from DVD again and created another virtual copy of its hard drive. Then he mounted both copies read-only onto another lab system and compared them. A few Windows Registry files were different, which was expected, but the newly created hard drive image also had three files not present in the first image. Which meant something must have deleted them off the first image, and that could only have happened when the virtual machine around it booted. Jerry swallowed. Whatever this was, it was sophisticated.

Jerry copied the files to a safe location and then uploaded them to Saphas Antivirus for analysis, along with an email detailing the investigative work he'd done so far. He pondered what he discovered for a few minutes as a sense of dread came over him. He dialed his cell phone.

"Hey, Dan, this is Jerry Barkley. That malware on Leah's workstation is nastier than I thought. It was targeted specifically at you. Somehow, it knew it was running in a different environment when I booted the clone I made, and it deleted itself. Call me back. This is a big deal."

His next call was to the FBI office he'd visited the day before.

"FBI," answered a brusque voice after four rings.

"Hi, I'd like to get in touch with either Ron Blackwell or Jake Channing."

"I'll take a message for you."

"This is urgent," Jerry said. "I think Iran is trying to attack us."

"Yeah, okay. I'll give them the message."

"Listen. I spent half my day holed up in a little room in your office yesterday, listening to your guys grill me about Iran. And now I think I know why."

"And I said I'll give them the message."

"Okay, thanks."

Jerry wondered what the odds were of Blackwell or Channing actually getting his message and acting on it. Given his past experiences with the FBI, probably not good.

THE TEACHER

The headlines were everywhere. "Ebola Back with a Vengeance," screamed *The New York Times*. "Minnesota Nurse down but Not out Yet," from *USA Today*. "Minnesota Nurse Has a Fighting Chance, Docs Say," from *The Wall Street Journal*. Network TV stations broadcast hourly updates, interviews with doctors, interviews with experts about what the doctors said in their interviews, and endless speculation about what might happen next.

In Tehran, Atesh took in all the coverage. The time had come.

Khalid Farooq, headmaster of the Ibn Idhari Academy of Muslim History in Blaine, Minnesota, stroked his neatly trimmed, salt-and-pepper beard. His eyes widened as he opened the email he'd both eagerly anticipated and dreaded. With more than ten years of being an Iranian agent in the United States, Khalid could count on one hand the number of messages from Alain.

Alain was not a real person. Alain was code for "Priority A," messages that needed immediate attention. The real sender was Atesh Zare, Khalid's contact with the Ministry.

The American NSA could search for deep, dark, encrypted messages all it wanted. This one would never trigger any alarms. If NSA agents traced it, they would find it came from a public internet café in Paris, France, a friendly country. Just one of billions of email messages traversing the planet every day.

Everything important was in the subject, "Winter will be harsh this year." His handlers called it a passphrase. The body of the message, about skiing in Switzerland, was meaningless. The real message was an encrypted attachment to an unsent email in the drafts folder for a different Gmail account.

To decrypt the message, Khalid logged in to the same Gmail account and copied and pasted the passphrase and message onto a website registered to a shell company in Paris. His handlers called it a Java applet and said it used a SHA-3 hash. Whatever that meant.

His fingers were more adept with turning pages of his well-worn Quran than manipulating computer keyboards and mice, and he needed a few tries to make it work. He sighed. Prayerfully, Allah, may his mercy be known, won't allow this technology in Jannah.

Finally, the decrypted message read:

> Greetings to you. Every day we say mamnū-
> nam to Allah for your dedicated service in
> the heart of the Great Satan, where even
> your few Muslim brothers and sisters are
> Sunni. At last, we will soon realize the
> fruit of your long labor.
>
> Please extend all courtesy and financial
> support to a few zealous American teens
> who will be coming to stay with you for a
> time. They will need lodging, food, and
> guidance. They believe they are being re-
> cruited by Yazid Kalil of the Daesh, but,
> in fact, we are recruiting them for a glo-
> rious mission in support of our own rev-
> olution. If successful, we will strike a
> blow to the Great Satan and start a war
> between America and the Daesh.
>
> You are to evaluate and supervise these
> recruits. Prepare them with your knowl-
> edge of the holy Quran to become martyrs
> for Allah and prepare yourself for a quick
> exit. Allahu akbar!

Stunning. After all the planning, all the meetings, all the observation. After living among the people of the Great Satan all these years, it was finally happening. Khalid's heart raced. He needed to know more.

He also needed to acknowledge and respond to the message. The process was the reverse of reading the original. He selected another passphrase, "Harsh winters make the snow more beautiful," and used a different Java applet to encrypt and save his reply. He attached the encrypted message to another email and left it in the Drafts folder of the shared Gmail account without sending it. Next, he composed an email from his Academy email account to Alain using the passphrase as subject, filled the body of that message with gibberish, and clicked the "send" button, signaling he had read and responded to the encrypted message.

```
Greetings in the name of Allah from the
heart of the Great Satan. It will be my
honor to serve the revolution. I look for-
ward to a successful mission. Perhaps we
should set up voice communication so we
can stay in close touch throughout this
important operation.
```

The coded response came back from Alain almost immediately—by itself a signal that this was big.

```
Agreed. Purchase several disposable cell
phones, each from a different store. Use
for yourself and guests as needed. Call
our VOIP phone in New York to be forwarded
to Tehran. Identify yourself in the usual
manner and speak in Farsi at all times.
```

The time was almost noon in Minnesota. With stores closing no later than nine o'clock, Khalid would need to hurry.

It was eleven at night in Minnesota, but half past eight the next morning in Tehran. Khalid heard a few clicks and then a phone ringing.

After a few seconds with a receptionist, Khalid heard the voice of Atesh himself.

"Khalid, it is good to hear your voice. You will be coming home soon."

"Thank you, Atesh. Why did Alain contact me?"

Atesh went on to describe more details of the operation.

Khalid's mind raced. Audacious was not a strong enough word to describe what Atesh proposed. "How will we do this?"

"I leave the operational details up to you.

"Your plan is bold," Khalid said. "I have much to do and little time."

"Yes," Atesh said. "And you will return home a hero very soon."

SUMMER JOB

It was graduation day at Sioux Falls Jefferson High School. Brian Cox sat in the second row of folding chairs on the auditorium main floor. Brian's parents and other families surrounded their graduating sons and daughters in raised perimeter seats. Dignitaries sat on the elevated stage and they all had to make speeches. Mr. Pedersen was last and, thankfully, about to finish.

"Ladies and gentlemen—and get used to that because you aren't boys and girls anymore—I want to leave you with one last piece of advice. Our world is filled with lots of different people. When you leave this place, you'll meet people who don't look like you, don't sound like you, and maybe don't even smell like you. Don't hide from it. Embrace it. Diversity makes us strong and homogeny makes us weak. I urge you. Seek out somebody different from you and make friends. Enrich your own life by learning about another culture and another way of life. And never, never, never give in to bigotry and hate."

Polite applause.

"And now, we have one more piece of business to take care of." He handed the mic to the school principal.

"Upon the recommendation of the Jefferson High School faculty, and by the authority of the board of trustees of the Sioux Falls School District, I confer upon each of you the high school diploma with the rights, privileges, and responsibilities thereon to appertaining. Please call the roll, and graduates, please line up."

Thunderous applause.

An attractive woman on stage right with a different mic started calling names in alphabetical order. "Mary Elizabeth Amundsen." Mary climbed the stairs to the stage, showed her ID, and then strode across the stage and accepted her diploma. While Mary accepted her diploma, the woman read the next name.

Brian's turn was coming soon.

"Denise Louise Chowden." Denise rushed onto the stage and blew a kiss to her parents as the principal handed her a diploma.

"David Wayne Cooper." David quietly accepted his diploma and shook hands.

"Brian Quasim Cox." As Brian stepped up onto the stage, somebody grabbed his foot and sent him crashing against the woman. Brian and the woman sprawled across the stage, Brian on top of her. Her mic crashed onto the stage, filling the auditorium with a deep boom, which morphed into a deafening screech until somebody turned down the sound system.

"Hey Muzzie. Too bad you can't talk to girls." Nobody knew who said it, but everyone in the auditorium heard it. A few students cackled.

Brian picked himself up and fumbled with his taquiya. "Sorry." He looked down, fighting tears, and glanced at the woman as some of the dignitaries helped her up and retrieved her mic. He stood for a second, not sure what to do, and then ran off the stage and out of the auditorium.

Brian's diploma came in the mail a week later. While he waited, he exchanged dozens of email messages with ISIS fighter, Yazid Kalil.

A few days later, when Yazid suggested an audio chat, Brian agreed.

Sitting alone in his bedroom, late at night in South Dakota, Brian's heart pounded as he heard a genuine freedom fighter's voice over his computer speakers. Brian looked up the time zone in Syria; it was already tomorrow morning.

"Brian Cox, Allah salutes you. I can feel that Allah has great things in store for you."

"I want to come to Syria to stand with you and fight the infidels and kuffar!" Brian said.

"Yes. It would be glorious. But we all have our duties, and Allah sometimes sends us down different paths. You speak perfect English, and we can use your skills with a project in the United States."

"I want to stand and fight next to you."

"Perhaps you will in time. But for now, we need you in your country. Can we count on you?"

Brian took a deep breath. "Yes."

"Good. I'm looking at a map of the United States. You live in Sioux Falls, South Dakota?"

"Yes."

"We need you in Minneapolis."

"What about my parents?"

"What about them?"

"What will I tell them about where I'm going?"

"Are they believers in our cause?"

"No."

"Tell me about your parents."

"We moved here from New York. My father works for a large bank, and he brought my mother and me here to this wasteland of infidels. He's some kind of high-up manager, and he spends most of his time at work. And I'm ashamed to say, my mother drinks alcohol."

"I see."

"I spend as much of my time as possible reading about my Islamic heritage. There has to be a better life than the hypocrisy my parents have chosen."

"There is, Brian. There is. The path of Islam you've chosen leads to paradise. But it's a difficult path, and it sometimes requires us to make difficult choices. This may be one such time for you. Are you prepared to make difficult choices?"

"Yes."

"Tell me what you want for your life ten years from now."

"I want to be millions of miles away from this den of infidels and hypocrisy. I want to be part of something glorious. I want to take revenge."

"Excellent. We have the same vision for the world. Perhaps the choice I will ask you to make will not be so difficult, then."

"What choice?"

"Leave your parents."

"What?"

"Leave your parents. Join our holy cause now. Help shape the world to the vision we both share."

"You mean, right now? But what about college?"

"Where do you plan to go to college?"

"My parents want me close. Dakota State University accepted my application."

"So, now you are presented with a choice. Immerse yourself even more into the decadent Western system you despise or rid yourself of its hypocrisy and shame and join our holy cause today."

"I . . . I could really do that now?"

"Yes. Right now, today. Leave this cesspool behind and join our cause."

"But what about my parents?"

"What about them?"

"They'll want to know what happened to me. Where I am. They'll call the police if I just disappear."

"Nobody said anything about just disappearing. Leave in the morning after your father goes to work. Tell your mother you found a summer job with a school in Minneapolis."

"How will I get to Minneapolis?"

"Do you have access to a car?"

"Yes."

"Do you have money for gas?"

"Some."

"Then it's settled."

INTERNET VIROLOGY

An email was waiting in Jerry's inbox the next morning from a Joanne Gittens with Saphas Antivirus in London.

```
Greetings from across the pond. Please phone
at your earliest convenience to discuss the
malware sample you emailed last night. It oc-
curs to me that traditional phoning might be
prohibitively expensive. If so, we can also
interface via Skype if you wish.
```

Jerry smiled. *I like these guys.* He started a video call, and Jgittens23 answered after a few rings.

On Jerry's computer monitor, Joanne Gittens looked tall and thin with messy blond hair. Yellowed Styrofoam cups on dusty shelves behind her may have held coffee in an earlier era. Books, papers with computer code listings, and clutter were visible all over Joanne's office.

"If you don't mind, I should like to eat my sandwich while we talk. It's been a long night. You caused quite a row with your email."

"Groovy. What do you make of my little malware sample?"

"How did you come across this wonderful piece of engineering?"

"It's a long story, but let's say the American FBI motivated me a few days ago. And as I said in my email, this thing looks like it's targeted specifically. Which scared me half to death."

"Have you shown this sample to your FBI?"

"No, not yet. I'm still waiting on a call back. But everything I've ever given the FBI ended up in a black hole. What did I find?"

"Jerry, I need to know, in detail, how you came across this code." Joanne looked serious. This was no game.

Jerry described what he'd done and how he isolated the files he sent. "This malware must be targeting specific environments, and when it saw my test environment was different than what it wanted, it got rid of itself."

"Ah. Jolly good. You kept a baseline to compare."

"Well, yeah. Doesn't everyone?"

"Unfortunately, no. You say you have another clone of another infected workstation?"

"Yeah. There are two infected systems. I sent you samples from New Brighton Transport because that one behaved differently than the original workstation."

"Would you mind sharing both disk images with us?" Joanne asked.

"I have a little ftp site here." Jerry typed a few keyboard commands. "I put copies of them there. Why don't you start grabbing them while we're talking? Just let me know when you get them so I can move them out of there once you have your copy."

"Excellent."

Jerry gave her connection details and watched Joanne start copying.

"So, how did I give you guys a long night?"

"What do you know of Stuxnet?"

"The stuff the NSA and the Israelis deployed in Iran to mess up their nuclear centrifuges?"

"Yes. It was supposed to be carefully targeted to only a few specific systems. But it managed to work its way out into the wild and the Iranians reported it to the antivirus companies. We've had its signature in our database since 2010."

"Are you telling me I have a Stuxnet sample here?

"Your sample matches our signature, yes."

Jerry's eyes widened. "You're sure about that?"

"As I said, you caused quite a row. We have a team still working on disassembly, but from what we've gathered so far, the malware appears to be driven by a dispatch table based on what we think are internal DNS names."

"Wow," Jerry said. "How would they get internal DNS names?"

"One of many questions we've been asking. The attackers must have phished every attack target to find this out. And then they tailored the attack to each target. The code we've disassembled so far branches to specific modules based on DNS names. So, the malware behaves differently depending on where it finds itself. You mentioned a company named New Brighton Transport?"

"Yeah. That was the computer that wouldn't act badly here at my place."

"Interesting. Would you be willing to try an experiment with us?"

"Sure."

"One of the DNS names was nbt.local. That may be your New Brighton Transport. Would you set up a subnet with internal DNS name, nbt.local, and see how it behaves?"

"Yeah, I can make that happen. Let me work on that, and I'll get back to you."

"And I'll message you when I finish uploading those hard drive images."

SCHOOL

Brian spotted the sign along Interstate 35 North. "Exit 48, County 12, County 28, Medford." This was his exit.

The text message instructions were precise:

```
At the traffic circle at the top of the
exit ramp, turn left onto NW 69th Street.
At the next traffic circle, exit left onto W.
Frontage Road heading south. Immediately past
the Medford Outlet Center, turn right onto NW
66th Street. After the Steele County 12 sign,
turn left into a cemetery. Park in the back on
the left side of the gravel road with your car
facing west. Wait for instructions.
```

Brian parked and waited.

"What have I done?" he said out loud. How could he abandon his home? His life?

"Hah, what life?" he said out loud again. A life filled with jocks who desecrate the ground they walk on? A life filled with sluts like Cheryl Samuels? A life living alone and a victim? No, here was a chance to change all that. To do something about it. To strike back.

"But what will father think when he comes home and I'm gone?"

Brian looked at the headstones. The nearest one read, "Here lies Abigail Finch, 1891-1952. May she rest in peace."

He looked up from the old headstones and noticed an old maroon cargo van pass the gravel road entrance, moving slowly west on the paved street. It stopped where the other side of the U-shaped gravel road met the paved street. A man got out and strode through the neatly mowed grass, across the headstones toward Brian's car. The van turned around and drove back the way it came.

Brian's cell phone buzzed. The text message read, "Unlock your passenger door and roll down your window." He followed instructions.

The man looked in Brian's passenger side window. He was muscular with short, dark hair. He wore hiking boots, blue jeans, and a short-sleeved green T-shirt.

"Brian?" he asked.

"Yes."

"Good. Please give me your car keys."

The man had an accent. "Why?" Brian asked.

"Security precautions."

"My father doesn't allow others to drive my car."

"You're free to leave right now if you want. If you wish to join us, give me your car keys and move to the passenger seat." He looked at Brian and waited.

In slow motion, Brian handed him the keys. He slid to the passenger seat.

"You made a good choice," the man said as he climbed into the driver's seat. He started the car and continued around the U-shaped path, back out to the road; he turned left, then right onto NW 32nd Avenue, behind the Medford Mall. He drove slowly north past two farm fields, a copse of trees, then another small farm field, scanning his rear-view mirror. He turned right onto NW 76th street and followed the frontage road to the right, now headed south.

No other cars were in sight.

"Why are we driving back and forth?" Brian asked.

"To make sure nobody follows us."

Apparently satisfied, he continued south past the traffic circle and into the McDonald's parking lot. He parked and turned off the ignition.

"Please come with me." They exited Brian's car and crossed to the other side of the building, where the maroon van was waiting. The back door swung open as they approached it.

"Nice to meet you, Brian," a passenger in the van said. "Please, climb in."

Brian glanced back at his muscular escort.

"If you wish to join us, please climb into the van," he said. "If you wish to leave, this is your last opportunity." He dangled Brian's keys in front of him.

Brian bowed his head and bit his lip. What was he thinking, driving more than two hundred miles to this place? What would Father say? He needed to leave and go back home! But no—he was tired of the constant humiliation from the letter jackets and the others back in Sioux Falls. And college at Dakota State University would be four more years of the same. Go home and lie down like a dog or join this group and fight? He lifted his head and climbed into the van.

"Excellent," the van passenger said. He was tall, with greying black hair and a neatly trimmed beard. He wore dark-colored clothes. His brown eyes were piercing, even behind his glasses. He reached out to shake Brian's hand. "I am Khalid," he said. "I will be your teacher for a time. May Allah be pleased with what we accomplish."

"I will follow you," Brian's escort said. He turned back toward Brian's car.

Khalid closed the van doors. Brian looked around inside the windowless van. Both the front bucket seats and the seat row in front of him were occupied, but the occupants did not look back. Khalid directed Brian to the middle bench seat.

"Please buckle your seatbelt and allow me to put this on," Khalid said, showing Brian a blindfold.

"Why are you blindfolding me?"

"It's a security precaution."

Brian felt that now-familiar fear rise in his gut. His mind transported him to shortly after his family moved to Sioux Falls. Father had encouraged him to go to a party. They looked like nice young men. Socializing didn't mean abandoning what you believe. That's what father had told him. Later, five of them tied a dark hood around his head, shoved him in the back of a truck, and dumped him in the middle of a cornfield.

"Don't freeze to death out here, Muzzie," one of them said. "And after you figure out how to get back home, you'd better not tell anyone about this." One of them punched Brian in the stomach before they left him writhing and puking into that hood. He listened to their fading laughter before tearing the hood off and finding himself disoriented and alone in the dark, surrounded by seven-foot cornstalks.

"Don't make me wear that!" he protested in the here and now.

"Brian, your training begins right here," Khalid said. "By joining us, you declare war on this enemy country. If you are captured, it is best for you if you don't know our location. I'm afraid I must insist you wear this blindfold while we travel. It's as much for your own protection as ours."

Khalid's logic made sense. Brian allowed Khalid to tie the blindfold behind Brian's head and then put a hood over the top.

"I can't breathe!"

"Yes, you can. Lean your head forward and point your nose down, not into the hood. It will only be on for a short time."

Brian leaned forward, pointing his nose down.

"Better?" Khalid asked.

"Yes."

Brian heard the van motor start. He felt motion. Slowly, he relaxed. Perhaps these men would be his new family.

Somebody tapped Brian's shoulder. "We've arrived."

Hands helped Brian exit the van. What time was it? Somebody guided him across a parking lot. He tripped—somebody caught him.

"Sorry about that. Steps coming. Step up. Step up again. Stop."

Somebody moved past Brian. A door whooshed open. He reached and felt a metal frame around a glass panel. Hands guided him through. The door shut behind him.

A few more steps. Right turn. And through another door.

The hood whipped off over his head. Others untied and removed the blindfold. Brian squinted in the bright florescent light.

"Welcome to your temporary home and your new family," Khalid said. "May Allah be pleased with what we accomplish during your stay here. Allow me to show you around."

Brian and Khalid stood in a reception area, with a windowed view outside the front of the building to Brian's right. A computer sat on a reception desk on his left, in the near corner of the back wall.

Khalid led Brian through the hallway opening in the center of the back wall. It was lined with lockers, with openings to classrooms on both sides. Brian noticed a dining room, at the end of the hall and on his right, where three people sat at a table. One, who looked older, made eye contact with Khalid and nodded as they walked past. Khalid nodded back.

Brian followed Khalid into the open space in back. An industrial-sized overhead door filled much of the right wall. Brian's car was against the left wall, next to two other cars.

"This place looks more like a warehouse than a school," Brian said.

"Yes," Khalid said. "This building was a warehouse before we rented it. We use this area for storage and physical education during bad weather."

"Where do we sleep?"

"We have temporary sleeping arrangements in the office suites you passed when you entered the building."

"What about showers and food?"

"Meals are catered. Showers, I'm afraid, are primitive."

A solid wall that looked like a temporary partition was on the left, with one closed door in the middle. "What's behind the door along that wall?" Brian asked.

"Expansion space."

"Were those my teammates in the room we walked past?" Brian asked.

"Yes. You will meet them soon. But first, a question. Are you prepared to devote your life to serving Allah?"

"Yes. I had hoped to serve Allah in Syria and become a true brother."

"You are already a true brother. Perhaps the day may come when you are needed overseas. But for now, you can best serve the cause of Allah here."

"How?"

"All in due time. But for now, you must be hungry."

Brian followed Khalid back into the dining room. Five long folding tables in parallel rows with attached benches filled the floor. An industrial sink and dishwasher were on the right, with clean dishes stacked on one side. The three people Brian saw sitting at the table earlier greeted him. Two looked like they were in their late teens or early twenties. The older one had dark hair and olive skin. His face was lined. He looked out of place wearing civilian clothes.

Brian started to introduce himself, but Khalid stopped him.

"A few ground rules for our new arrival," Khalid said. "For your own protection and ours, none of you are to tell any of the others about details of your former lives, such as where you lived or your real names, in case you are caught. You will refer to each other by nicknames only."

Turning to Brian, Khalid said, "I will give you the nickname Owl because your glasses make you look wise for your young years. Meet Cypress, Lion, and one of my assistants we will call Walter."

Cypress was overweight. Lion looked like the stronger of the two.

"You will learn much about each other over the next few days. I will give you details of our mission at the appropriate time. We have much preparation to do. And Owl, I need to take your picture."

"Why?"

"For your Minnesota driver's license. Please stand against this wall and smile." Khalid fumbled with his cell phone, looking perplexed. Khalid continued tapping. Walter chuckled.

"May I help?" Brian said, walking toward Khalid. Khalid took a breath and handed his phone to Brian. Brian tapped the appropriate icons. "You can adjust your flash with this button. And tap right here to take the picture." He handed the phone back to Khalid.

Walter made eye contact with Khalid. "Impressive."

Brian grinned.

"Thank you," Khalid said. "I'm afraid I am not the most up-to-date with technology."

Brian stood against a blank, beige-colored wall and smiled while Khalid snapped a few pictures.

"Excellent," Khalid said. "And now I will let you become acquainted." He nodded to Walter, who nodded back.

Late that night, after the new recruits were in bed, Khalid walked to the warehouse area, unlocked the door along the middle wall Owl had asked about earlier, and entered the other side of the building. A few fluorescent lights in the ceiling fought the darkness, revealing four men sitting around a table, each hunched over a laptop computer. One looked up. He was in his early 40s, fit and trim. All the men around the table were in their 30s and early 40s and represented the best of Iranian Special Forces. All entered the country on commercial flights from Paris using the best false French passports the Iranian Embassy could produce. All were in the country on business trips. Or so said the paperwork.

"We're working out the first diversion logistics right now," the team leader, Tabor, said. "How are your recruits?"

"All eager to serve our cause," Khalid said.

Tabor snorted. "You mean the Daesh cause, don't you?"

"But they'll die serving our cause," Khalid said.

"It's a pity," Walter said. "I've gotten to know some of them. They're no different than me when I was their age."

"And if the situation was different, maybe Khalid could teach them the difference between Shia Islam and Daesh perversions," replied Tabor.

"I admit, I'm also feeling regret," Khalid said. "Owl was helpful today."

"When any of us begin to enjoy killing, we lose our humanity and become monsters," Tabor said. "But we are all trained soldiers, and we've been given a mission."

"I know," Walter said, "I'll do my duty when asked."

Khalid and the others nodded.

"How much time do we have?" Tabor asked.

"A few days at most," Khalid said. "The American nurse entered the hospital two days ago. The blood samples will be ready to move soon. A week perhaps."

"Timing will be tight," Tabor said.

"Yes. But doable. Insha'Allah."

"The information gathered by the Science Ministry is proving invaluable. This is the ideal situation to make our move," Tabor said, studying Google Maps routes in northern Minnesota from Hermantown to a wooded area between Ely and Babbitt. "There can be no clearer signal that Allah is with us. This area holds one of the largest undeveloped mineral deposits in the world. One company operates a mine at this site and takes regular deliveries of explosives to extract precious metals. We can take what we need from one of the delivery trucks for our project and stage an accident that will shut down that mine for months. We will deprive the Great Satan of the precious metals it needs to build more weapons and computers and have industrial ANFO for our project."

"I am only a humble Muslim cleric," Khalid said. "What is ANFO?"

"You are much more than a cleric, my friend," Tabor said. "ANFO is ammonium nitrate mixed with fuel oil in a precise ratio. Mining companies use it to blast holes in rock."

"How do we detonate it?"

"We need a heat source to set off a small amount of blasting powder. When the blasting powder explodes, it creates a heat and pressure wave that explodes the ANFO. A truckload of that material in an enclosed space could cause an earthquake."

"What do we use for a trigger?"

"A cell phone."

"What of the truck driver?" Khalid asked.

"Ah, yes. We need a supply of ketamine."

"Ketamine?"

"Yes. It is a drug that causes short term amnesia."

"This is a controlled substance, is it not?"

"Yes, but available over any number of online, offshore pharmacies. Order it quickly from a few sources and pay whatever premium they ask for expedited delivery. We will also need syringes and needles. And rubber gloves for later."

"Very good," Khalid said. "The recruits and I will acquire the vans in the morning and start work on preparing them."

"Excellent," Tabor said. "Also, order some flash powder online."

———•———————•———

"Time to wake up," Khalid's voice blared over the intercom. "Please dress and assemble in the cafeteria in fifteen minutes."

Brian sat up in his makeshift bed and looked out the window. It was barely light outside.

When he made it to the cafeteria room, Cypress and Lion were already seated at the same table closest to the door, eating their breakfast. Khalid was at the next table with the man who met Brian earlier, along with three other men who also looked like soldiers.

"Owl, please see to it you are not late again," Khalid said, looking up. "I apologize for the food we must endure here. I miss food from home."

Brian dropped some bread in a toaster and spooned eggs onto a paper plate. "Scrambled eggs and toast are fine. My mother makes sejouk all the time. It's too spicy for me."

"What does she use for sausage?" Khalid asked.

"Chicken mostly," Brian said.

Khalid nodded. "At least it's halal. It's better with lamb or beef as the base. Hurry with your breakfast. We have much to do today." Now addressing all the recruits, he continued, "Your mission and training begin today. Meet Tabor, your team leader. Please introduce yourselves with the code names I gave you earlier."

With breakfast finished and the dishes cleaned, Khalid stood.

"Gentlemen, by joining with us, you have declared the Great Satan your enemy and sworn your allegiance to Allah. It seems appropriate that each of us tell the group why we chose to join this cause. Following our introductions, we have a short mission today to acquire some cargo vans. I'll start and then call on each of you."

"I started this school a few years after 9/11," Khalid continued. "I wanted to teach students the true and glorious history of Islam and be a beacon of light against the dark forces oppressing Muslims here. I failed. My students and I endured all manner of constant harassment and attacks. When somebody tried to burn down my house and destroy this school and the police did nothing, I abandoned my house and took up residence here, at this school. And now I dedicate my life to teaching young Muslims how to protect themselves and defend our homeland. It is a calling from Allah.

"The men with me are my trusted assistants. Each will take you under his wing and mold you into a true soldier of Allah. We may all die from this glorious cause, but we will meet in paradise and perhaps reduce the persecution here. That will be our reward.

"Lion, why don't you go next."

Lion, with his blonde hair and blue eyes, looked like an all-American weight lifter, with bulging muscles over his whole body. "I was a professional body builder," he said. "I used the money I made from endorsements and competition to pay for graduate school, where I studied comparative religions and theology."

Lion paused and chose his next words carefully. "I have no wish to harm anyone, but I believe we need to build a whole new society that enforces the first verse of Surah One: 'Praise be to God, Lord of the Universe, the Beneficent, the Merciful and Master of the Day of Judgment.' Only this will wipe away the scourge of fear, greed, and oppression I see every day in America."

"A worthy goal and well said," Khalid said. "But do you understand that to accomplish our goal, believers may need to spill blood?"

"Yes," replied Lion. "An unfortunate reality, but necessary to achieve the greater good."

"Excellent. Your education serves you well. We will use your knowledge to supplement our training here. Cypress?"

Cypress, overweight with brown hair, carried a far-off look in his hazel eyes. "I thought Muslims worshipped Allah, not God."

"Allah is God," Lion said. "We seek assistance from him alone, and he guides us to the right path and grants us blessings if we stay on his path."

"Well said, Lion," Khalid said. "Cypress, Allah is the name we give to the one true god."

"That sounds good to me," Cypress said. "Those *Dabiq* articles were cool. I want to be a bad-ass terrorist."

"Are you willing to die for our cause?" Khalid asked.

"No way! I want to make the other guys die for their cause!"

The rest of the group laughed nervously.

Khalid paused and smiled. "And if we make our enemies die for their cause during our efforts, no doubt Allah will be even more pleased."

The group laughed again, more at ease now. Something about Cypress seemed off to Brian, but he could not figure out what it was.

"Owl, that leaves you," Khalid said.

Tears formed in Brian's eyes as a movie in his mind replayed the events that led him here. He wiped his eyes.

"I've been picked on and humiliated for the last time. For everyone who made my life miserable, I hope the last thing they see is me watching them as their lives slip away."

"Hey, I like this guy," Cypress said. "I figured you for a wimp."

"Shut up!" Brian said. "I'm not a wimp!"

"I didn't say you were," Cypress said. "Dude, I'll be right there next to ya." He pantomimed spraying the room with machine-gun fire.

"You will all have your opportunity for revenge," Khalid said. "But for proper revenge, you need to learn discipline."

Now addressing the whole group, Khalid said, "For today, we have a simple mission: to pick up some used cargo vans and bring them back here."

Cypress pounded a fist into his other hand. "When do we start kickin' some ass?"

Khalid took a breath. "Cypress, please, control your outbursts. To answer your question, we will start our operations after we're prepared. And one of the first elements we need for our preparations are three full-sized cargo vans. But these vans cannot be associated with anyone in our group. That's why we need to make driver's licenses for each of you."

"Cool. Like, real spy stuff?" Cypress asked.

"Something like that," Khalid said. "It is to protect all of us."

"It's about time. I was going stir-crazy."

"How long have you been here?" Brian asked.

"Who knows? A few days maybe?"

"What about everyone else?" Brian asked.

"A couple days," Lion said.

"And are we recruiting more team members?" Brian asked.

"No. This is our team." Khalid looked at Cypress. "At least for now. We may expand later if our first missions are successful."

Lion stroked his chin. "How will we acquire the vans?"

"There are a few Craigslist ads," Khalid said. "You will negotiate with the sellers and buy the vans with cash."

"Where do we get the cash?" Cypress asked. "Do we rob a bank?"

Khalid smirked. "No, we don't rob a bank. We have a sufficient supply of cash."

"What about title transfer and insurance and all those things?" Lion asked.

"The power of computers these days is truly amazing," Khalid said, looking at his assistants. One assistant smiled and brought some papers to Khalid. "Lion, you are John Denney, and you live in a place named Big Lake, Minnesota. Cypress, you are Joe Morgan. Here are your automobile insurance cards and Minnesota drivers' licenses." He handed the papers to Lion and Cypress. "Memorize your new names for your mission today. And do not lose those. Owl, having joined us only yesterday, we will have your package ready in a few days. You and I have a different mission today.

"Lion and Cypress, you will split into teams, each led by one of my assistants. One of you will pose as a son or younger brother, negotiate with the seller, acquire the van, and drive it to a suitable spot out of sight of the seller, where you will park it. Your team leader will blindfold you and return you and the van here. If the seller wants to transfer the title and wishes to accompany you to a license bureau, you will do so without protest. The van will be registered to your fictitious identity and will be untraceable later."

Cypress fidgeted. "I hate the blindfolds. Why do we have to keep using them?"

"As I told all of you earlier, the blindfolds are for our safety," Khalid said. "If you are captured, it is important you not know our location."

"Dude, if somebody tries to capture me, I'll just whack em."

"I'm sure you will, but we will still practice operational security."

"Whatever, man."

"What's your mission for me?" Brian asked.

"Reconnaissance," replied Khalid. "But first, Tabor and Walter, please set up your teams. Owl, come with me."

The meeting ended as the group split into teams. Khalid led Brian back through the hallway to the warehouse area, carrying a laptop.

"Owl, I need your help with some computer issues."

"Glad to help. What do you need?"

"I believe there's an application where we can look at satellite images of buildings?"

"Sure, Google Maps. It's a website."

Khalid lifted the lid on his laptop and started it. After logging in, Brian showed Khalid how to launch Google Maps and explore the satellite imagery.

"Truly amazing," Khalid said. "First, I would like to explore MSP Airport." They navigated around the website, focusing on the parking ramps. They also looked at US Bank Stadium, Target Center, and other sites, always focusing on parking. Khalid stroked his beard as they looked at the images taken from the sky.

"What are you interested in?" Brian asked.

"A suitable target. Or targets."

"For what?"

"Unimportant for now," Khalid said, navigating around the map on the screen with the laptop touchpad. "But what is important is that we strike a blow for Allah."

Brian watched Khalid struggle with the laptop touchpad. Khalid always seemed to overshoot his destination on the map on the laptop screen and then had to slowly navigate back to it.

"You're looking for parking ramps to bomb?" Brian said.

"Yes."

"But how does bombing parking ramps strike a blow for Allah?"

"It's part of a larger plan."

Brian raised his eyebrows. Maybe the vans would be used for bombing. This was no longer pages in an online magazine. This was real. And it was exhilarating.

"A real mouse may be helpful," Brian said. "Do you have a USB mouse nearby?"

"What is that?" Khalid said.

"Just a normal computer mouse. I saw a computer in the front lobby. Why don't I get a mouse from it, and we'll use it back here on your laptop for your searches?"

Khalid looked at Brian. "Yes, that sounds like it might be helpful."

"You're right; this is much better," Khalid said later after Brian connected a mouse to the laptop. "But none of the places we've checked so far are suitable."

"What are we looking for?"

"A parking area close to a large building."

"My parents drive to the Mall of America sometimes. It has two parking ramps on either side."

"That may be useful," Khalid said as he used the new mouse to center on a satellite image directly above the Mall of America. "No. The parking ramps are too far away. Ah—but what's this? I see a Patterson Blu hotel on the south side and a JW Chariot on the north side. He clicked on some more pictures. "Perhaps they have parking below the buildings. How do I see a view from the street?"

"Just use 'Street View,'" Brian said. "Let me show you."

Brian drug the yellow stick-figure icon on the map to Killebrew Drive on the south side of the mall. A few seconds later, they both looked at a picture of the Patterson Blu hotel.

"Look at the windows on the first three floors. They're different than the upper floors." Brian clicked the plus sign in the lower-right corner of the screen to zoom in. He noticed cars and support pillars inside a few openings. "Those aren't windows; they're openings. That's a parking ramp!"

"Truly amazing," Khalid said.

"I wonder if the hotel on the north side also has parking below the hotel," Brian said as he navigated the view to the north side of the mall. "But we can't be sure. Look—the street view is from 2011, before it was built, and the satellite view is from when it was under construction."

"Owl, you have been extremely helpful. We'll need to physically visit these hotels to find out more."

"Thank you. Can we find a way to bomb my high school, too?"

Khalid's expression changed. He turned his head away. "I'll see what we can do."

"What's wrong?" Brian asked

"Nothing. I'm going to get some coffee and pray. Would you like to join me?"

HIJACKING

Aamir "Izy" Aziz was ready for work. Up before dawn and dressed in his usual flannel shirt, blue jeans, and work boots, he leaned over his sleeping wife and kissed her goodbye.

"When are you coming home again?" she asked.

"I should be back tomorrow night, Allah willing."

"And where are you going?"

"I drive an empty trailer to Hermantown. I leave from there and deliver my load to a mine near Ely, then return to Hermantown and bring the loaded trailer back here."

"I hate it when you drive explosives all over the country. That stuff scares me, Aamir."

"Don't be scared. It's my job. And we have all kinds of safety procedures. And unlike your mother, this stuff is stable."

"After what she's endured, it's a miracle she's still with us."

"It's just that when her passport comes through, we'll need to find a place for her to live."

"She can stay with us. At least for a few months, until she's settled."

"I love you."

"I love you, too. Don't forget to kiss Kayla and Amira. Maybe when you return, we will create a third child."

Izy smiled. "Maybe I can be late this morning."

His wife laughed. "The later you start, the later you return. Go to work. I'll be here waiting for you tomorrow night."

He kissed his wife again and left the modest family house on the east side of St. Paul and drove to work, eager to get back home. As he drove away, he noticed a maroon cargo van parked in front of the pharmacy across the street. He turned on his radio and drove to work at the New Brighton Transport St. Paul terminal to pick up his trailer.

A few minutes later, he left the St. Paul terminal and turned onto the I-35W North ramp toward Duluth and the Hermantown terminal. He noticed another maroon cargo van in his rear-view mirror. A country tune played on the radio. The sun rose on his left. He put on his sunglasses.

"Izy, can I ask you a question?" It was the Hermantown terminal supervisor, Levi Greenberg, again. He was tall and thin, with black wavy hair. His nose reminded Izy of the Egyptian pyramids. He was always full of questions. He handed Izy a clipboard with the necessary delivery paperwork.

"Sure, Levi, what is it?"

"Why do these terrorists want to blow up everything? You lived over there. What is it with these guys?"

Izy stopped walking around the delivery truck and looked at his watch. "I don't have time right now. How about we hash it over when I get back in about five hours?" He continued checking the truck, looking at the tires and various valves and gauges.

"What's the rush to get out of here? Hot date tonight?"

"No, not tonight."

Levi looked at Izy, curious.

"Tomorrow night. At home," Izy said.

"Ohhhhh!" Levi said, laughing. "And you're spending the night here."

"Gets me home faster tomorrow."

"Okay. But seriously, Izy, you're not going to turn into one of those radicals, are you?"

Izy stopped, turned, and faced Levi. "Look, Levi, I've told you a thousand times. I brought my family here to get away from all that. Over there, we'd have a knife at each other's throats. I want no part of that."

Levi nodded and smiled. "Have a good trip, Izy. I'll see you back here later. We'll go have a beer."

"Sounds good," Izy said as he climbed into the truck and started it.

"And remember to turn on your GPS this time."

"Right," Izy said as he flipped a switch. "Satisfied?"

"Do you see him on your display?" Levi asked into a walkie-talkie to a dispatcher inside the truck terminal.

Izy heard a garbled answer.

"Yeah, now I'm satisfied," Levi said.

"Good. Hasta-LA vista, baby."

Izy put the truck in gear and rolled out of the terminal. Another maroon cargo van was parked across the street. This must be maroon cargo van day. They're everywhere. The driver was on a cell phone. It reminded Izy of the times he'd called his wife on his own cell phone. He rarely pulled over—but he always made sure traffic was light before dialing. And he used the hands-free option to talk. But still, the van driver set a good example.

Half a block later, in his side mirror, a silver Toyota rushed up to his rear bumper and then fell back. That driver also had a cell phone to his ear. Dude, learn from the guy in the van before you get yourself killed. Why do Americans always say words like "dude"? But it made the language rich, and Izy delighted in the informality.

Izy settled in for the rest of the trip. He always enjoyed the birch trees on the last leg of the trip along two-lane State Highway 169. He liked to roll his windows down and smell the fresh pine in the air. Especially on a sunny day like today. Yeah, that beer and a good talk with Levi was sounding better and better. And tomorrow night would be even better.

Approaching Armstrong Lake, Izy noticed a silver Toyota in his rear-view mirror. The same one? A man's arm came out of the driver's side window and attached a magnetic, flashing red light to the top of the car.

What in the world?

The car flashed its headlights, and the driver in Izy's mirror signaled for him to pull over. Izy looked at his speedometer. He wasn't speeding. I wonder what he wants. He signaled and turned into the Armstrong Lake side road, making sure he was safely off the highway before stopping.

The Toyota stopped behind the truck. In his mirror, Izy watched the cop step out and put the light back inside. Then the cop said something on his radio. Well, wait a minute, that looks more like a cell phone than a radio.

A maroon cargo van turned down the same road, drove slowly past Izy, and parked in front of the truck. The officer from the Toyota in back approached Izy's rear-view mirror on foot. He drew his weapon.

"Please step out of the truck," commanded the officer from behind Izy's open window.

Izy stepped down and faced the officer standing at the rear of the truck, gun drawn.

"What's wrong, officer?"

"Looks like you might have a taillight problem," said the officer.

"I know that accent," Izy said. "It's Persian. What's going on?"

The officer said nothing for a few seconds. Something stung Izy in his right shoulder. He felt dizzy and staggered. Hands caught him as he fell.

Izy woke with a start. What time was it? His head hurt. His shoulder was sore. He stepped out of the truck and stretched his legs. He was in a turnoff next to a lake. Why? He trudged to the main road and saw the sign: Armstrong Lake.

Memories started to come back. A police officer, a sting in the shoulder, and . . . now. He inspected his arm. No obvious wound. He looked at his cell phone. No service and no way to call for help. What happened to the last hour?

He climbed back in the truck and started it. This load needed to be delivered. Maybe the guys at the mine could help figure out what was going on.

The gravel road leading to the open pit mine curved left, doubling back on itself, and began gently sloping down to the entrance. Izy rounded the next curve past the Rare Metals Mining sign, and saw the back wall of the open pit rise up, four hundred yards away and thirty feet below ground.

The demolition crew supervisor was waiting, checking his watch. Other crew members stood around or sat on the ground, waiting. Izy stopped. The supervisor climbed onto the driver's-side running board. "Hey, Izy, how ya doin'?"

"I'm not sure," replied Izy.

"Did you get lost or what? The dispatch station said the GPS showed you here an hour ago."

"I don't know what happened," Izy said. "I remember talking to a police officer, and then I woke up in the truck parked on the Armstrong Lake turnoff."

"Get some help, man. It's called a blackout."

"Dude, I'll have a couple beers with friends, and that's it."

"Uh-huh. Let's get unloaded. I have a whole crew standing around burning money."

"Hop in."

The supervisor climbed up into the passenger seat, and Izy followed the gravel road against the left side of the pit toward the back wall of the mine. At the back wall, he swung to the right, now with the driver's side and truck hydraulic tubes against the rock face. Workers had drilled the usual twelve-inch diameter holes every few feet into the rock face. The next steps: fill those holes with ANFO, detonate it to move the mine wall back a few more feet, and extract precious metals from the rubble.

Izy manipulated controls on the truck to direct the end of a hydraulic tube into the first hole. Men positioned the tube inside the hole. One man gave a signal, and Izy pressed another button to release the material through the tube, filling the hole with explosive.

"Seriously, Izy, get some help, man."

"I don't know what happened. The cop pulled me over. I turned into Armstrong Lake Road, . . . and then I woke up. It's weird."

"I don't smell any booze on you."

"Because I didn't have any."

Izy moved the truck to the next hole.

"But wait a minute. There was another vehicle. A van. And the cop—I thought he was on his radio, but it was a cell phone." Izy felt his shoulder. "They shot something in my . . ."

The explosion sent seismic tremors more than one hundred miles away.

MISSING TRUCK

Jerry Barkley sat up in bed, looking over his sleeping wife at the alarm clock on her nightstand. No, the sound was different. He groped for his ringing cell phone. "You do know it's almost midnight, right?"

"One of our trucks blew up and killed thirty people. You're gonna help me figure out what happened."

"Dan?" Jerry asked.

"Yeah. I'm on my way home from Izy's wife and family. I had to tell them he's not coming home." Dan's voice broke. "We were friends."

"Wait a minute. Who's Izy?"

"He was one of our drivers. Don't you watch the news?"

"Sometimes I sleep at night."

"Turn on CNN."

"Hang on a second." Jerry fumbled for the lamp next to his bed and turned it on.

"What's going on?" Lynn asked. She drew a pillow over her head.

"Not sure." Jerry found the remote and tuned the TV to CNN.

It was an earlier interview with a geology professor at the University of Minnesota in Duluth:

> We felt the ground shake. Our seismograph recorded it at
> around a magnitude 5.0, which is unprecedented here. At first,
> we thought we'd found a newly discovered fault line. It was only
> later, when the radio reports started coming in, that we realized
> that's where our seismic activity came from. It was more than
> one hundred miles away and still registered here in Duluth.

Lynn snatched her head out from under her pillow. "What is going on?"

"Wait a minute," Jerry said into the phone. "Are you telling me one of your trucks blew up in a mine explosion?"

"Our truck was carrying about twenty thousand pounds of industrial explosives. Somebody blew it up and killed Izy and about thirty other people. I need you to help me find who did it."

Jerry rubbed his eyes. "Dan, I'm an IT consultant, not a crime scene investigator. I watch packets fly across the internet."

"You said Leah Anderson's workstation is sending stuff to Iran the other day, right?"

"Yeah."

"Well, Leah dispatches trucks. What was she sending to Iran?"

"I don't know. I didn't dig into the content; I just watched the packets. I recorded some of it. Have you talked to the police yet?"

"They showed up at Izy's house after I got there," Dan said.

"So, why are you calling me?"

"Because this doesn't add up. They're saying Izy was a terrorist 'cause he's Muslim. They're saying he blew himself up on purpose in that truck."

"Who's 'they'?"

"ISIS. Those nutcases in Syria. They're calling Izy a hero."

The TV cut to another reporter:

> A few minutes ago, an ISIS representative left this chilling social media post: "We relish in the glory of our brother and hero, Aamir Aziz, now in paradise after destroying your precious metal mine and sending many infidels to their fiery deaths. We can hit you anywhere and anytime we choose. And we will hit you again. And again. Until the Great Satan becomes a tiny Satan and a shadow of your former self."
>
> Calls to Aziz's family were not returned. Aziz's employer, New Brighton Transport near St. Paul, Minnesota, put out this statement: "We mourn with the families of our employee and the people killed today in the truck explosion. We will fully cooperate with the authorities to get to bottom of this and bring the perpetrators to justice."

"Who is Aamir Aziz?" Jerry asked.

"I told you. Our driver. Izy was his nickname. He was Palestinian. He brought his family here from the Gaza Strip a few years ago."

"And he was a terrorist?"

"No. We were friends. He didn't have a terrorist bone in his body."

"So, why did he blow up the truck?"

"He didn't. You're going to help me figure out who did."

"Wait a minute. You're sending data to Iran."

"Yeah . . ."

"Well, Iran is Shiite. ISIS is Sunni. Sunnis and Shiites hate each other's guts. So, if you're sending data to Iran, how does ISIS know your driver's name?"

"Good question. Don't you think it's suspicious you found us talking to Iran right before our truck blew up? And that those nutcases know our driver's name? You seemed like a guy who wanted to get to the bottom of things the other day. So, help us get to the bottom of this. Think of it as one of your consulting gigs."

At the Ibn Idhari Academy of Muslim History, Brian Cox surveyed the news on the internet from the computer in the front lobby. The mine explosion story was everywhere.

He found a video from a TV station up north interviewing the wife of one of the dead miners. An anguished woman with dark hair and skin color similar to Brian's sat with the interviewer on a brown couch, partially covered with a sheet. The couch sagged in the middle.

"Tell me about your life with your husband."

"I was a waitress at Fortune Bay Casino and he worked construction. We got married and lived in a duplex near the reservation."

"Bois Forte Band? Vermillion Lake?"

"Yeah. We found out the mining company was hiring when I was pregnant with Meoquanee, and so we moved to Ely."

"How old is she?"

"She's four. She looks just like her dad."

The camera panned back to show mother and child. Mom wiped a tear and put her arm around Meoquanee.

Meoquanee looked up at her mom. "Mommy be brave?"

"Yes, honey. And you be brave too." She stroked Meoquanee's hair.

"We'd heard about *Native Mob* guys from the Cities showing up and trying to recruit. They're from different Bands; some Fond Du Lac Ojibwe, most Mdewakanton Sioux. They all wear baggy pants and baseball caps. They look like boys trying to be thugs. Why would anyone around here care about their drug wars down in Minneapolis? But they said there was nothing up here for our people and anyone who joined them down there could get rich. My husband told them he'd put an air-nailer through anyone from that gang who came near us. After the explosion, I thought they did it to get back at my husband."

"What will you do with your husband gone?"

"I don't know. I don't want to move back to the reservation. I—I don't know what we'll do."

"Do the children know?"

"Meoquanee does, but she doesn't understand it. The younger ones keep asking when Papa is coming home." She teared up as the camera zoomed in on her face. "And then to find out somebody from the Middle East did this. Why does anyone in the Middle East care about a mine in northern Minnesota? Why would anyone do this?"

The reporter looked into the camera. "That's a question we're all asking. This is Sharee Campbell, reporting from WELY TV, Ely, Minnesota."

The video ended.

Brian wiped a tear. They were all kuffar, weren't they? Didn't all kuffar persecute people like Brian? But what about that lady? It didn't look like she mistreated anyone. If anything, it looked like she was victimized herself. But she was kuffar. And kuffar need to accept Allah. But what if nobody told her family about Allah? Something was wrong.

Brian shut down the computer and plodded back to his makeshift sleeping bag to think and pray.

FOR THE FAMILY

In the east side of St. Paul, Dan pointed out the Aziz home to Jerry and then parked his car behind a police car in front of the house.

The house looked out of place between a Hmong funeral home to the left and a small apartment building and Asian food market on the right. Window-mounted air conditioners on the first and second floors would struggle to keep the inside bearable on this humid summer afternoon.

TV news crews were setting up in the family medical center parking lot across the street, cameras aimed at the house. Thick cables ran to vans with satellite dishes on top.

Reporters milled around on the fresh concrete city sidewalk between the curb and a narrow strip of grass in front of the Aziz home. A three-foot chain-link fence with a gate in the middle, covered in spots with vines, surrounded the property. Photographers snapped pictures of the gnarled oak tree shading the mostly dirt front lawn.

Dan and Jerry strode through the media swarm, through the gate, and up the uneven and cracked concrete walkway to two wooden steps that used to be painted brown. They climbed the steps to a wooden front porch where the brown paint was in better shape. Tan vinyl siding covered the house and knee wall around the front porch. The roof had brown shingles, and the brown painted trim matched the front porch, giving the house exterior a tasteful look.

They stepped into a small hallway with a well-worn wooden floor. The Aziz family lived in the downstairs apartment. Dan knocked.

A petite lady with dark hair and red-rimmed eyes answered.

"Farah, I want you to meet Jerry. He's my friend I told you about yesterday."

"Come in," she said.

Jerry took in the Aziz living room as they entered. With curtains drawn on all windows, a lamp on a corner table provided the only light. An old green couch behind a coffee table leaned against the front wall. Against the living room back wall, a TV sat on a table, tuned to a news channel with a reporter talking about the Aziz family from the sidewalk in front of the house.

Farah walked across the room and turned off the TV. She straightened and faced Dan. "Who murdered my husband and made us look like terrorists? What are we supposed to do with newsmen across the street watching our house? Why is my husband dead?" She began crying again but then angrily dashed the tears from her eyes.

Dan walked across the room and hugged her. Jerry stood silently, unsure what to do with his hands.

After a few seconds, Farah separated from Dan. She turned to Jerry, "Would you like some zanjabeel?"

"What's zanjabeel?" Jerry asked, lifting his chin, surprised. "Wait, I'm sorry." He took a step back and lifted his hands, palms up. "I'm sorry, no, please, don't fix me anything. I am so sorry for what happened to you and your family. I don't like intruding on you this way." He looked toward the door and back to Farah.

Farah smiled weakly. "You are not intruding. Dan is our friend. You are Dan's friend. So, you are our friend."

"Dan, I'm sorry, but what can I possibly do to help?" Jerry took a step toward the door.

"Farah, maybe you should tell Jerry your story."

"He does not know?"

"No. And it's important. I think the Iranians murdered Izy, and Jerry's going to help prove it."

"What?" Jerry asked.

"Izy. I never liked that nickname," Farah said.

"That's what he wanted us to call him," Dan said. "He wanted to fit in."

"And his given name, Aamir, does not fit with your American culture?"

"Farah, Jerry found an infected computer at our company talking to Iran. That's how Jerry and I met."

"Iran? No. It is not possible," Farah said.

"They wanted revenge," Dan said. "They hate Israel."

"That does not explain murdering all those other people," said Farah.

"Hang on a second," Jerry said. "I'm lost."

"Please, sit," Farah said, gesturing to the couch.

Farah sat in the middle of the couch. Jerry and Dan sat on either side.

"We are from the Gaza strip," Farah said. "We lived in a flat in Gaza City until five years ago when we immigrated to this country. What do you know of the Gaza strip?"

"It's in the news all the time. It's that strip of land on the bottom-left corner of Israel next to Egypt, right? You guys are Palestinians, but there are also West

Bank Palestinians, and both groups are fighting. You elected Hamas, while the West Bank Palestinians elected the more moderate guys, I forget their name."

"Fatah," Farah said. "Fatah and Hamas are enemies." She almost spat out the words. Then her eyes softened. "Our grandparents lived in what is now Israel. But now we are herded like sheep into little pockets in Gaza and on the West Bank. We have every reason to hate Israel. But the ancestors of today's Israelis also lived on that same land. So, we fight and die over this land and attitudes harden with every new generation, every new murder, and war never stops."

She continued, "Five years ago, three Israeli soldiers were in Gaza, pretending to be Palestinians. But a few Hamas fighters figured out who they really were and fired at them. The Israelis found cover, but all were severely wounded. My husband is, was, an ambulance driver."

Farah paused, fighting tears at the mention of her husband. Dan looked for a tissue to offer, but she waved him off and wiped her eyes. "We are angry with Israel and the United Nations for the injustice they did to us. But that anger does not mean murdering Israelis. Despite what your press says, not every Palestinian is a radical terrorist. My husband saw three human beings, wounded, and in danger. Without help, they would die. Many in Gaza would cheer at their deaths, but we have no wish for anyone to die. So, he helped them into his ambulance and tried to take them to a hospital in Gaza. But no hospital would take them. So, he drove to the Eraz crossing, and a helicopter brought them to a hospital in Tel-Aviv."

"I can't imagine having to live that way," Jerry said. "Your husband was a hero."

"Our neighbors did not see it that way," Farah said. "When my husband turned back from the crossing to reenter Gaza and come home, an angry mob had already formed. He begged the Israelis to allow him to cross into Israel, and the Israeli soldiers at the gate agreed. He had just saved three of their comrades. One hour later, a man visited us and convinced me my husband had sent him and that we were in mortal danger. He asked us to pack whatever belongings we could put in his car, and we left. We never returned."

Jerry felt the intensity in Farah's eyes, pleading for help, for answers. His thoughts raced: I'm an IT contractor, not a counter-terrorism expert. How am

I supposed to figure out how your husband died? "How did you get here, to Minnesota?"

"When I reunited with my husband in Tel-Aviv, the Israelis expressed their gratitude to us. But we could not live in Israel as Israelis. It was agreed we would go to the United States under a political asylum program. We are both fluent in English, and we both wanted to live as far away from any Middle Eastern conflict as possible. My husband is, was, a driver, not a hero. And I am a mother. We just want to live in peace. We thought, nobody cares about Palestine or Israel here. Perhaps our children can grow up and help make the world better." Farah looked down, toying with a thread in her shirt.

"And that's where we came in," Dan said. "We're always looking for drivers, and we did some deliveries for the INS at the Canadian border. Somehow, the government heard about us and asked if we'd sponsor this family and give him a job. We said yes."

Farah looked back at Jerry. "Dan helped us set up a computer at our house and has been a wonderful friend. So, you see," Farah said, eyes glistening, "my husband cannot be a terrorist. Somebody murdered my husband and dozens of other people and is trying to make my husband responsible for all of it. We tried so hard to escape all this and now," she burst into tears, "it strikes the heart of our family."

Farah sobbed. Dan put his arms around her shoulders. Jerry looked down at his hands.

Farah wiped her eyes, this time with a tissue, and stood and faced both Dan and Jerry. Her eyes hardened. "I have known grief and agony my entire life. I am used to it. But I will not rest until I find out who did this to my husband and those innocent people and why."

Dan nodded. "We'll find who did this. That's a promise."

"Um," Jerry said, "I don't know what I can do to help you. I'm sorry, but as I said, I'm just an IT consultant."

"You have a few tricks up your sleeve," Dan said. "You found that malware on our computers. Dig deeper. Figure out what we're sending to Iran and who set us up."

"I don't have ESP," Jerry said. "Leah got rid of the original email, remember?"

"I don't know what any of that means, but I am grateful for your help," Farah said.

———•———

The doorbell rang a few minutes later. Farah answered it.

"Farah Aziz?" asked a man with a receding hairline wearing a suit.

"Yes," Farah said.

FBI Agents Blackwell and Channing introduced themselves. Blackwell showed his badge to Farah.

"How may I help you?" Farah asked with a hint of fear in her voice. She looked at Dan for guidance. Dan rose and walked to her side.

"May we come in?" Blackwell asked. Blackwell and Channing made eye contact with Jerry.

"Yes, of course. Are you acquainted?" asked Farah, standing aside and looking at Jerry as they entered.

"We spent some quality time together," Jerry said. "You guys look good in your suits. Did you get the message I left the other day?"

"I don't recall," Blackwell said. "May I ask why you're here?"

"Funny, I was about to ask you guys the same thing," Dan said.

Channing asked, "Mrs. Aziz, may we ask you some questions?"

Farah squeezed Dan's hand. "Why does the FBI want to ask questions of me the day after my husband was murdered? Aren't the statements I gave to the police enough?"

"We're just trying to get to the bottom of his death," Blackwell said. "A goal I'm certain we all share."

"Very well. Ask your questions," Farah said.

"In private, please."

"No. You may ask your questions with my friend Dan present. And his friend Jerry."

"Okay. Was your husband involved with any terrorist groups?" Channing asked.

"No!" Farah said. "Of course not!"

"Did he have any communications with anyone associated with ISIS?"

"No!"

"Was he ever away from home for extended periods of time?"

"Of course he was. He was a truck driver."

"So, there were times when he was away and you were unable to account for his whereabouts?" Blackwell said.

"Now, just hold on right there," Dan said. "Aamir Aziz was my friend and worked at my company. He was no terrorist. He was a victim."

"Maybe," Blackwell said. He looked at Channing.

"Did you talk to your husband between two and four o'clock yesterday afternoon?" Channing asked.

"No."

"You understand, we can pull phone records and verify the time and duration of every call you've had, right?"

"Then pull your records. My husband did not call me yesterday afternoon. He does not call while driving unless it's an emergency. And then, he pulls over, out of traffic, to make the call."

Channing continued. "New Brighton Transport took a call from the mine supervisor at approximately three thirty yesterday afternoon; he was wondering where their delivery was. The dispatcher said their GPS showed your husband arriving at the site at three, half an hour earlier. But he wasn't there. The GPS unit stopped transmitting, and the mine explosion occurred at 4:07p.m., so your husband was roughly an hour late arriving. How do you account for the missing hour?"

"I don't know," Farah answered.

"Wait a minute," Dan said. "You talked to our dispatchers?"

"Yes," replied Blackwell. "Before we stopped here."

"And the GPS unit on Izy's truck gave a wrong position report?"

"It reported him at the mine an hour before he actually arrived there, yes," answered Channing.

"That doesn't make any sense," Dan said.

"Anything can be spoofed," Jerry said, rubbing his hand over his bald head. "Those GPS devices listen to signals from the satellites, figure out where they are, and then send position updates, right?"

"Yeah, that's how they work," replied Dan.

"What if somebody drove the route ahead of time and recorded the GPS signals?" Jerry said. "And then they could replay the GPS signals to the receiver on the truck and maybe block the real satellite signals. The GPS receiver on the truck would report its position based on bogus GPS signals, instead of real ones from the real satellites."

"But why?" Farah asked.

"To buy time," replied Dan. "We thought he was onsite because that's what the GPS told us. We didn't find out differently until the mine supervisor called, a half hour after the GPS said he was already there. And it would have taken another half hour to alert people."

"None of that tells us who or why," Channing said.

"Mrs. Aziz, who was your husband mad at?" Blackwell asked.

"He was angry at many people in Gaza City who wanted to murder innocent people. And many radicals in Israel who took advantage of the situation."

"Have you been in communication with people from where you used to live?"

"My mother," answered Farah. "She is old and doesn't have the mental capacity she once had. She lives with my brother and his wife in Gaza City. She is diabetic, and we're trying to find a reliable supply of insulin for her."

"What about the rest of your families?"

"Aamir has two sisters and a brother. His parents are dead. I have my mother, brother, and his family. Of course, we want to get them all out."

"It must be frustrating."

"Yes, it is."

"Frustrating enough to kill himself and thirty other people in an explosion?"

Farah's eyes glistened.

"That's enough," Dan said. "Why would somebody who's trying to get his family out of a bad situation blow himself up? Do you guys have evidence or warrants or anything like that?"

"I believe the St. Paul police were granted one yesterday evening," Blackwell said. "That warrant also applies to us. We have authority to search this house."

"I can do nothing to stop you. But I beg you to let me grieve in peace for my husband."

"Look, we all want the same thing," Blackwell said. "We want to find out what happened to your husband. But the St. Paul police told us you were less than forthcoming. Do you understand how this looks when you play games with the police?"

Farah's face turned red. "I did not play games with the police."

"Do you know what the penalty is for interfering with a federal investigation?" Blackwell asked. "People died in that explosion."

"My friend died, too," Dan said. "And her husband. And now you guys barge in here and accuse him of being a terrorist. How do you expect her to act? Unless you guys are here to arrest somebody, I think you should leave now."

After Channing and Blackwell were out the door, Dan said, "Farah, thank you for having us. We'll stay in touch. And if there's anything . . ."

"Yes, thank you," said Farah. "You have been so kind."

As they drove away, the news played on the car radio: "A social media post with a short video from a Yazid Kalil credits ISIS with the Northern Minnesota explosion yesterday that killed dozens." The announcer played a sound bite from the video: "We will strike you at will in the heart of your country and devour the spirit of your Great Satan in the name of Allah!" The announcer then gave the latest update: "Law enforcement officials suggest the video is credible. The president is ordering tightened security at airports, power plants, and other critical infrastructure."

"Except ISIS didn't do this," Dan said. "Iran did. You watched the packets. You uncovered this yourself."

"And what am I supposed to do about it?"

"Finish what you started. You're not in this alone anymore."

"What does that mean, 'Finish what I started?' I've given malware samples to Saphas, and I tried to report what I found to the FBI. What else am I supposed to do?"

"Keep digging," Dan said. "I'm your customer now. Send me the bill."

MOA RECON

Brian, Cypress, and Lion followed Khalid into the warehouse area at the Ibn Idhari Academy.

Brian looked through the open driver's side window in one of the vans. The interior was lined with plastic and filled with off-white pellets. "What's that stuff? Smells like fuel oil."

"That," Tabor said, "is the reason we acquired the vans."

"Man, it stinks in here," Cypress said.

"Cypress is right," Khalid said. "The odor could be a problem."

"Burns my eyes," Lion said.

"I'll see if I can find some scents to mask it," Tabor said. "And let's roll up the windows and see if that helps."

"We'll see you when you return," Khalid said. "Insha'Allah."

Tabor nodded. "Yes, Insha'Allah."

Tabor and Walter climbed into an empty van while Khalid walked to a door opener and pressed a green button to open the door. The humid air only reinforced the fumes. Khalid pressed the red button to close the door as the van disappeared down the street.

"Where are they going?" Lion asked.

"Reconnaissance," Khalid said.

Brian smiled. He knew their likely destination. And that had to be explosives in the vans. This was really happening! This wouldn't be like the mine explosion where poor people died. This time, rich people who exploited believers would die. Brian could barely contain his excitement as he furtively glanced at Khalid.

But he also felt a nagging doubt. Weren't Brian's own parents rich? Yes, but they were believers, not kuffar. But how would they know nobody in those hotels was a believer?

"Let's finish our history lesson, and then we'll break for lunch," Khalid said, as he opened the hallway door back to the classrooms.

The group trudged down the hall to the classroom where they'd spent the past two days in a crash course in Muslim history.

After they were seated, Khalid asked, "What do we know about the Crusades?"

"They were holy wars between Christians and Muslims around eight hundred years ago," Lion said.

"Yes," Khalid said. "Between 1095 and 1250, Christians tried to wipe out our Muslim ancestors at least seven times. Our ancestors had to arm themselves and fight back or die at the hands of infidels. Our ancestors paid for our right to exist with their blood."

"Christians say they want peace. Why did they start these wars?" Brian asked.

"Because we had something they wanted," Khalid said. "One thousand years ago, while Europe was convulsing through the Dark Ages, our ancestors led the world in mathematics, astronomy, medicine, optics, physics, literature, music, technology, and every discipline important to humanity."

Khalid continued. "Today's algebra and trigonometry came from Muslim scholars. Our understanding of gravity and physics and astronomy did not start with Isaac Newton but with Muslim scholars hundreds of years before Newton, Kepler, Copernicus, and other Europeans. Our ancestors led the ancient world in nearly every academic discipline. And our reward? Deceptions, lies, forced conversions, relocations, and mass murders. We hear on today's Western news programs about atrocities they call ethnic cleansing. Who do you think started that? Westerners."

"But why?" Brian asked.

"Because they wanted our land and our knowledge."

"Still, that was eight hundred years ago," Lion said. "Ancient history."

"Yes, the Crusades were hundreds of years ago," Khalid said. "But that was only the beginning. What can you tell me about the year 1492?"

"Columbus?" Cypress said.

"Yes, but there was a more sinister event in Spain early that year that we don't read about in Western history books. That was the year Christians conquered Granada, the last remaining Muslim city in Spain. By 1499, Granadans were presented with a choice: convert to Christianity or leave. By 1609, even many of those who converted to Christianity were forcibly exiled and murdered.

"And as for Columbus and the Christian march west, look no further than the Native Americans who were on this continent first, before the European invasion. It's a history filled with suffering and oppression, from the same country that spouts freedom.

"And now, today, after stealing our knowledge and land in earlier generations, America and the West are back at our gates again, this time for oil. That's the real reason America has crusading armies across Iraq and Syria. They have always claimed to represent peace and freedom, but, historically, it's been from the barrel of a gun. Today, it's from a video-controlled drone that murders innocent Muslims in their homes.

"Owl, the Americans you've met hate you, not so much because you're different but because you represent an obstacle in their way. They want global domination and will kill you and your family to get what they want. You join us not only for revenge but also to defend our way of life and your family. To the death, if necessary."

"I don't wish to die," Lion said.

"I want the other guys to die," Cypress said.

"Nobody wishes to die," Khalid said. "But let me describe the paradise that awaits you when you die defending our honor."

"I heard we get seventy virgins," Cypress said.

"Well, there's that." Khalid smiled. "Although it's not universally accepted that we'll have seventy virgins available to us, we will have servants to take care of all our needs and wants, including sexual. Let me read you the first few verses from Surah 56 in the holy Quran."

Khalid picked up a well-worn book bound in leather with markers on several pages. "I generally like to read in the original Arabic, but this English translation is reasonable. Starting in Surah 56, verse 1, it says,

> When the day of resurrection and judgment occurs—there is no denying that it will befall—it will bring down some and raise up others. When the earth is shaken with convulsion and the mountains are broken down, crumbling and become dust dispersing, you become of three kinds: Then the companions of the right—what are the companions of the right? And the companions of the left—what are the companions of the left?"

"What does that mean, companions on the left and right?" Cypress asked.

"The companions on the right are believers. Companions on the left are nonbelievers and infidels," Lion said.

"You are correct," Khalid said. "Let's continue, starting with verse 10:

> And the forerunners, the forerunners—those are the ones brought near to Allah in the Gardens of Pleasure, a large company of the former peoples and a few of the later peoples, on thrones woven with ornament, reclining on them, facing each other. There will circulate among them young boys made eternal with vessels, pitchers and a cup of wine from a flowing spring—no headache will they have therefrom, nor will they be intoxicated—and fruit of what they select, and the meat of fowl, from whatever they desire. And for them are fair women with large, beautiful eyes, the likenesses of pearls well-protected, as reward for what they used to do. They will not hear therein ill speech or commission of sin—only a saying: 'Peace, peace.'"

"Wait a minute," Cypress said. "We'll have little boys to feed us food and wine and girls we can take to bed?"

"That's what it says," Khalid said. "You can drink all the wine you want and never get intoxicated and take your choice of beautiful women to bed with you. But you don't need to be a leader, just a believer. Let's pick it up again at verse 26:

> The companions of the right—what are the companions of the right? They will be among lote trees with thorns removed, and banana trees layered with fruit and shade extended, and water poured out. And fruit, abundant and varied, neither limited to season nor forbidden, and upon beds raised high. Indeed, we have produced the women of Paradise in a new creation and made them virgins, devoted to their husbands and of equal age, for the companions of the right who are a company of the former peoples and a company of the later peoples."

"Wow!" Cypress said.

"What about those forbidden thoughts and feelings?" Brian asked.

"Deny yourself in this life to indulge in the next. And, Owl, here is your revenge. Continuing with verse 40: 'And the companions of the left—what are the companions of the left? They will be in scorching fire and scalding water and a shade of black smoke, neither cool nor beneficial.'"

Khalid put his book down. "Gentlemen, what do you think of all that? Is it worth the struggle?"

"Yeah," cried Cypress.

Brian and Lion nodded quietly.

"Excellent," Khalid said. "I will leave you to study your Qurans, and we will gather for questions later."

●———●

Alone after dinner in his makeshift sleeping bag, Brian set down his holy Quran and glanced at his prayer rug, rolled up neatly in a cubbyhole. Khalid had said its Arabic name was *Sajada* when he gave one to each recruit. And Khalid had taught Brian more about his Muslim heritage here in the past few days than a lifetime of living at home. Khalid was a wonderful teacher, and this experience was exhilarating.

But doubt also nagged Brian. He unfurled his prayer rug and laid it down on the floor, with the head facing east toward Mecca. As Khalid taught, he stood at the rug foot and raised his hands to his shoulders, palms facing up. "Allahu akbar. Allahu akbar. Allahu akbar. Peace and blessings on the Prophet. Allah, please forgive me for not knowing the right way to pray to you yet. I come to you in supplication the best I know how."

He kneeled on the rug and touched his head to the ground.

"Allah, please guide me. Khalid talked about European Christians who murdered the people who were on this continent first. But didn't we do the same thing to that lady's family in the video you guided me to earlier? What did she mean when she said she might have to move back to the reservation? Was she Native American? Her family didn't look like they ever persecuted anyone. But now her husband is dead. Does that mean we persecuted her family? But they

135

were kuffar. Downtrodden maybe, but still kuffar. And this is war. And war has casualties. It's no different than when Christians made war against your Prophet. Allah, please help me sort all this out."

He stood, lifted his palms again, and finished. "All Praise belongs to Allah, cherisher and sustainer of the worlds."

He rolled his prayer rug up, tucked it back in its cubby hole, and crawled in his sleeping bag. But he couldn't fall asleep.

•————•

"And one of your recruits suggested these targets?" Tabor asked later that evening. Khalid, Tabor, Walter, and the rest of the Iranian Special Forces team sat around a card table in the locked office area next to the warehouse, looking at uploaded cell phone photos and Google Maps satellite views of the Mall of America.

"Yes," Khalid said. "Owl. He is an impressive young man. I wish we did not have to sacrifice him."

"This is the only way," Tabor said. "You know we cannot risk letting him get close to us."

"I know. But it's a pity." Khalid paused. "What are your thoughts about the target?"

"It has challenges, but it's doable," Tabor said. "The Patterson Blu hotel is on the south side, facing Killebrew Drive, and the JW Chariot hotel is on the north side, in front of a large outdoor parking lot and the Ikea furniture store. Both have parking ramps under the hotels and offer two-hour free parking for mall visits. Drive into a ramp, press a button on the ticket machine, and take a ticket. Anyone can get in anonymously."

"That is promising," Khalid said.

"Yes," Tabor said. "We should park the vans in an upper level, as near to the hotel center as possible. Both ramps have large enough spaces to handle cargo vans. We must assume it's all on video, so we should acquire different license plates for the vans to make them more difficult to trace."

"We can use our recruits for that," Walter said.

"Yes, an excellent idea," Khalid said. "They're eager for action."

"And what about timing?" Tabor asked.

"The CDC doctor leaves the hospital in the afternoon," Khalid said. "So, your team should have ample time to get into position. What if they close the airports?"

"Then the CDC doctor will not be leaving anytime soon," Tabor said. "And even if they close MSP airport, the smaller airports will stay open."

"And your reconnaissance of Anoka County Airport?"

Tabor brought up a Google Maps satellite photo. "We will do the blood sample handoff here." He pointed to a spot near what looked like some maintenance hangars. "It is a blessing from Allah. We can bring anything we want into that airport, even drive cars right up to the runways."

ONION LAYERS

"Hey, Dan," Jerry said into his cell phone. The Minnesota midafternoon sun shone through his basement office window. "I just finished talking to the antivirus team in England. They disassembled the code from Leah's workstation. And all I can say is, wow. The stuff on Leah's workstation is unique to you."

"What do you mean?"

"That code has custom modules for dozens of individual trucking companies and every single one of them is unique. Yours had a bunch of database queries apparently looking for scheduling information and routes and drivers. The others also had queries looking for similar information, but the databases and syntax were different. Which means the attackers must have specific knowledge about what software packages each of these trucking companies use."

"How did they get all that?"

"Who knows. Probably the same way they got inside Leah's workstation at your place. Anyway, the antivirus team has a copy in their lab of everything I had running. Leah's workstation clone is talking like mad to the Maverick Marketing clone I told you about, and the antivirus group is analyzing the packets."

"Let me know what your antivirus guys come up with."

"I will." An incoming call beeped in Jerry's ear. "Uh-oh. Let me call you back. The caller-ID says it's the Twin Cities FBI."

"This should be good," Dan said.

"When I get my one phone call on the way to Gitmo, I'm calling you." Jerry pressed the answer button on his cell phone.

"Interfering with a federal investigation. Aiding and abetting terrorism. Obstruction of justice. And I'm just getting warmed up. You're playing a dangerous game, and I want to know why."

"Good afternoon to you, too, Agent Channing."

"We know you're exchanging data over the internet with an enemy of the United States. You were less than forthcoming when we gave you an opportunity to explain yourself in our office. And now, we know you're in contact with a suspected terrorist's family."

"Well, why don't you come and arrest me, then?"

"We're considering it."

"Well, come on over. I assume you know where I live."

"Do you know how expensive legal battles are? What will your family do after you're bankrupt?"

"Maybe they'll call the TV stations and tell everyone how the FBI is abusing its power."

"Do you know what it's like to have media camping out in your front yard and asking your family questions about how you're helping terrorists? You live in a nice school district. It would be a shame if your family has to move."

"Is intimidation just instinct with you guys or is this what they teach you in FBI school?"

"Do you know what prison is like, Jerry? Don't bend over in the shower. What if your cellmate's a serial killer?"

Jerry laughed. "Abuse your power and you'll be the one going to prison. Maybe I'll come visit."

"Don't mess with us, Jerry. It'll go badly for you. We've learned a lot about you these past few days. You went to college, so you must be a smart man. Smart people know when they're out of options. I suggest you start talking."

"Did you get that line from an old movie? What do you think I've been trying to do? Did that bozo give you the message I left the other day? If you want to investigate something, why don't you investigate why the country of Iran is stealing data from trucking companies across the country as we speak."

"How do you know that?"

"Because I built a little honeypot here, and I've been watching the packets fly back and forth. That's the TOR traffic we talked about in your little room the other day. You guys told *me* it was going to Iran. And I've been meaning to ask—how did you know?"

"We have traffic monitors."

"That's a load of crap. I wasn't born yesterday. There's no way to trace it through TOR. That's why TOR exists."

Neither said anything for about thirty seconds.

"I really do have information you need. And I want to help. But after watching you guys take five years to work an embezzlement case after the FBI jerked me around when I tried to report a cyberattack back in 2000, after my $14,000 credit fraud problem disappeared into your bureaucratic black hole, and after I busted my butt to help you guys out in the Bullseye breach case, I don't know if you're another bureaucratic bozo or not."

"So, now, in addition to impeding a federal investigation, you're threating to withhold vital information?"

"You win the prize, Agent Channing. Before you send me to Gitmo, I'll tell you this—you're chasing the wrong people if you think ISIS was behind that mine explosion."

"I'm working up your arrest warrant right now."

"Are you recording this call? When you guys put me on trial, play this part back. You said it yourself. It was a New Brighton truck. And the Iranians penetrated the New Brighton network. They probably have all the schedules for all the deliveries. They knew about that explosives delivery, and they probably blew up that truck."

"The cleaner theory is the driver was a suicide bomber."

"Except that he wasn't."

"If you have evidence to prove it, I'm listening."

"Last time I checked, it's on you to prove he's guilty. If you railroad his family and me, you'll miss what's really going on here. Maybe we can figure it out together."

After a few seconds of silence, Channing said, "Why don't we meet?"

"You know where I live. Maybe we'll do a video call with Joanne Gittens with Saphas Antivirus. They're disassembling the malware I found, and you might want to warn the trucking industry. Ever heard of Stuxnet?"

"No. What's that?"

"It was malware the Israelis and the NSA built to mess with the PLCs controlling Iran's nuclear centrifuges starting around 2008 or so. Only the antivirus companies sniffed it out because it got onto systems it wasn't supposed to get onto."

"Okay . . ."

"Okay, well, pass along my congratulations to your buddies at the NSA. Their code's in the wild and it came back home. I have a copy of it inside a virtual machine right here in my basement. Which is another clue leading back to Iran."

Jerry waited for a response.

"Still working on that arrest warrant? Joanne tells me this malware has modules specific to lots of companies. It knows when it's running in any one of those environments, and I've seen it kill itself when it finds out it's somewhere else. Whoever's behind this knows details about each of the companies it targets."

Jerry waited for what felt like hours on the phone. Finally, Channing responded.

"Okay, hotshot, I have a question for you. Where are they going to hit us next?"

"How would I know?"

"You're the one listening to all the traffic. Where are they planning to strike next?"

Jerry stood. "What makes you think they're planning another one?"

"Because they didn't blow up twenty thousand pounds of ANFO in that mine explosion."

"What?"

"ANFO, hotshot. It's the explosive that was in that truck. According to New Brighton Transport records, it was carrying twenty thousand pounds of the stuff. But the blast was only big enough for ten thousand pounds."

"Holy crap."

"Welcome to my world."

TO A LONG AND HEALTHY LIFE

Heather Magnussen's time in the hospital was a blur. First the fever, spiking to 104, then chills, then vomiting and watery diarrhea. Days and nights blended together as an endless stream of people in isolation suits constantly checked every detail of everything in her room. The fever broke on day eleven. And now it was day fourteen, and she was in front of a bank of microphones and cameras.

"I'm proud to report that Heather Magnussen is winning her war against Ebola," the lead doctor on her care team, dressed in blue hospital scrubs, said. The news conference was in the hospital auditorium, with local and national news crews covering the event. "We'll keep her here for another few days for monitoring and then send her home to recover for a few months."

"How do you feel?" asked a reporter.

"Alive!" answered Heather. "And grateful."

Another hand went up in the audience. The lead doctor pointed to the raised hand, and then looked at Heather and smiled. "I believe this gentleman has a question."

Mike stood. Heather put her hands over her mouth. Her eyes glistened, and she screamed with surprise and delight.

"Heather, I was wondering if you felt like wearing this ring I showed you last month?" He held up the wedding ring. "And I brought some other people with me who wanted to say hi."

A video image appeared behind the podium, replacing the white background on the projector screen. Heather's doctor gestured for her to turn around as the image of the entrance to the Port Loco hospital, where she had spent the most fulfilling and painful weeks of her life, came into focus.

Heather's eyes widened when she saw the new, home-made welcome sign: "Lahai Taylor Hospital. May all who enter here find healing and comfort." Tears filled her eyes.

The image blurred as the camera twirled and faced the operator. It was Clemence, Heather's Médecins Sans Frontières supervising doctor, smiling. "Bonjour, Heather," he said. "We are overjoyed you are improving. We wanted to show you the impact you made during your time here."

"Can they see and hear me?" Heather asked.

"Oui, we can hear and see you quite well," Clemence said.

Heather waved, now laughing and crying. Clemence waved back. "We brought a few special friends who are eager to talk to you," he said as he spun the video camera back toward the Lahai Taylor sign.

Heather recognized the two women who stood together in the foreground in front of the sign. Tears flowed down her cheeks.

"Heather," the oldest said, "please do not cry. This is a happy time."

"I am so sorry," Heather said. "We did everything we could, but we could not save Lahai."

"I know," the older woman in the video said, "and I miss my granddaughter. But she is in heaven now, and one day, we will all be together."

The other woman, closer to Heather's age, spoke. "Heather, I loved my sister and my niece more than words can describe. And that demon named Ebola took them away from us too early. But God teaches us that life here on this earth is only temporary, but life in heaven will be forever. So, what is a few years of waiting when we will spend eternity together?"

Lahai's grandmother continued. "Until we see my youngest daughter and granddaughter again, we are dedicating this place to their memory and to the work your wonderful team started. We will beat back this demon while we work to spread the word of God throughout this region. So, you see, this is a happy time. Lahai served her purpose here on earth, and now she is in a better place with God."

Tears streamed down Heather's face. Unable to talk for several seconds, she was finally able to say, "Thank you."

"Mike, would you do the honors?" Heather's doctor asked.

Mike walked up to the podium and put on a pair of rubber gloves. He turned to Heather. Somebody held a mic close. "Heather, you are the love of my life, and I can't wait for our marriage to begin."

Heather held out her left hand, and Mike slipped the engagement ring over it.

"I want so badly to kiss you, Mike!" Heather said.

"No physical contact yet, not for another few days," Heather's doctor said. "And I'm afraid it will be several months before you can consummate that marriage."

Everyone in the room laughed, many through tears. The two women in the video image clapped.

"We have the rest of our lives," Heather said.

DEFECTOR

During the final keynote presentation at the University of Minnesota epidemiology conference, Benjamin Donovan's cell phone chirped with a text message from his supervisor. Since he was already in town, what were his thoughts on staying an extra couple days to meet the Ebola nurse and hospital staff and bring back a blood sample? And a carrot—he would fly home on a charter, instead of flying in a commercial cattle car. It was an easy decision. "Of course—great idea!" he texted back.

●━━━━━●

In Tehran, Atesh finished reading an intercepted email.

```
Ben, thanks for changing your plans so you
could meet with the Ebola patient and shep-
herd her blood sample home day after tomor-
row. We made arrangements with a charter
company named Locke Air to bring you home.
Instead of wading through security at MSP,
you'll fly out of the Anoka County Airport di-
rect to Atlanta.
```

Atesh, aka, Alain, left a coded, one-sentence message in the Gmail account shared with Khalid Farooq.

```
Begin phase two in two days.
```

Bahir Mustafa stared at a computer monitor in his office in Tehran, studying his botnet heat map and trying to figure out why two control nodes were so close together. Had Atesh done something to the system he'd built over more than the past decade?

The algorithm was supposed to be simple. Whenever a new drone came online, it contacted the home server and awaited instructions. The home server decided whether this new drone was a candidate for promotion to control node, based on hop count and geographical proximity to other control nodes. If it passed those tests, the next series of tests probed whether the home server could completely control it. If the new drone passed all these tests, the home server promoted it to control node, where it played an important role, relaying commands to drones and responses back to Tehran. But this new control node in Minnesota, in a city named Eagan, was within ten kilometers of another control node in a city called Burnsville. Why?

He typed a few commands and squinted at the screen, stroking his chin.

The evidence was unmistakable. The Eagan node and the Burnsville node were duplicates. Bahir stood and paced. It was unlikely this was Atesh's doing. It had to be Americans. Somebody in the United States was infiltrating his botnet network. But who? And why?

He sat again and brought up another window with code listings. It had been a long time since he'd done this. He studied it for a few seconds and found what he was looking for. Next, he brought his heat map window into the foreground and expanded the details around this Eagan rogue control node. He issued the appropriate command, and the dot representing the rogue control node disappeared from the heat map.

After spending hours in front of a keyboard, staring at packet traces and trying to make sense of it, Jerry Barkley had a headache. And a vague sense of dread in his gut.

"I build firewalls. I'm an IT guy, not a counter-terrorism expert." It was time for a break. He pushed back the office chair he'd scavenged from a yard sale ten years ago, stood, and stretched. He needed some pretzels and pop. And maybe he could find a *Star Trek* rerun. He glanced back down at the computer monitor and stopped.

"That can't be right."

He looked closer—there was no mistaking it. The flow of data to Iran had just stopped. And the flow from Leah's workstation clone had also stopped. Jerry sat, clicked some mouse buttons, and typed a few keyboard commands.

"No way."

He brought up the Maverick Marketing virtual console and opened a window to search for the malware files on that virtual machine. He did the same for Leah's workstation clone. No mistaking it—all trace of the malware on both systems was gone.

"Well, isn't that special?"

He quickly composed an email to Joanne Gittens.

```
Hey, Joanne—did that malware disappear from
any of the systems in your lab? It just
self-destructed here.
```

Jerry walked upstairs, sat on the couch, and turned on the TV. Romulans were about to invade the Federation, and only a few crew members from the *Enterprise* stood in their way. The couch felt nice. Jerry sipped his pop, set the can down, and leaned his head back.

He woke up two hours later. A show about British car enthusiasts was on. The pop can was still full. He turned off the TV, stood, stretched, and trudged back downstairs.

A reply from Joanne Gittens was waiting.

```
No, our malware samples are unchanged.
```

I wonder . . . He tried a video call. After a few rings, Joanne Gittens appeared on Jerry's computer monitor.

"Hey, Joanne, you look tired."

"I haven't slept much these past few days, thank you very much."

"You and me both. Anyway, I was thinking—our friend just communicated with us. All that malware is gone from the test systems here."

"Yes. You mentioned that in your email. That is troubling."

"Well, it is and it isn't. Our friend knows about me, and he murdered around thirty people here. That's the troubling part. But I also know about him, and maybe that's an opportunity."

"How so?"

"Maybe we can communicate with him."

"I hadn't considered that. It could offer us some advantages, couldn't it?"

"Yeah. You've disassembled that code, right?"

"Most of it. Our friend employs some fascinating tactics."

"Great. So, here's what I was thinking. Can you replace some of his malware code to send a message back to his home server?"

"Good heavens! Yes, we can!"

"Groovy. I'm going to revert my test systems here back to their snapshots. I'll get back to you with the message I want to send."

"Did you really just say, 'Groovy'?"

"Yes, I did."

Bahir Mustafa leaned back in his chair and stroked his beard. Again. How could that Eagan control node be back? He reviewed his earlier self-destruct steps and then sent the appropriate commands again. This time, he would watch closely to make sure it succeeded.

What was this? A spike in inbound network traffic? And that control node was still active. What happened to the self-destruct command? Maybe the diagnostic logs would show something.

He opened another window and navigated to the directory holding his diagnostic logs. New lines appended to the bottom of his diagnostic log file at lightning speed. Dozens of times every second. It had already consumed another 5 percent of his log partition. It would quickly fill up and bring everything to a halt if he didn't find a way to stop it. Bahir's eyes widened. Were the Americans counterattacking?

Line after line repeated,

```
Say hi to your buddy Allah after we fry you.
Send another self-destruct signal to turn
this flood off.
```

After a few seconds, Bahir sent another self-destruct command. Shortly after that, the traffic flood stopped. But not before one last message:

```
You murdered thirty innocent people. We're
coming for you.
```

The system went silent. But did not disappear from the heat map.

What murders?

Bahir's fingers tingled as he started a Google search. He grew more alarmed with each article. From the *St. Paul Pioneer Press*: "At Least 30 Dead in Ely Mine Explosion." From *The Washington Post*: "ISIS Takes Credit for Latest Terrorist Attack."

Why were the Americans blaming him for an ISIS attack? Iran was Shiite. ISIS was Sunni. They had to know where he was.

The lead sentence from one of the articles was key: "A Yazid Kalil took credit for yesterday's bombing in the name of ISIS in a social media post . . ."

Bahir found Kalil's social media profile and started looking through posts. They all were carefully worded not to reveal anything of substance. Kalil's pictures—here posing with an AK-47, there posing with a knife, all showed backgrounds with no distinguishing features.

Only one conclusion was possible. Yazid Kalil was a fake.

And the Americans knew it.

●—————●

In his basement, logged on to the Maverick Marketing virtual workstation clone as the administrator, Jerry stared at its console screen. His gaze drifted across the icons in the Maverick Marketing desktop screen and lit upon something unfamiliar: a new text file on the Maverick Marketing desktop named "NotMe. txt." Jerry opened it with Notepad.

```
I am not responsible for those deaths. I am
also a victim. And I also know how to find you
in Minnesota.
```

Jerry sat back in his seat. "No way. This isn't happening." He appended some text to the end of the file and saved it.

```
OK, scumbag, come meet me in the real world.
I'm in command of a fleet of flying US drones
looking down on you right now. Save us the
trouble of blowing you up where you sit.
```

Jerry fumbled with his cell phone. His hands shook. He took a deep breath and dialed.

"Agent Channing, you are not gonna believe what's going on here."

•———•

Jerry's unfinished basement walls were filled with green spray foam insulation, covering the wiring and sealing the house from the outside. The office area was set off by two tables, one along the back wall under a window, the other perpendicular. Beyond the perpendicular table was a large table saw, covered with spare wood and parts from long-forgotten house projects. Both tables were piled high with old PC parts, printouts, CDs, DVDs, and clutter. A metal shelf held a few servers, some with covers off and in various states of disrepair. Wires were everywhere, bundled in places with twist ties taken from old bread packages in an unsuccessful attempt to provide order.

Channing's gaze stopped at a set of plywood shelves, where books with titles like *Building Linux Firewalls*, *Hacking Exposed*, and dozens of others were stacked haphazardly.

"Do you read this stuff?" Channing asked.

"Most of the books are obsolete," Jerry said. "But the fundamentals are still the same."

"How do you keep track of it all?"

Jerry laughed. "I don't have the resources of the United States Federal Government, so I have to be more creative. What I do down here isn't for the faint of heart, but I make a living."

"So, you've having a conversation with this guy. I'll give you points for having a pair," Channing said. "Show me what you've got."

"Let's see if he's added anything in the past few minutes."

Jerry sat in his surplus office chair, clicked on the file, and gestured for Channing to sit in an old kitchen chair to read the responses he had traded with Bahir:

```
If you blow me up, you will never find out who
is behind your bombing.

I think you're behind the bombing, and now
you're trying to save your skin."

I did not know there was a bombing until now.

OK, so what's your story then?

I run a botnet your law enforcement calls the
Zagros network. I have no interest in terror-
ism or murder. These are bad for business.

If you didn't blow up that mine, who did?

Atesh Zare.
```

```
Who is Atesh Zare?

What do you know of Iran?

I know we're about to turn where you live
into a bomb crater if you don't give me some-
thing I can use.
```

"Impressive," Channing said. "This is the guy who runs the Zagros botnet?"

"Apparently. What's special about that?"

"It's one of the more sophisticated ones we've been tracking."

"So, that's the traffic pattern you guys found coming out of here?"

"No comment. And he thinks you're a cop?"

Jerry laughed. "Nah, I told him I'm US military and sending a fleet of drones his way." Jerry directed Channing to the relevant dialog.

```
How do I know you are who you say you are?

You don't.
```

"And that was a few minutes after I called you," Jerry said to Channing.

The last modification date on the document updated. Channing closed and reopened it. The new last line said,

```
I wish to talk face to face.
```

"Holy crap," Jerry said. "That's new."

Channing typed another line onto the end of the document:

```
What do you suggest?
```

He saved and exited.

Within seconds, the access date on the file updated again. Channing opened it.

```
I suggest a Skype meeting. What is your user-
name?
```

"I need to call my boss," Channing said. "Why don't you set up a throwaway username? And we need to set up a background for the video. I can't believe we're doing this."

●────────●

Jerry called upstairs. "Anne, would you come down here please?"

Jerry's daughter appeared a few seconds later. "Yeah? Why do you have plywood in front of the bookshelves?"

"Because I don't want to give the guy we're about to call any clues about where we are."

"Who are you talking to?"

"The guy who blew up that mine in Ely. Except he says he didn't do it."

"Huh?"

"I need you to put your boys in front of a TV and tell them Grandpa will be unhappy if they make any noise for the next few minutes. And then I need you to record us talking to this guy over video."

"Okay." She had that curious look in her eye. Jerry knew she was used to her dad's cockeyed ideas.

"Anyway, use my cell phone. But stay out of the picture and stay quiet. Do not let this clown see you. And keep the dog upstairs."

●────────●

The Skype call from Alma123 for CnlBarkley came in a few minutes later. The name, CnlBarkley was Channing's idea. General would be too easy to verify and Major would not have the authority to command a fleet of overseas drones.

Jerry sat in his office chair, took a deep breath, and clicked the "Answer" button on his screen.

A dark-haired man with a neatly trimmed beard appeared in the screen. Behind him in the background was what looked like a typical office, with a window on the left side of the screen and some plants on the sill. Outside the window was dark.

"Can you see and hear me?" asked the man in the image.

"Just fine," Jerry said. "And you have about thirty seconds to tell me why I shouldn't tell my drone crew to bomb you into the Stone Age."

"Please, no, I beg you; hear me, please."

"Why don't you start with your name."

"My name is Bahir Mustafa. I am a system administrator at the University of Tehran. My father was American; my mother is Iranian. My father left us when the Shah was overthrown. Colonel Barkley, who is with you?"

"This is Special Agent Jake Channing with the FBI. He's interested in what you have to say."

"I wish to live in the United States," Bahir said. "I want to leave this place. I admit, I use my botnet to make money. But it has been compromised by members of my government to commit murder and possibly even cause a global war. I have no desire for murder or war. Bad for business."

"So, just leave," Jerry said.

"They are watching. I can't."

"How do you know?"

"They watched all my internet traffic. And now I see Basij motorcycles always close by."

"How do you know they aren't monitoring this call right now?"

"I am routing it through the satellite system I recently installed."

"Why are you letting your government use your botnet?" Channing asked.

"I spent a week in Evin prison at their hands, and I'm only alive now because they need me to operate my botnet. They'll kill me when I am no longer useful."

"You said a man named Atesh Zare is behind all this? He is framing ISIS. Is that right?" Channing asked.

"Yes. Atesh Zare is with the Ministry of Science and Technology. He is behind this attack."

"Do you have proof?" Channing asked.

Just then, the sound of a dog thundered across the upstairs floor. Loud barking and banging noises resounded through the basement. Jerry recognized the sound of the dog lunging at a squirrel just outside the upstairs glass patio door.

"What is that noise?" Bahir asked.

Jerry and Channing glanced at each other.

"That was one of our canines," Jerry said.

Anne stifled a laugh.

"Now, more to the point," Channing said, "What proof can you provide to back up your claim?"

"I have no proof to offer, other than the evidence you have already seen. You have a copy of one of my control nodes. You have seen the network traffic from various transportation companies. I have also analyzed this traffic. The compromised systems are sending delivery schedules to Atesh, and he is attacking them."

"I need more than that if you want me to find a way for you to live here," Channing said.

"You're a malware expert," Jerry said. "Why not get inside this Atesh's computer and see what he's up to?"

"That is not possible," Bahir said.

"Then I don't see how we can help you," Channing said.

"Wait—please! Many more people will die if you do not help me."

"Get us the proof we need, and we'll talk some more," Channing said. "We'll reconvene this time tomorrow."

●————●

"I amaze myself sometimes." Frank "Duceml" Urbino stood at the first tee on a golf course near Miami and loosened up with the other guys in his foursome. "Last Thursday, I'm out in the Lambo, top down, parked at the liquor store. I come back out and this drop-dead, gorgeous blonde is sitting in the passenger seat. I don't know where she came from or who she is, but I know I want to get to know her better. A lot better. I walk up to my car, and she's sizing me up, you know, and she says, 'Hot wheels. But will it last?'"

"She did not," one of the men in the group said.

Urbino's cell phone rang. He pulled it out of his pocket. The caller ID displayed, "Alma."

"Excuse me, gentlemen," he said. "Duty calls."

"I have to hear the rest of this," another man laughed.

Urbino walked away from the first tee, phone in his ear.

"Duceml, I call you because I just find out our last project kill many people," Bahir said. "And I need your help."

Urbino stood near some trees between the first tee and the clubhouse with his back turned. "Your English is better than that. How does a spam campaign kill people?"

"Forgive me. My English escapes me when I am upset. Have you read articles about mine explosion in your US state, Minnesota?" Bahir asked.

"Yeah, I heard a little about it," Urbino said. "What's that got to do with me?"

"That spam campaign targeted transportation companies in your country," Bahir said. "One of our Ministers use that information to blow up that mine. And he make it look like ISIS did it."

"Global politics is not my strong suit," Urbino said. "Why do I care about any of this?"

"Because it could start World War III."

Urbino paused. "Look, Alma, you told me one of the reasons we get along so well is, we don't ask questions. And now you're telling me people are dead because of our little spam campaign?" He paced back and forth in front of the trees.

"Yes. And more will die soon. The mine bombing only first step. Bad for business. For both of us. I need your help."

"What do you need from me?"

"Who do you know in your free country who can draw sexually explicit pictures?"

Urbino stopped dead in his tracks. "Are you nuts?"

OUTRAGE

Atesh forced himself to reread the email from Defense Minister Farid Rahimi:

```
I am horrified and outraged by the drawings on
this website. I am ashamed to even repeat the
website name, www.faridsux.com. I wish to find
who is responsible for this website, and I
will personally deal with this outrage to Is-
lam. You will not discuss this with your su-
periors or anyone else, and when you find the
information I need, you will send it to me
via my personal Gmail account. You will also
delete this email and purge it from your sys-
tem. I want no record of any of this outside
the Gmail mailbox I mentioned above.
```

Atesh clicked on the link to visit the offending website. The cartoon caricatures of the Minister of Science, Research, and Technology, Atesh's superior, with other men were revolting. An insult to every standard of decent behavior in the world. A whois lookup showed the domain name registrant hid behind a veil of privacy. But the website IP address belonged to a web hosting site in Florida. Typical American perversion.

●───●

In another neighborhood in Tehran, a few blocks away, Bahir Mustafa smiled as a dot lit up on his display screen, signaling a special new addition to his botnet army. He would need to work fast. Bahir had underestimated Atesh the last time, and it cost him a week in Evin prison. This time, a mistake would cost his life.

But his life was over anyway. As soon as he was no longer useful to Atesh, some Basij radical on a motorcycle would murder him in a hail of bullets. Or secret police would roust him out of bed and throw him back into Evin prison, never to leave alive. So, even if Atesh found this specially crafted piece of malware on his computer, it would only hasten the inevitable. Hopefully, the key logger program would stay hidden long enough to yield the login credentials Bahir needed before he removed it. He had to congratulate Duceml on the artwork.

Early the next morning, Atesh needed to update his superiors on the progress to date. Everything was set. The mine explosion had gone flawlessly, leaving almost ten thousand pounds of ANFO explosives for the next diversion. The American CDC doctor would be scheduled to travel from Atlanta to Minneapolis to pick up the virus samples soon, and the recruits staying with Khalid Farooq, who still thought they were working for the Daesh, would be ready. It was time for Khalid to set up the diversionary operation.

Atesh sat in front of his computer and noticed the login screen. After logging on, a window popped up:

```
Your computer was recently updated. Windows
recently downloaded and installed an import-
ant security update to help protect your
computer. This update required an automatic
restart.
```

Atesh launched Outlook and composed and sent his status update email.

Bahir's computer beeped. The key logger listener was capturing a session on Atesh's computer.

He had Atesh's login credentials.

Bahir rubbed his eyes and immediately started Outlook Web App, connecting to Atesh's mailbox. Atesh had just sent a new message.

Bahir's jaw dropped. Had Atesh and all those ministers of idiocy gone mad? This plot was unthinkable. And yet, also an opportunity.

And a threat. The key logger program on Atesh's computer had done its job. It was time to remove it. He had Atesh's login credentials and could check Atesh's email anytime. Unfortunately, removing it required another reboot. Bahir would remove it tonight, disguising it as another three o'clock in the morning Windows update. Windows Updates two nights in a row were unusual, but hopefully would not arouse Atesh's suspicions.

●————●

Something electronic chimed in Jerry Barkley's upstairs bedroom. "Boop-bee-boop, beep-boo boop, boop bee-boop, beep boo boop . . ."

Lynn Barkley jerked awake in bed beside Jerry. "What's that noise?"

"Huh?" Jerry asked.

"That noise—what is it?"

"Oh, crap, that's a video call from Bahir." Jerry leaped to his feet, now fully awake.

"And why is somebody calling you at this time of night?"

Jerry fumbled for his reading glasses and stumbled to the table where he had set his laptop overnight.

The ringing stopped.

"Jerry, why is somebody making your laptop beep at four o'clock in the morning?"

"Because it's Bahir's early afternoon. Something's up. He's six hours early. I gotta take this."

"Whatever," Lynn said as she rolled onto her side.

"Don't go back to sleep yet. I need your help."

"Huh?"

"This is important. I'll need you to record this."

"What's important?"

"The call we're gonna do. I'll need you to record it so I can play it back for the FBI."

"Like that cell phone thing you did with Anne yesterday? With somebody in the house while I was at work you never told me about?"

"Yeah. We need to document the conversations with this guy."

"You want me to hold your cell phone and take a video of you doing a video call with some guy named Brian?"

"It's Bahir. And yeah. It's important. It's national security. It could be life and death."

Lynn rolled onto her back and sat up. "It was important when you forgot to pack pants on your Boston trip fifteen years ago. It was an emergency when you couldn't find your shoes after I put them in the closet. It was life and death when you lost your car in the mall parking lot. And now it's national security for me to make a cell phone video of you talking to some guy at four in the morning? When I have to get up at five for work? You know I don't know anything about that cell phone. Now, leave me alone and let me sleep!" Lynn rolled back over on her side.

"Lynn, this guy is from Iran. More people could die if we mess this up."

"What?"

"You heard me. This guy knows who blew up that mine up north and killed all those people."

"Why are you in the middle of it?"

"I'll tell you about it later, but right now, I need your help."

Jerry put on a pair of sweatpants and a T-shirt and walked down the two flights of stairs with his laptop and cell phone to set up in the makeshift video studio from earlier. Lynn followed. He adjusted the laptop webcam to only show the plywood background and made sure the toys from when his grandsons played in the space earlier were out of view.

He took out his cell phone and dialed Agent Channing's cell number. After several rings, somebody answered.

"FBI."

"Hi. This is Jerry Barkley, and I've been working with Agent Jake Channing on a case. He must have forwarded his phone to you guys. I need to talk to him right now."

"Agent Channing is not available."

"You better make him available. The guy who bombed that mine in Ely is trying to do a video call with me right now."

"Yeah, okay, I'll take that down and leave a message."

"Do you guys not watch the news? I just told you I'm about to have a conversation with the guy who knows something about that mine explosion in Ely."

"Uh-huh. Give me a call-back number, and somebody will get back to you."

Jerry repeated his phone number. "When will I get a call back?"

"After I give them the message."

"And how long will that be?"

"Shouldn't be too long."

"Okay, thanks."

A few minutes passed.

"Great. Just great. Somebody's trying to blow up the country, and I'm on my own."

"Shouldn't we give them a few more minutes to call back?"

"No. We can't wait any longer. Bahir is probably climbing the walls right now."

Jerry launched the camera app and handed his cell phone to Lynn. "Tap this red button to record. And tap the big grey button here to stop."

"Jerry, I'm scared."

"So am I." He hugged her. "Ready?"

Lynn nodded.

"Here we go." Jerry took a deep breath and returned the video call. The same man answered, looking more disheveled this time.

"Colonel Barkley, I have the proof you asked me to deliver. I am pasting a copy of an email correspondence between Atesh Zare and his boss, Minister Kashani, in another text file on the desktop of the machine you cloned. I have a great deal of correspondence that will interest you. Too much to paste into that text file. I placed all the documents on my website. I'll paste the URL in the chat area. I allowed directory searches for user barkley, password colonel, so you should be able to retrieve all of them immediately."

Jerry started navigating to the website.

"Wait. Do not access that website from your computer. Do it from a throwaway system. I put some, shall we say, special programming into that website."

Jerry smiled. "I'll bet you did. I have a virtual machine handy. Let's see what you've got."

Jerry started up a virtual machine and navigated to the website from there.

"Forty-five gigabytes. You've been busy. This will take a while to get here through your satellite."

"I'm not routing that website through the satellite."

"Won't your friends see it?"

"I packaged it all into a few encrypted gzip archives. They won't be able to decipher it. I'm pasting the passphrase into our chat."

"Got it," Jerry said. "But they'll see a spike in traffic. And they'll know where it's going."

"Yes."

Jerry and Bahir locked eyes. "Route it through your satellite," Jerry said.

"Not enough bandwidth. This is the only way," Bahir said. "What is the Mall of America?"

"It's the biggest shopping mall in the United States."

"They plan to bomb it."

"What?"

"They stole the explosives and bombed the mine to destroy the evidence. Now they plan to bomb the Mall of America. But it's another diversion. The real target is the Ebola virus."

"Wait a minute. I don't get it."

"You have an Ebola patient in a hospital in your city, yes?"

"Yeah. It's all over the news."

"A doctor from your Center for Disease Control is planning to visit the hospital and retrieve a blood sample later today, your time. While your authorities are responding to the Mall of America bombing, Atesh's team will steal that blood sample, infect some recruits who think they are fighting a war for ISIS, and send them to populated areas where they will start an epidemic."

Jerry's jaw dropped.

"That's why you need this information quickly."

Jerry nodded and started the download. "What do you have for upstream bandwidth?"

"A hundred megabits."

"I have forty for downloads here. It should take two or three hours to copy."

"And now I need to leave. I used that website to plant a key logging program in Atesh's computer. He will realize it soon, and when they see encrypted information going to you, I will die. I have more information you will find useful, but it will die with me if I remain here."

Jerry leaned back in his chair. "Let me see what I can do."

"Thank you."

After terminating the call, Jerry checked his download progress. The smallest archive was already here. He decrypted and unpacked it and skimmed the documents; many were in what looked like Arabic or maybe Farsi. He picked one document at random and found an online translator.

```
My dear Atesh, let me be the first to con-
gratulate you on a job well done. You struck
a blow to the Great Satan and found a way
to blame it on our enemy. Your enthusiasm
and creativity inspire us all, and you are a
credit to our revolution. The Supreme Leader
himself expresses his gratitude. And now, the
next phase begins.
```

It was signed, "Mahmoud."

"Oh, wow," Jerry said. "Oh, wow."

Jerry dialed Agent Channing's cell phone again.

"FBI." It was a different voice.

"Listen, I tried to call Agent Jake Channing a few minutes ago. A lot of people will die today if you blow me off again."

"Sir, making terroristic threats is a crime."

"I'm telling you somebody is about to blow up the Mall of America and a lot of people will die. Call that whatever you want."

"Please hold, sir."

"You're kidding, right?" But it was too late; Jerry heard a click and found himself on hold. He put his cell phone on speaker and set it down.

"What now?" Lynn asked.

"England. I wonder if England has an embassy in Iran." He looked at Wikipedia and found it. 198 Ferdowsi Avenue, Tehran. There was even a published telephone number. And they were about as likely to listen as that FBI knucklehead.

But maybe . . .

He started another video call to Joanne Gittens.

"Good morning, love. It's not even sunup on your side of the pond. What brings you up this early?"

"You know that code you modified for me? Well, it worked. I made contact with the guy. His name is Bahir Mustafa. He thinks I'm a colonel in the US Military."

"Well done! We have been trying to identify this chap for several years. Do you have a picture of him?"

"I should have taken some screen shots. But forget the picture. We have bigger fish to fry. I'm downloading a ton of documents, including emails from guys in the Iranian Government who plan to blow up the largest shopping mall in the United States, which happens to be just a few miles from here. And get this—he got all this stuff by planting a key logger in the computer of an Iranian honcho named Atesh Zare."

Joanne's eyes widened. Joanne moved her face closer to the camera, filling Jerry's screen.

"Bugger me! Definitely a 'bigger fish,' as you Yanks say! How can I help?"

"I'm copying all the content from Bahir's website right now. It's forty-five gigabytes and will take forever to grab from here. So, download it directly from Bahir's place. I'm pasting the URL, login credentials, and gzip passphrase in the chat. We need to get him out of the country. He thinks I'm a colonel and have the power to do that. Britain has an embassy in Tehran, maybe right down the street from the university where Bahir works."

"And you want to hide him in the British Embassy, possibly even spirit him out of the country?"

"Yeah, something like that."

"And how do you propose we do that? You do know we're an antivirus company and not the British Government, yes?"

"Well, that embassy has a phone number. Maybe they'll listen if we both call together."

"Why doesn't your government call my government to work all this out?"

"I'm waiting on hold with the American FBI right now." Jerry held his cell phone in front of the webcam.

Joanne nodded. "Ah, of course. But we can't just call the Embassy and tell them they need to bring this chap in. The lines are not secure. The Iranians will know about it the minute we bring it up."

"Oh, yeah, you're right. What if we call your government in London? You're a big company over there. Maybe they'll listen to you guys. The clock's ticking."

"Let me see what we can do."

As the call terminated, Jerry heard a siren in the distance. Multiple sirens. Getting louder.

He flew up from the basement to the main floor and stared out the front window as four police cars maneuvered into positions in the cul-de-sac in front of his house. Dancing blue and red lights reflected off the neighboring windows. He looked down at his cell phone, still on hold with the FBI. "You've *got* to be kidding me."

Lynn stood behind Jerry at the foot of the second-floor stairs, her bathrobe alternately bathed in blue and red light. "What's going on?"

Squad car doors opened, and police officers took up positions, guns aimed at his front door. "Looks like the FBI and I had a misunderstanding."

"Now What?"

"Maybe I'll invite 'em in for coffee."

"You think you can charm your way out of everything."

"Got any better ideas?"

Jerry walked out the front door. Lights came on in all the nearby houses. Faces peered out the windows. "Does anyone want coffee? I don't drink the stuff, but we can put some on for you if you want."

"Show us your hands," somebody shouted into a megaphone.

"Jerry lifted his hands, one hand still holding his cell phone."

"Drop what's in your hand, right now!"

"Do you know how expensive these are?"

"Drop it, now!"

"How about I put it down, gently, right here? Can you guys live with that?"

Guns clicked.

"For God's sake, guys, it's a cell phone. I'm not a threat to anyone. I'm putting it down in this chair."

Jerry slowly placed the cell phone in the green plastic chair on his front porch and then lifted his empty hands again.

"Would anyone mind if I go back inside and grab some shoes?"

"Turn around and walk backward toward us."

Jerry rolled his eyes.

"Do it, now!"

"Jerry turned and started walking backward down the driveway. He tripped over the front bumper of Anne's car, parked halfway down the driveway.

He started to get back on his feet, but two officers wrestled him to the ground in the yard next to the driveway. Face down in the grass, he felt a knee in his back. Somebody handcuffed his arms behind his back.

"Jerry Barkley, you are under arrest for making terroristic threats against law enforcement officers and the Mall of America," somebody above and behind him said.

Somebody lifted him by the shoulders and walked him toward the police cars. "You have the right to remain silent and to refuse to answer questions. Anything you say may be used against you in a court of law. You have the right to consult an attorney before speaking to the police and to have an attorney present during questioning now or in the future."

"We don't have time for this!"

"If you cannot afford an attorney, one will be appointed for you before any questioning if you wish. If you decide to answer questions now without an attorney present, you will still have the right to stop answering at any time until you talk to an attorney."

Jerry rolled his eyes. "No good deed goes unpunished." He stumbled. Two officers caught him.

"Knowing and understanding your rights as I have explained them to you, are you willing to answer my questions without an attorney present?"

Jerry spat grass and dirt from his mouth and tried to wipe what he could on his T-shirt, with his arms handcuffed behind him. "Please tell me you guys are more competent than the FBI."

Several officers entered Jerry's house as the officers escorting Jerry stuffed him into a squad car and drove away.

●———————●

A uniformed officer escorted Jerry, still handcuffed, from one of the holding cells in the back of the Eagan police station to a small interview room at the end of a short hallway. He sat Jerry next to a desk, back to the wall, facing one-way glass on the opposite side of the room. A plainclothes detective was waiting. Sounds echoed over the tiled floor and tan concrete-block walls.

Plainclothes read Jerry his Miranda rights again. "We are recording this session, and you acknowledge your willingness to talk with me, is that correct?"

"Yes."

"May I call you Jerry?"

"Well, what else would you call me? Will you take these stupid cuffs off?"

"Not until I evaluate your mental state."

"Okay, here's my mental state. I'm frustrated and royally pissed at bureaucrats who won't listen."

"And that's the kind of talk that will keep you in those handcuffs. So, why don't you tell us what's going on?"

"What do you think I've been trying to do? Let me cut to the chase. I have credible information about a group of Iranians who plan to bomb the Mall of America and kill a bunch of people. Today. It's the same group that blew up that mine in Ely. But the bombings are only a diversion. They also plan to unleash an Ebola epidemic across the country."

"Do you have any evidence to back up this claim?"

"As a matter of fact, yes. It's all in my basement."

"Where in your basement?"

"In my office."

"Are you willing to show us?"

"Do you think I went through all this because I love getting jerked around? I'm downloading it all right now, and I'll put a copy of it on my ftp site. You're welcome to all of it."

"What's an ftp site?"

"Think of it as a document repository."

"On a computer?"

"No, in my toilet." Jerry paused and shook his head. He looked down, closed his eyes, and then looked back up. "Sorry. That's frustration. I have several physical and virtual systems connected to the internet, and I have a bunch of documents from a guy in Iran who is in the middle of it all."

"We're dismantling your equipment and bringing it in. You can set it up here and show us."

Jerry shook his head. "No. Tell me you're not doing that."

"Why?"

"Because lots of people might die."

"Are you making another threat?"

"Do you still beat your wife?"

"What's that supposed to mean?"

"It means, I never threatened anybody, so how would I make another threat? But in the spirit of full disclosure, I'd like to wring an FBI dispatcher's neck right now."

Plainclothes sat back in his chair, stroking his chin.

Jerry leaned forward. "Listen. I'm the good guy here. We don't have time for this crap. Tell your guys if they shut my systems down, you tip off the wrong people and lots of bad things could happen."

"Jerry, try to see things from my point of view. We were called out on a suspect believed to be making terroristic threats. And now you're telling us you're in communication with the terrorists and gathering information about them. Is that right?"

"Yeah, that sums it up. I was a few minutes into a three hour download when you guys showed up and hauled me away. What time is it?"

"I'm asking the questions here."

"Well, the clock is ticking, and we need to see that data."

"It's 5:20. And that leads to the obvious question: what made you decide to take it upon yourself to save the world and not contact law enforcement?"

Jerry shook his head and laughed. "And the obvious answer is, I did try to contact law enforcement, and look what happened."

RED TAPE SUNRISE

Thirty miles away from the Eagan police station, FBI Special Agent Jake Channing reached to turn off his alarm clock. But the alarm wasn't ringing. He fumbled for his cell phone and knocked it to the floor. It stopped ringing. He swung his feet to the floor, yawned, and rubbed his eyes. He picked up the phone and checked the caller ID. It was the call center. He stretched and then punched in the numbers to call back. This better be important.

"This is Agent Jake Channing. Why are you guys calling me at—what time is it? It's five thirty in the morning."

"Agent Channing, sorry to wake you up. This is Patrick. We got a call from the Eagan police a few minutes ago. They have a Jerry Barkley in custody, and he claims he knows about some Iranians who want to blow up the megamall. He says he's working with you."

"Why is he in custody?"

"Apparently, he called the office earlier, and we thought he was threatening to blow up the mall."

"And nobody thought that was important enough to call me?"

"We left a message for the agent on call overnight. You're off shift, but after thinking about it, I figured you'd also want to know."

"I'm on my way to Eagan as soon as I get dressed. And I want to talk to the Eagan police on the way. Text me a phone number."

● ━━━━━━ ●

Jerry Barkley's mood grew darker after answering the same questions over and over and over again. Who was he working with? Why was he making threats? What did he want? Did he know that threatening to blow up a shopping mall was a felony? And his favorite, over and over and over again, what medications was he on?

At least they'd taken the cuffs off. But with a warning—if he tried anything violent, the cuffs would go right back on.

"I've told you everything I know. Every minute that goes by is more wasted time. What's going on with my equipment?"

Somebody popped their head in and motioned for the detective. A uniformed officer escorted Jerry back to a holding cell.

"How do I wake you guys up?" Jerry asked in the hallway. The uniformed officer guided him into the holding cell. "Why am I stuck in here when somebody is trying to attack us?" The officer closed the door. Jerry peered through the small shatterproof glass window and pounded on the closed door. "I'm one of the good guys!"

He paced the room. Bahir Mustafa in Iran was waiting for a rescue. Electronic copies of dozens, maybe hundreds, of documents with details about an imminent terrorist attack were beyond his grasp. Joanne Gittens would be contacting the British Government. And he was stuck here, in a police holding cell, sitting on a padded shelf twiddlintg his thumbs and staring at a stainless-steel toilet, unable to do anything about any of it.

That was the key. Unable. At least for now. Sooner or later, somehow, some way, this would get cleared up and maybe then he could help put a stop to the nightmare that was coming. He sat, folded his hands in his lap, closed his eyes, and took a few deep breaths, willing his heart to slow down and the adrenaline to stop flowing. The time for action would come. But not now.

That sleeping shelf was right out of a Klingon warship in a *Star Trek* episode. Except for the padding. And, just like Jean-Luc Picard, he'd slept in less comfortable places. He put his legs up and his head down and stared at the ceiling. What about creating a diversion by jamming a paper clip into an electrical outlet to create a short circuit? He'd seen that in a movie somewhere. With any luck, it could disable the door lock and he could get away in the confusion. The problem with that plan was, it required electrical outlets. What about dismantling the light fixture in the ceiling? That lead to the other problem; the plan needed paper clips. He fell into a fitful sleep.

At the crack of dawn, Taneka Martin scrambled to dress in her nicest business clothes. She slipped into her four-year-old son's bedroom and watched him. After a few seconds, she picked him up.

"No, Mommy, I stay in bed."

"Not today. We're going to see grandma."

"Why?"

"Mommy has a job interview."

"I want to stay in bed."

"I know, baby, but you can sleep in the car. And at grandma's." She carried him to the car.

"What's a job interview?"

"It's where the people I want to work for ask me lots of questions."

"What questions?"

"Manager stuff. Maybe about what I'd do if all the hotel rooms were full." She strapped him into his car seat.

"What's manager stuff?"

"It means I'll be the second-shift boss."

"I want to go back to bed."

"You have your sippy cup right next to you and Mr. Puff Puff right here." She showed him his cup in the car seat cup holder and handed him a worn stuffed animal.

"I want to go back to bed!"

"Baby, you can sleep in the car and at grandma's. And I'll pick you up after my interview at the Patterson Blu."

"I go back to bed."

"I know, baby. If I get this job, you won't have to get up early anymore. And you and I will be able to spend lots of time together. But today is special." She closed the backseat car door and slid into the driver's seat.

"I go back to bed."

"I know, baby. Pretty soon."

Shortly after sunup, two vans entered the parking ramp of the 8200 building in the Normandale Lakes office tower complex in Bloomington, Minnesota, seven miles from the Mall of America. The vans proceeded to an upper level of the ramp, far away from any entrances. The white van backed into an out-of-the-way parking space while the blue van waited. The driver of the white van got out, locked the doors, climbed into the blue van, and they drove away.

●———●

Westbound drivers on Interstate 494 in front of the Mall of America lowered their visors against the sunrise reflecting off the Ikea building in the northern mall parking lot as they inched along in the stop-and-go rush-hour traffic. Local talk radio blared in many cars: "It's another top-ten weather day on tap, a great day to enjoy the Minnesota outdoors if you can sneak away from work."

Morning Mall Stars worked on their daily exercise routines inside the Mall of America, briskly walking the perimeter aisles in front of stores that would open in a few hours. Many had been walking for years and greeted each other as old friends as they exercised. Some planned to meet later for coffee and conversation.

At the Patterson Blu hotel on the south side of the mall, workers set up chairs in a conference room, getting ready for an afternoon corporate sales conference. With a theme of "Knock It out of the Park," every chair would have a plastic bat with a St. Paul Saints logo for participants to take home to their kids.

Breakfast smells wafted through the JW Chariot hotel restaurant on the north side of the mall. Business people sipped orange juice and mingled with out-of-town shoppers as they waited for stores to open.

Nobody noticed the maroon cargo vans driving into both the Patterson Blu and JW Chariot parking ramps. At each ramp entrance, a driver extended a hand, pressed a red button, and waited for the machine to print a ticket. The van in the Patterson Blu ramp proceeded to a parking space on the top parking ramp level against the inside wall, as far away from the south-facing openings as possible. The van in the JW Chariot ramp also parked on the top ramp level, near the elevator underneath the lobby and restaurant.

Video surveillance at both ramps showed drivers exiting the vans, each carrying a shopping bag and wearing loose-fitting pants, long-sleeved shirt, and a baseball cap. Neither driver looked up into the ceiling video cameras, so facial features were never visible as they walked out of the ramp. Just a couple more mall walkers.

Each van carried a faint odor of fuel oil, but nothing so unusual as to attract attention, especially this early in the morning. The ramps were almost empty, so even if someone noticed the odor, nobody would give it a second thought because the vans looked old and in need of repairs.

Video cameras inside the mall picked up men wearing baseball caps entering, one from the south entrance, the other from the Sears store on the north side. Both made their way into the nearest restroom. A few minutes later, video showed a muscular, dark-haired man wearing shorts and a T-shirt leaving the restroom near the south entrance and another man, similarly dressed with dark hair, leaving the north restroom. Both carried shopping bags. Neither looked up.

Both men made their way separately out the north mall entrance toward the Ikea store. Beyond the view of any mall security cameras, the first man climbed into a blue van near the Ikea store. A few minutes later, the second man climbed into the same van.

———•———

The Eagan police station holding cell door opened.

"Mr. Barkley?"

Jerry sat up and rubbed his eyes. "What time is it?"

"About five minutes to seven," the detective said, walking into the room, looking sheepish.

"So, I've been holed up here for almost two hours now?"

"Mr. Barkley, we owe you an apology."

Jerry noticed Channing behind the detective. "Good morning, Jerry."

"Did somebody finally get my message to you?"

"Yes."

"Good. Apology accepted. Where's my phone? Did anyone warn the megamall?" Jerry pushed past Channing and the detective into the hallway. "And we need to take care of Bahir, your Zagros botnet guy. What did you guys do with my stuff in my basement?"

"What stuff?" Channing asked.

"All my equipment."

"Mr. Barkley, I'm sorry. We had to execute the search warrant, and we dismantled some of it before the FBI called and asked us to stop," the detective said.

Jerry shook his head. "Just Great. Bahir got into Atesh's email and took forty-five gigabytes of stuff."

"Do you know what it was?" Channing asked.

"I was starting to download it all when, um, I got interrupted. Maybe our guys at Saphas in England grabbed a copy. I need my cell phone."

A uniformed officer brought in a bag with Jerry's personal belongings.

"Would you believe I'm still waiting on hold with the FBI?" Jerry said as he attached his cell phone and belt clip to his sweat pants. "I think I'll hang up now. And by now, the Iranian Government probably already knows what he did. We need to get him out of there."

"Let's get the State Department working on that," Channing said.

"Hey—great idea—why didn't I think of that three hours ago?" Jerry said. He smacked his palm into his forehead. "Oh, wait a minute—I did, but then you guys hauled me away. Why are we still standing here?"

A distant boom sounded. The building shook.

MALL OF AMERICA

The JW Chariot kitchen staff and patrons died first. First, a deafening boom. Less than a millisecond later, the first floor rose and buckled and collapsed into the upper level of the parking ramp, tossing people on the first floor through the air like rag dolls. After the ovens and grills from the kitchen dropped into the parking ramp, nothing impeded the natural gas flow through the pipes. Within seconds, the gas exploded in a fireball in what was left of the first floor. Surviving gas pipes became flamethrowers, spewing fire through the devastation and consuming drapes, wood, and anything combustible in its path.

The steel and concrete columns holding up the building—weakened from the explosion in the basement—began to buckle. People in upper floors felt the building sway. Most thought the first concussive blow was an earthquake, but only a handful would survive to describe the scene as floor upon floor collapsed into a growing mountain of twisted rubble.

The van near the Ikea store drove away, blending with traffic on American Boulevard, now filled with stopped cars as drivers gaped at the devastation. Nobody noticed the van passenger texting on his cell phone. Most other drivers were also calling, texting, or snapping pictures of the grisly spectacle a few hundred yards away.

Mall walkers and employees heard the explosion and felt the vibrations. Most thought it was a rare Midwest earthquake and tried to laugh it off. But as the JW Chariot collapsed, taking a section of the north side of the mall with it, everyone in the mall realized something was dreadfully wrong. This was no earthquake.

The van followed American Boulevard East to 24th Avenue South and turned right at the stoplight. It drove south along the east side of the mall, through the Killebrew Drive intersection, and continued slowly south on East Old Shakopee Road. As the van passed the Homewood Suites hotel on its right, the driver and passengers heard the second explosion through the open windows.

Taneka Martin parked in the Patterson Blu ramp, next to a maroon cargo van near the elevator, and opened her car door. First a boom and then a deafening rumble filled the air. The open car door flew out of her hands and then swung back against her body. She caught it and held on. The car shook with the parking garage floor. An earthquake? Don't those only happen in California? She turned her head, searching for cracks in the concrete, and said a silent prayer for the parking ramp to stay intact. The shaking and rumbling stopped after a few minutes. Other than a car alarm from another floor, all was silent.

Earthquake or not, she needed that job. She checked her makeup in the car mirror and looked down at her blouse and pantsuit. No damage. The earthquake would be a good icebreaker for the interview. She stepped out of the car and closed the door.

She noticed a faint fuel oil smell as she locked her car but didn't give it any thought. Maybe that van had an oil leak. Then something buzzed. It sounded like a cell phone on vibrate. It was coming from the van. The one that smelled like fuel oil. Somebody must have left . . .

•————•

Cars filled Killebrew Drive in front of the Patterson Blu parking ramp as people drove to work in nearby office buildings. This ramp was above ground with openings facing the street. Drivers traveling westbound in front of the hotel all instinctively looked to their right when they heard the second, louder boom. It was the last sight they ever saw as an onslaught of concrete chunks, some as large as a city bus, flew away from the ramp and slammed into vehicles, followed by the pressure wave from the blast that lifted cars and slammed them into traffic in the eastbound lane.

Unlike the JW Chariot, the Patterson Blu parking ramp wrapped around the hotel lobby, restaurant, and meeting rooms, all underneath five hundred guest rooms. The explosion obliterated the concrete wall separating the lobby from the parking ramp, destroying the restaurant and lobby. Dozens of people were killed, and dozens more were maimed by shattered glass spraying the street.

Similar to the JW Chariot, ruptured gas lines triggered fires and ignited everything that would burn. Unlike the JW Chariot, the Patterson Blu explosion created a large air corridor from the above-ground parking ramp openings facing south above Killebrew Drive, through the parking ramp, lobby and restaurant rubble, and out the shattered restaurant windows facing the mall to the north. The air intensified the natural gas fires, which superheated the building, causing car gas tanks to rupture, which set off secondary explosions to feed a growing inferno, now fueled by both gasoline and natural gas. As the fire grew, it sucked air in through the shattered restaurant windows and parking ramp openings, setting up a mini firestorm inside the building and pushing flames up through blast holes in the parking ramp ceiling and into the guest floors above, consuming everything in its path as it grew in intensity.

The building support columns absorbed heat from the growing inferno and conducted it both up and down, weakening the structure as they heated up. It took almost thirty minutes, but the Patterson Blu hotel eventually collapsed into a mountain of rubble on top of any initial blast survivors in the lobby and kitchen area as people trapped on upper floors tried and failed to escape.

By the time the building collapsed, rescue crews were arriving and good Samaritans and blast survivors worked to free people trapped in cars on Killebrew Drive. But when the Patterson Blu collapsed, the skyway above Killebrew Drive also collapsed, killing dozens more would-be rescuers and commuters who had survived the initial blast but were trapped in cars under the skyway.

Security staff on duty inside the mall quickly found the morning mall walkers and, without information about what was going on outside and with the north entrance under apparent attack, ordered them to shelter in place in Nickelodeon Universe in the center of the mall. A bomb could destroy the glass skylight above the mall, raining shards of glass down on the mall walkers, but the walking routes around the perimeter were deemed even more risky. A few mall walkers refused to cooperate and left out of the south entrance shortly after the JW Chariot collapse at the north entrance. It was a fatal mistake and bad timing. Seconds after walking out the south entrance door, the Patterson Blu exploded, killing most of them and splattering their remains against the south-facing mall wall. The few survivors of that blast who could still walk worked their way down the mall driveway to Killebrew Drive and tried to help trapped drivers. They died when the skyway above them collapsed.

The Patterson Blu, with five hundred rooms, and the JW Chariot, with 341 rooms, were both about half full that day. The final death toll from the blasts in both buildings and subsequent collapses, including the casualties on Killebrew Drive, the mall walkers who ignored the shelter-in-place directive from mall security, and two heart attacks, was 592.

At the Eagan police station, Channing and the police officers stopped dead in their tracks and stared at Jerry after the first explosion.

"Oh, no! No, no, no, *no, no!*" Jerry walked, and then ran, out the door to the parking lot. Still barefooted, he led the others around the police station and looked northwest, toward Bloomington. A plume of smoke rose in the distance.

Northbound rush-hour traffic slowed and stopped on Pilot Knob Road. Drivers' eyes registered shock as they looked toward the growing plume of smoke. Many fumbled for cell phones. Some turned on blinking hazard lights. Jerry, Channing, the detective, and other police officers watched the smoke rise, open mouthed.

"We could have stopped this!" Jerry stormed back across the grass and back into the police station. "I need a ride home. The megamall is a diversion."

The second explosion shook the ground again as the van in the Patterson Blu parking ramp detonated.

"This is nothing compared to what happens if they get that Ebola blood sample. Why are we still here?"

Tabor and his passengers in the blue van continued south on Old Shakopee Road, turned right onto 86th Street, and took side streets over the seven miles back to the Normandale Lakes parking ramp. They entered the parking ramp where they left the white van earlier and parked in an out-of-the-way spot. They locked the doors, climbed into the white van, and drove away.

LITTLE CHICKEN LITTLE

Bahir Mustafa was becoming more alarmed by the minute. Colonel Barkley had told him to wait near his Skype connection. That was more than three hours ago.

"Jerry, where have you been?" It was Joanne Gittens on Jerry's cell phone.

"In police custody," Jerry said, barely looking at Joanne's face on the screen of his phone. "Long story. Were you able to get anyone in your government?"

"Yes. That's why I've been trying to call you. I have a Sir Nigel Holbrooke with the Foreign and Commonwealth Office waiting for a confirming call from your government. I explained the situation and forwarded your documents to him. By now, the foreign secretary himself has them."

"That's great. Text me his phone number. Listen, Joanne, they bombed us. They blew up the Mall of America."

Joanne nodded. "Yes, we've just heard. Jerry, we've been reading what you captured, and we have more details on the Ebola outbreak."

"Good, because I don't have any of it yet. What did you find out?"

"He managed to pilfer this Atesh's whole PST file."

"He got the whole PST file? Really?"

"Yes. And more. It seems Atesh uses two Gmail accounts to pass messages back and forth with agents in your country. Apparently right in your Twin Cities. With one, he passes a decryption passphrase as a subject, and then he puts the encrypted message in the other."

"Pretty slick."

"It's ingenious. Do not underestimate these people."

"Okay, give this to me in English," Channing said.

"I thought we just did," Jerry said.

"Well, simplify it for me."

"Okay. Microsoft Outlook is an email program. It keeps sent and received emails in a PST file. That's just the name Microsoft gave to the file format. Sometimes these are cached copies of emails on an Exchange email server; other times, they're the real emails. Either way, if we have a PST file from Atesh's computer, we probably have all his correspondence with Iranian Government officials."

"Okay, and what's the deal with Gmail? Why does he use Gmail if he has Outlook and a government email server?"

"For correspondence with his guys in the field. They won't have access to Iran's government email server, so they need a publicly accessible email location. But since it's public, they also need encryption."

"Yes, they do," continued Joanne over the phone. "And we cracked it."

"Oh, wow!"

"Yes, we said something similar."

"How does he encrypt Gmail messages?" Channing asked.

"He does it with two Gmail accounts, right?" Jerry said.

"Yes, absolutely brilliant," Joanne said over the Skype connection. "With the first, he sends a subject and gibberish for the message body. That subject is key. Literally. They calculate a 512-bit SHA-3 hash value from that email subject and use that as the encryption and decryption key to the real message. They exchange decryption keys in clear text, right under our noses, but nobody notices because it looks like normal email conversation. They never send the encrypted message; they deposit it into a drafts folder in the other Gmail account and reference it there."

"So, nobody suspects anything because they're separate accounts, right?" Channing asked.

"Right! O, love! It really is brilliant."

"Let's not go gaga over these guys," Channing said. "They just murdered I don't know how many people."

"Yes, of course," Joanne said. "And that leads to what we found. They're planning to steal that Ebola blood sample. Today. A CDC doctor happens to be in your city, and he's visiting your Ebola patient to retrieve a blood sample."

"That's what Bahir told me a few hours ago. Is there more?"

"The terrorists plan to steal the sample and kill the doctor on the charter flight to Atlanta. I'm afraid we don't have more specifics."

"How current is all this?" Channing asked.

"Let me see, the timestamp on the newest gzip archive is 8:07 GMT."

"About three in the morning our time," Jerry said. "If they noticed my C&C node offline, plans could change."

●———●

Bahir paced in his office, checking and rechecking his watch, glancing out the window, and listening for Basij on motorcycles. His server logs showed two downloads of his data. One to the Eagan control node, the other to someplace in England. He deleted the logs. If Atesh and his minions had not already copied them, there was no need to make it easy for them to find. Finally, a video call from Colonel Barkley.

"Colonel Barkley. I was wondering what happened to you. And your control node disappeared."

"It's been busy here, Bahir. They bombed the Mall of America."

"I am sorry," Bahir said. "I gave you the best information I had."

"I believe you," Jerry said. "When our control node went dark here, did that tip off anyone?"

"It is not possible to know."

"Okay. Agent Channing and I have an exit strategy for you."

"Thank you."

Jerry picked up a piece of paper and read from his notes: "Proceed immediately to the British Embassy at 198 Ferdowsi Avenue. Do you know how to get to that address?"

"Yes."

"Good. When you get there, go to the right side of the main gate and tell the guard you're looking for Simon Paddington. This is important. The guard will ask you what your business with Minister Paddington is. You need to tell him these exact words: 'The sky is falling.' He will ask you if you are Chicken Little. You must reply with, 'Just a little chicken.' Got that? Anything else and they'll turn you away."

"Yes. The sky is falling. Chicken Little, little chicken. Yes, I can remember that."

"Good. How far is it?"

"Not far. I should be able to get there in about thirty minutes."

"Good," Channing said. "Assume you're being watched. How do you normally go home?"

"I live near here. I usually walk or take the Metro."

"That's the mass transit train, right?"

"Yes."

"Okay. Instead of walking directly to the Embassy, take the Metro to your normal stop. Go home. Change into comfortable clothes and pack an overnight bag. Turn off the lights and leave from a back door. Blend in with the crowd at the Metro station. You forgot something at work and you need to go back. Act the part. Watch for anyone who may have gotten off the train with you earlier."

"To make sure nobody is following me?"

"Exactly. When you get off the train, make your way toward the Embassy but not on a direct route. Keep them guessing where you're going because once you deviate, they'll try to intercept you."

"Okay. I will set off immediately." Bahir paused and peered into the camera. "I am not a violent man. How do I fight back in case they try to apprehend me?"

Jerry and Channing exchanged glances. "Get rid of that white shirt," Channing replied. "Wear dark clothes. You may need to hide. And try to get your hands on a cane or something you can use as a club in case you need it."

●———●

Packed Metro trains and busy stations during the Tehran evening commute made it easy to blend in with the crowds, both for Bahir and his potential followers. On the street, heavy car traffic on Taleqani Street and Hafez Avenue acted as a shield against Basij murderers on motorcycles. Bahir continued walking south on Hafez Avenue, using a cane and faking a limp. It wasn't much of a disguise, but maybe it would make a murderer looking for somebody in good health think twice.

Car traffic thinned after crossing College Bridge over Enghelab Street, and with the Russian Embassy now on his left, it was time for a decision. Should he continue south on Hafez Avenue and hope for heavier car traffic or turn left onto Nofel Loshato Street, keeping the southern side of the Russian Embassy on his left? Would being in front of a foreign embassy offer protection? It was a shorter walk to Ferdowsi Avenue and the British Embassy this way. He turned left.

Only a few blocks to go. But now the street was empty. He should have stayed on Hafez Avenue. What was he thinking? The Basij were fanatic murderers. They didn't care about foreign embassies. And nobody in a foreign embassy would care about a murdered Iranian outside their walls. Just another political dissident in a country full of political dissidents.

He quickened his pace as a motorcycle whined in the distance. He broke into a run and crossed Bobby Sands Street. The British Embassy was on his right. But no gate—only walls. The motorcycle was getting closer.

The old embassy entrance was only a few feet away. Why did those fanatical idiots rename this street after an embarrassing Irish protester, forcing the British to change the main entrance to their embassy to Ferdowsi Avenue? A fitting death for an Iranian political dissident, on a street the Iranian Government named after an Irish political dissident.

He dove behind a tree on Bobby Sands Street as a motorcycle zoomed by on Nofel Loshato Street—and then slowed. It really was a Basij thug. Looking for him. The motorcycle continued slowly with the rider searching the right side of the road.

Bahir still had a chance.

If he could stay behind the trees on Bobby Sands Street, he could make his way to Jomhouri Avenue, go left, and then left again on Ferdowsi Avenue. If the motorcycle didn't turn around too soon and come looking.

Bahir worked his way south, behind trees and against the British Embassy wall along Bobby Sands Street, away from the motorcycle. Now he was halfway down the street. The motorcycle sound faded. He might live through this night yet. Oh, no. The whine of the engine was getting louder—he must have turned around. Headlights. Now pointing down Bobby Sands Street. And not enough tree cover.

One large tree. It had a wide trunk. Bahir dove behind it. The motorcycle came closer. Slowly. Slowly. Weapon extended. Too slow to jam the cane in the motorcycle spokes. Plan B.

The motorcycle inched down the street. Bahir kept snug to the tree, circling to the north as the motorcycle inched south, keeping the tree between himself and the headlight. He shifted the cane to his right hand. There would be only one chance.

Bahir lunged from behind the north side of the tree, extended his cane, hooked it around the rider's arm, and pulled with every gram of strength he could muster. The gun flew out of the thug's hand and clattered onto the street. The motorcycle wobbled when the rider's other hand wrenched the handlebars, but his attacker recovered. Bahir lunged for the gun at the edge of the street while the rider jumped off the motorcycle and came at him. Bahir grabbed the gun and fired. The gun recoiled as the sound echoed off walls and the thug's right arm went down before he could strike. He fired again. This time, the thug dropped.

Bahir staggered to his feet and watched the expanding pool of blood under the Basij thug's lifeless body. As if they had a mind of their own, his legs started running. He was an observer, watching and analyzing as he ran for his life. Curious—he wasn't winded, even after running the rest of Bobby Sands Street, around Jomhouri Avenue, and up Ferdowsi Avenue. There was the gate. And the guard.

"May I help you?"

Bahir's hands started to shake. His knees were weak. The street was spinning. He reached for the bars on the gate and slid down to the sidewalk.

"I say, bloke, you look white as a sheet! Do you speak English?"

"Basij."

"I'm sorry sir, I didn't hear you."

"Um, I want to see, um, dead Basij. On your other wall! I want to see Chicken Little!"

"Would you be looking for someone, sir?"

"Yes. Not Chicken Little. You're supposed to say that. I'm just a little chicken. I want to see, um, I don't remember who I want to see. You have a dead Basij murderer on the other side of your compound! And others coming. Let me in! Please! I am Bahir Mustafa. The sky is falling on Mr. Paddington! I am not a soldier! Atesh Zare is a pig!"

"Not exactly protocol, but I believe you. Let me help you up. And I'll take that weapon if you don't mind. Who is Atesh Zare?"

Two more motorcycles drove slowly down Ferdowsi Avenue. Both riders stared at Bahir as the British guard helped him through the Embassy gate. Bahir stared back. One rider lifted his right hand and extended his thumb and pointed his index finger at Bahir. The universal symbol of all who play war. Bahir lifted his right hand, kissed the tip of his middle finger, and extended it toward the riders. Another universal symbol as they slowly rolled past and zoomed away.

"Best not to provoke them, chap."

BLOOD SAMPLE

"It was glorious," an elated Khalid Farooq said. He shook hands with Tabor and the other soldiers as they exited the white van in the warehouse at the back of the Ibn Idhari Academy. "All the television stations are covering it. And blaming the Daesh. Allah is pleased."

"We need to dispose of the cell phones," Tabor said. "But first, to make sure they never turn on again."

Tabor grabbed two 4X4 posts stacked against the inside wall and set them end to end in the middle of the floor, with about a two-inch gap between them.

Khalid handed him an ax and smiled. "You enjoy this too much."

Tabor laughed. "Reminds me of chopping wood when I was younger."

Tabor placed the top and bottom of his cell phone on each end of the 4X4s with the middle of the phone over the gap. He swung the ax. It smashed the middle of the phone, spewing electronic debris everywhere. Khalid swept it up, putting half the debris in one box, half in another.

Each soldier took his turn at his phone. Tabor finished off Khalid's phone. "I'll dispose of these in restaurant trash bins. Shall we gather your recruits?"

Khalid brought all the recruits into a classroom and asked them to sit. "The mission for which we recruited all of you begins today. You have all pledged your lives in service to Allah. And now Allah has spoken and chosen you for a great honor. He wants you to be the instruments that wipe out the Great Satan."

"The three of us? Wipe out America?" Lion asked.

"That's right," Tabor said. "With some help from us."

Khalid and Tabor exchanged glances. Khalid nodded. "You've all heard of Typhoid Mary?" Tabor asked.

"Typhoid who?" asked Cypress.

"Mary Mallon worked as a cook one hundred years ago in New York. She carried the typhoid pathogen and infected people everywhere she worked. They called her an asymptomatic carrier, meaning she carried the pathogen and was contagious, but it didn't hurt her body."

"So, you're going to make us into Typhoid Mikes?" Brian asked.

"Similar, yes," Tabor said. "We have a method to introduce a pathogen and antidote into your bodies, which will cause you to infect everyone you contact. You will experience a mild fever and some flu-like symptoms after a few days and then recover. We will release you into crowded venues such as shopping centers, concerts, sports events, and so forth. You will come into contact with large numbers of people and pass the pathogen to them. They will come into contact with other people. But they will get sick because their bodies don't have the antidote."

Khalid continued. "You will be known as true Islamic heroes everywhere and will make history. You will pass a scourge to the infidels who ridicule you and defile our beliefs. You will start a movement that spreads across this continent, coast to coast. I envy all of you because you will carry a weapon more powerful than any firearm or even a ballistic missile, and not even the most powerful army in the world will be able to stop you."

"What's the catch?" Cypress asked.

"We need to acquire a blood sample today," Tabor said. "We will add the antidote to the blood sample, which activates it, and then inject you with it. After that, your time with us will end. We have a fund of two million dollars for each of you, which will generate an income stream to handle expenses. You will attend as many public events as possible, eat in crowded restaurants, travel on airplanes, and live in hotels. You will leave a legacy every day."

"Wait—how does making people sick further the cause of Allah?" Lion asked.

"Gentlemen, you will do more than make people sick," Khalid said. "The pathogen we're introducing into you will kill eighty percent of the people exposed to it. Once the disease ravishes this country, our armies will conquer the rest. You will be welcomed and remembered as heroes of the cause."

The room was silent for a few seconds.

"Are we together?" Khalid asked.

"Yes!" Cypress said.

"It's a good plan," Lion said.

Brian nodded without saying a word.

"Excellent," Khalid said. "Words cannot express Allah's gratitude or how proud I am of you."

"Cypress, you will fly to Los Angeles and visit San Diego and San Francisco," Tabor said. "Lion, you will visit New York City and Boston. Owl, you will visit Chicago and Kansas City first and then return to Minneapolis after stopping in Sioux Falls. With outbreaks in major cities across the country, the authorities will have an impossible task of finding the source. By the time they learn of the outbreak, it will be too late to stop. And I leave you in Khalid's capable hands until I return. Allahu akbar!"

"May Allah be with you as you collect blood samples today," Khalid said. "We will devote today's prayers to your safe mission and return."

"Insha'Allah," Tabor said.

It was prayer time. Khalid's instructions were clear. Recruits should clear their minds and pray to Allah for a successful mission. And praise Allah for playing such a key role. Brian finished praying, rolled up his prayer rug, and wandered from his room into the hallway. Khalid and two of his assistants stood in the warehouse area in back, speaking quietly. They turned and headed toward the wall in the middle of the building.

Brian moved down the hallway into the warehouse area. The door in the middle wall swung shut. Khalid and the two soldiers must have gone in there. Brian glided to the door and put his ear to it. He heard Khalid's muffled voice on the other side and the voices of the two soldiers. What was on that side of the building he wasn't supposed to see?

Those nagging doubts nibbling at the back of Brian's mind were now monsters, devouring everything in their path. Yes, kuffar like letter jacket and Cheryl Samuels deserved to die. But a whole country? Wasn't this operation just like European Christians who brought disease and murder to the Native Americans who were on this continent first? That poor lady in the interview—this epidemic would kill her and her children.

Why did they need a poison blood sample to deliver an antidote? And if he became a carrier of this poison for the rest of his life, what would stop him from infecting believers?

Khalid and the soldiers were still in that other room. Nobody would notice if he looked something up on the internet in the front lobby. He turned on the computer. It was old and had no password. Brian searched for "epidemic" and found references to Ebola II. He'd heard about Ebola, but that was long over. And Ebola II was the one raging in West Africa. Here was an article about a nurse, right here in the Minneapolis area, who had it. She was in a hospital, not far away. It must be her blood sample they planned to steal.

As for the antidote, one article summed it up: "There are no commercially available Ebola II vaccines. Supportive therapy with attention to intravascular volume, electrolytes, nutrition, and comfort provides the best benefit to the patient."

Brian looked over his shoulder. Khalid and the others were still not visible. He turned off the computer and quietly stood. He opened the office door into the main building hallway and strode through the glass doors to the outside. He ran. It didn't matter where.

Dr. Benjamin Donovan's cell phone chirped with a text message from an unknown phone number.

```
In Mpls for the conference and a family vis-
it, wondered if I could catch a ride back
to CDC on your charter. Hoping to pick your
brain. If okay with you, I'll make arrange-
ments. Danush Bagheri.
```

Of course this would be okay. Ben welcomed the company. Truthfully, the job of transporting the Ebola blood sample belonged to a courier, not a seasoned doctor, but with the conference in town anyway and a chance to talk to the Ebola patient, he was happy to do it. He texted back:

```
Looking forward to meeting you, Danush. Wel-
come aboard.
```

Jerry surveyed his basement office. "I can't believe the mess they made with my systems. I need to set it all back up and start that download again."

"No time. We have to get to that hospital in Fridley."

"Don't you want a copy of all this stuff from Bahir?"

"Your British friends have a copy, don't they?"

"Yeah."

"So, put on some socks and shoes and let's go."

"Hello, this is Dr. Benjamin Donovan. I'm away from my phone right now, so please leave a message."

"Dr. Donovan, this is Special Agent Jake Channing with the FBI in Minneapolis. It's urgent that we speak, and whatever you do, don't get on that charter flight. Please call me back as soon as you get this."

"No answer, huh?" Jerry said, sitting in the passenger seat of Channing's car.

"We'll meet him at Unity Hospital."

Heather Magnussen sat up in her hospital bed, watching breaking news on a thirty-year-old TV mounted on a stand high on the wall opposite her bed. "Mom, wait, turn that up, please."

Somebody knocked on the hospital room door.

"Come in." Heather's mother responded.

"Miss Magnussen?" Dr. Donovan asked.

"Yes, I'm Heather Magnussen."

"I was eager to meet you," Dr. Donovan said. "I'm Benjamin Donovan with the Centers for Disease Control. I spoke on the phone with, I believe, your mother."

"Nice to meet you," Heather said. "And this is my mom, Ellen."

"It's a pleasure to meet you," Ellen said. "I want to thank you for helping save my daughter's life."

"I wish we could take credit, but the people here at the hospital did the heavy lifting."

"Dr. Donovan, have you been watching the news?" Heather asked. "Somebody just bombed the megamall."

"No, I've been driving with the radio off. What happened?"

Heather gestured at the TV. Ellen turned up the sound with the remote control.

"I'm in Skycam seven above Interstate 494," a news announcer on TV said, "and we're looking down on what was the north entrance to the megamall. Yes, there—yes, let's get a zoom shot on that. As you can hopefully see, the JW Chariot hotel on the north end is reduced to rubble. Just demolished. It's gone. And you can see the collapsed north entrance to the mall, as whatever demolished that hotel also wiped out the north mall entrance. Looking south toward Killebrew Drive, and, yes, can you see that? We're aiming at what used to be the Patterson Blu hotel in front of the south entrance, and just look at the carnage along Killebrew Drive and the fallen skyway on top of several cars."

Jerry and Channing found Wing C of Unity Hospital in Fridley, Minnesota, and rode the elevator to the fourth floor. Channing showed his FBI badge to the uniformed police officers and medical staff in the nurse's station. Room nine was at the end of the hallway on the left. Someone had taped a note to the door: "Only family and friends allowed. No physical contact."

A TV blared behind the door with coverage about the megamall bombing. Channing knocked. The sound muted.

A muffled voice behind the door said, "Come in."

Channing pushed the door open.

A clear plastic curtain hung from a track in the ceiling, acting as a makeshift isolation shield between Heather's room and the door. Jerry and Channing stopped outside the curtain.

"May I help you?" a middle-aged woman asked. She stood with an African-American man near a younger woman in the bed.

"You must be Dr. Donovan," Channing said.

"Who are you?" Dr. Donovan asked.

"I'm Special Agent Jake Channing with the FBI." Channing took out his badge and showed it to the group. "May we come in?"

"I guess," the middle-aged woman said.

"Mrs. Magnussen?" Channing asked, looking at the middle-aged woman.

"Yes, I'm Heather's mom, Ellen Magnussen. What's this all about?"

Channing and Jerry parted the curtain and entered the room. Channing said, "We have reason to believe Heather is the reason terrorists bombed the megamall and the mine in Ely a few days ago."

Heather's jaw dropped.

"What?" Ellen asked.

"I'm sorry," Jerry said, looking at Heather. "The Iranians want a blood sample. The bombings are a diversion. You're the target. Well, not you so much as your blood."

"And you are?" asked Ellen.

"Jerry Barkley. I'm an IT contractor."

Channing continued. "Dr. Donovan, under no circumstances should you bring that blood sample to your charter flight this afternoon."

"How do you know about my flight plans?"

"You're scheduled to leave from Anoka County Airport this afternoon at one on a charter flight to Atlanta where you'll meet CDC colleagues and deliver Heather's blood samples for storage and study," Jerry said. "We know all this because we penetrated the Iranians' email after they penetrated your CDC email."

"Iran—what?" Ellen said. "The news channels say ISIS did those bombings."

"Yes, they do," Channing said.

"Okay, so, how do you fit in?" Ellen asked, looking at Jerry. "Did the FBI contract with you to do a bunch of cyber-sleuthing?"

"Um, not exactly, no," answered Jerry.

"Our relationship isn't important," Channing said. "What is important is that we take these guys down, and we need your help."

"What do you need from us?" Heather asked.

"Wait a minute," Ellen said. "None of this makes any sense."

"Listen, you guys," Jerry said, "I'm sorry we barged in on you like this. I know I must look pretty wild-eyed right about now. That's mostly because I haven't slept much these past several days while I've been tracking these guys and that's because they want to kill us. Iran is behind all this, and they want Heather's blood to start an Ebola epidemic in the United States. They're framing ISIS."

"Okay, I'll stay away from the airport," Dr. Donovan said. "You could have just called."

"We tried," replied Channing. "And we need you there to draw them out."

"In that case," Dr. Donovan said. "Why don't I just bring a fake sample? They can steal it; you follow them and arrest them; and we deliver the real blood sample later. They can store it here in the hospital indefinitely."

"I was thinking along those same lines," Channing said. "We know they plan to steal it on the plane, but we don't know how."

"Oh, no," Dr. Donovan took out his cell phone and fumbled with it. "Yes, here it is."

He showed Channing the text message from Danush Bagheri.

"That's our guy," Channing said.

"Unless they changed their mind when my C&C server went down."

Channing paused. "Oh. Now I see your point. They'll know something's different here, but they won't know why."

"Right. And they might dream up some other way to steal that blood sample."

A woman walked in. "Sorry to interrupt. I'm Avery Sawyer, Chief of Internal Medicine. Dr. Donovan, may I see you for a moment?"

"Sure, what's up?"

"Miss Magnussen, this concerns you, too. Do you remember if the paramedics who worked on you in the ambulance were properly suited and gloved?"

"I think so," Heather said, "although I wasn't the most observant that day. Why?"

"One of them is complaining of flu-like symptoms."

"Oh, no," Dr. Donovan said.

"And it might just be an influenza bug. But we're not taking chances. Dr. Donovan, I read your paper about contact tracing from the 2014 outbreak, and we could use your expertise to help us quickly ramp that up here. We were hoping we could persuade you to stay for a few more days."

"Yes, of course. Let me alert the team."

"We could have an Ebola outbreak right here? Because of me?" Heather said.

"Not directly caused by you, no, but we may be looking at an Ebola situation, and we'll need to contain it quickly," Avery said.

"Yes. Minutes and hours count. I'll help in any way I can," Dr. Donovan said. Turning to Channing, "Under the circumstances, there's just not a way to get on that flight."

"Thank you," Avery said. She turned to leave.

"Hold on," Channing said to Avery. "What's the security like here? Nobody checked our IDs."

"We have uniformed police, especially around the ER."

"What would stop somebody from impersonating a doctor or a nurse and extracting a blood sample?"

"The nurses watch the floor, and they keep an eye on who's coming and going."

"What if somebody slips past them?"

"That would be difficult."

"Nobody challenged us. Even when we stopped and asked directions."

"Wait," Ellen said. "Are you saying somebody could sneak in here and steal a blood sample from my daughter?"

"It's possible somebody already did."

"We should be able to reconcile that by looking at Heather's chart," Dr. Donovan said. "Heather, if you remember somebody doing a procedure and it's not in the chart, that's a suspect."

"Yeah. And I'll make sure nobody gets in here unless they're authorized," Channing said. "How soon do you need, Dr. Donovan?"

"This afternoon will be fine."

"Good." Turning to Jerry, Channing continued, "Jerry, would you and Dr. Donovan stand back to back?"

"Huh?" Jerry asked.

"Just humor me. You guys look like you're built similarly."

Jerry and Dr. Donovan exchanged glances. They shrugged and stood back to back.

"About the same height. Same build," Channing said. He looked at Avery.

She nodded. "Yeah, about the same. Where are you going with this?"

Jerry held his light-colored arm against Dr. Donovan's dark-colored arm. "I don't like this idea. We look way different."

"I'll bet makeup can fix that," Channing said.

"Are you proposing Jerry get on that charter in my place?" Dr. Donovan asked.

"No one's getting on that flight. But I'm thinking about sending him to the airport, yes," Channing said. "You have to handle a possible outbreak. I was planning to follow you to the airport, but I need to stay here and keep this room secure." Now turning to Avery. "Ma'am, does the hospital have a way to make Jerry the same skin color as Dr. Donovan to fool some terrorists? And can we do it before you need him?"

"I know we work with makeup artists for some of our long-term patients. Let me see what I can find. But I think so, yes."

"Good. And let's keep this quiet."

"Wait—are you nuts?" Jerry asked. "Doesn't the FBI have guys trained for this kind of stuff?"

"We do, but they're all busy with a terrorist bombing. If we can figure out a strategy to make him think you're Dr. Donovan and play this out safely, are you onboard?"

"I'm an IT guy, not a superhero."

"Yesterday, I watched you convince one of the smartest botnet masters on the planet into believing you're a US Military colonel over a video call from your basement. And that was after you tracked him down."

"What?" Heather asked.

"Long story," Jerry said.

"And before that, you faced down two FBI agents trying to intimidate you."

"Well, it was pitiful. It sounded like it was right out of an old movie."

"What's going on?" Ellen asked.

"Jerry's the reason we know about all this," Channing said. "Jerry, these guys want to use her blood to murder thousands of people. It's a fifty-fifty shot whether they try to steal it here or on the flight. I can arrest people here. I need your help at the airport."

"There's gotta be another way."

"You tell me what it is."

Jerry opened his mouth but couldn't think of anything to say.

"I can fill that charter terminal with trained agents but not this whole hospital. And we don't have time to get an agent ready to replace Dr. Donovan. Are you gonna finish what you started?" Channing asked.

"If you can fill that charter terminal with trained agents, why not use one of them as your Guinea pig?"

"Because Dr. Donovan needs to leave from here, at the hospital, and drive over there. For all we know, they might have people watching the place."

Jerry looked down.

"Well?"

Jerry bit his lower lip and took a deep breath. "For the record, this sucks. If you want me to go eyeball to eyeball with a terrorist, I hope you have some James Bond stuff in the trunk of your car."

TAKEOFF

"Hold still," the makeup artist told Jerry. They were still in Heather's hospital room, but the empty bed was pushed out of the way to set up a makeshift makeup studio.

"I still don't get what we're going to do about the hair," Jerry said.

"One step at a time," the makeup artist said. "You wouldn't believe what we can do for cancer patients. Compared to that, this is a piece of cake. How does the skin look?"

"Amazing. Put a wig on, and you guys could be twins," Channing said, looking at Dr. Donovan and then back at Jerry. "Now, let's go over the plan again."

"You know there are a bunch of assumptions behind this plan of yours, right?" Jerry said.

"And that's why we have so many contingencies," Channing said.

"We call it spaghetti code in my world," Jerry said.

"Still works better than making it up as you go along, right?"

"Yeah, okay. So, I meet what's-his-name . . ."

"Danush?" Dr. Donovan said.

"Yeah, Danush Bagheri, that's right. The terrorist with the made-up name. If he's there, I'll meet him somewhere in the airport. I make nice, and we'll both pretend we attended this conference at the U of M. Doc, I need some medical words."

"Call me Ben."

"Okay, Ben—thanks—I do need some medical words so I sound like I'm you."

"I have a conference agenda in my backpack," Ben said.

"You have a backpack?" Jerry asked.

"Yes."

"Which reminds me, we should swap clothes. What's your waist size?"

"Thirty-eight."

"Good, that works. I'd hate to fight a terrorist with my pants too tight."

Heather and Ellen smiled. Channing was more serious.

"You're not fighting anyone. You'll walk in, make contact, and then you need to use the men's room. That's it."

"One more question—why don't we let the charter company know?"

"Everyone in that airport will be an armed, law enforcement agent."

"It's a shame we don't have a way to make Danush's buddy believe Danush is handing him the sample. You could follow him to their base and nail all of them."

"You'd have to get on the plane for that to happen, and you're not getting on that plane."

Still in Heather's room, Dr. Donovan handed Jerry his rental car keys.

"We should recruit you for our church drama team," Jerry said to the makeup artist.

"Not to pat myself on the back, but you turned out well."

"Did I tell you guys about the time I played a computer nerd in a skit?" Jerry asked.

"I'll bet that was a stretch," Channing said.

Heather and Ellen chuckled. "Are you really on a drama team at your church?" Ellen asked.

"Yeah. It's been a while since we've put on anything."

"I was in a play in middle school," Heather said. "I forgot my lines. Scared me to death."

"Just another skit," Channing said. "A couple lines and then you're done."

"Right," Jerry said. Turning to Dr. Donovan, "Where's the car?"

"Level B, section seven."

"And everything's in my backpack?" Jerry asked.

"Yeah. You're set," Channing said.

"Okay." Jerry shouldered his backpack.

"Oh—I almost forgot," Channing said. He fumbled in his pocket. "Here. This might come in handy."

"Aw, Agent Channing, I'm touched," Jerry said. "My very own pocket knife."

"It's only a loan," Channing said. "I want it back when this is all over." Channing extended his hand. Jerry shook it.

"My friends call me Jake."

Jerry put the knife in his pocket. "I'll bring this back in about an hour."

●────●

Along the tree-lined street, the chain-link fence, topped with barbed wire and surrounding the entire Anoka County Airport, looked imposing. But a small sign attached to Gate A on the southeast side of the airport said what was important: "Drive close. Gate opens automatically."

Just inside Gate A, a man in coveralls trimmed trees on the left side of Airport Road. His truck was parked a few feet away.

After dropping off a passenger at the charter building on the other side of the airport, an older van drove slowly up to Gate A. The gate opened, and the van drove in. The gate closed behind it. Just another vehicle driving onto Airport Road. After the van passed, the driver looked in his rear-view mirror. The man trimming trees turned toward the gate and away from the van. It looked like he took out a walkie-talkie from his coveralls and said something into it.

The van slowly worked its way past several buildings with a few cars parked in front and past a few planes that looked like WWII-era relics parked in the grass. One was missing part of its tail. All looked rusty. Weeds grew up around the tires under their wings.

The van weaved around hangars and businesses and stopped briefly near a taxiway on Oregon Avenue between two rows of airplane hangars. The rows between hangars were named after American states. After studying the taxiway for a few seconds, the driver turned around and made his way to the parking area near the Stratosphere Aviation building. He parked near a few other vehicles and waited.

• ———— •

The Locke Air main building looked more like a corporate conference center than an airport terminal. It stood behind a small parking lot with plenty of spaces, a well-manicured lawn, and an overhang that covered a circular car drop-off area. Large, tan bricks of various sizes stylishly covered the support columns and building faces. Jerry parked Dr. Donovan's rental car and entered the building through the glass double doors.

He paused and took in the scene. The inside was spacious, with a ceiling at least twenty feet high. If a beach and the ocean were outside, this could have been a resort hotel lobby. But the gleaming corporate jet parked on the asphalt behind the glass double doors in back, combined with the fantastic view of the countryside and airplanes coming and going through the floor-to-ceiling glass back wall, was equally impressive.

A muscular man with dark hair and wearing a large backpack stood at the back of the lobby and made eye contact. He smiled and strode forward on the tan carpet and extended his hand.

Showtime. Jerry smiled and sauntered across the tiled walkway connecting the front and back doors to meet him, putting his best church-drama-team acting skills to work. Until today, he never imagined he would use all those hours of acting and improv practice this way.

Glancing to his left, Jerry found the restrooms and a hallway leading to a conference room. Adjacent to the hallway was a large, carpeted waiting area, set off from the main lobby by a glass wall. Two men in business suits sat in chairs in the waiting area facing the main lobby.

On his right, two men inside stood behind a desk inside a glass-walled office, looking at a computer display and gesturing. A plaque on a wooden door said, "General Manager."

Behind the general manager's office was another hallway with a sign that read, "Crew Lounge."

They met in the middle, in front of a reception desk that covered most of the wall space on the right side of the room. It had a computer, phone, laser printer, and plenty of work space, all behind a wrap-around, polished countertop that would work in the nicest of home kitchens.

"Danush?

"Dr. Donovan—nice to meet you." He had a slight Middle Eastern accent. They shook hands. He had a firm grip. But not too firm. He smiled. Jerry fought the butterflies in his stomach.

Next to the reception desk at the back of the room, three people in business suits huddled in plush chairs arranged around a low table. One glanced up at Jerry and back down.

"May I help you?" asked the young lady behind the reception desk.

It's just another improv. All over with a couple more lines. "Yes, ma'am. I'm um, Dr. Benjamin Donovan," stepping toward her with Danush, "and I'm here to pick up my charter to Atlanta. This is Danush Bagheri, and he'll be riding with me."

The two men in the waiting area behind the glass rose and moved toward the conference room hallway door.

Other people around the lobby exchanged glances. Jerry swallowed. Don't look at them. Keep smiling.

"Um, can I use your restroom?" Jerry asked.

"Sure, it's right over there." The receptionist smiled and pointed across the room.

"Thanks."

Danush's eyes darted. He grabbed Jerry's arm and wrenched him close.

"Hey, what . . ."

"Silence!" shouted Danush. He pulled Jerry away from the reception desk toward the middle of the room. "One hostile move from any of you and this doctor dies."

Jerry turned toward Danush, trying to free his arm. Danush's handgun was pointed at his face. He ducked. One of the men emerged from the hallway next to the restroom and drew a weapon, but Danush saw it first and fired. The agent dropped, a pool of blood forming under him. The other agent dove for cover back down the hallway. Danush fired two more rounds. The first shattered the glass panel in the front of the waiting area. The second went through the waiting area drywall and exited in the hallway. The other agent went down with a thud.

Jerry tried to wrestle his arm free, but Danush's fingers clamped around it like vice grips. In one lightning-fast motion, Danush jerked Jerry's arm toward him, released his grip from Jerry's arm and grabbed Jerry around his neck. Now with Jerry's head secure in one arm, he put the barrel of his weapon against Jerry's head.

During the commotion, one of agents from the low table in the back crept behind Danush to wrestle him down. Danush's left leg flew backward. A sickening crack echoed through the room. The agent went down, his leg now bending at an unnatural angle at the knee. The other two agents reached for their weapons, but Danush turned and fired first, pulling Jerry around. They both died before hitting the ground. The wounded agent moaned in pain as Danush kicked his weapon away.

Two seconds, three agents dead and two disabled. This wasn't how we planned it. Jerry struggled to free himself. Danush tightened his grip.

"Although none of us have met, I believe we are all acquainted. Dr. Donovan is getting on that plane with me. I will release him once we are safely away from this place."

The receptionist reached for the desk phone. Danush obliterated it with another round. Pieces flew everywhere.

Two agents emerged from the general manager's office, weapons drawn. "You're not going out that door," one of the agents said. "You are surrounded by at least a half-dozen agents aiming at your head."

"By my count, only you and your partner and this young lady are left standing," Danush said. "Dr. Donovan, I assume the blood sample you're carrying is fake?"

Jerry swallowed and looked around the room. Blood and bodies everywhere. He shivered.

"Um," Jerry closed his eyes. That agent from the general manager's office—Jerry had seen him before. But where? Jerry tried to control the shaking in his hands and the urge to throw up. He took a deep breath. "Um, no, I have the real blood sample."

"What?" the agent facing them said.

"Um, that's right," Jerry said. "And I'm not Dr. Donovan. My name is . . . George Baker." Now Jerry remembered that face. This would be fun in another setting. "And you know it, Blackwell! Ten years in the agency getting dumped on. Don't worry, you were just the latest supervisor. So, yeah, I switched the fake sample with the real one back at the hospital." He tried to turn his head toward Danush. "I presume your real name is not Danush?"

"Shut up!" Danush said.

"I guess it doesn't matter what your name is. I'm tired of America bullying its way around the world. And I'm tired of getting dumped on by supervisors like him. I've seen too many innocent people go down. I'm on your side!"

Blackwell's face hardened. "You'll never get away with this, Baker!"

Jerry met his gaze. "We're gonna land somewhere and finish what these guys started!" Turning to Danush. "Nice and easy, let's go out that door and up into the plane. You're a pilot, right?"

"Yes."

"Good. We'll get in the air and find a way to finish this."

"Baker!" shouted Blackwell as Danush pulled Jerry toward the back exit.

Danush stopped. "I am a soldier doing my job. Please forgive me." He fired at Blackwell and his partner. Both agents went down.

"Drop your weapon!" It was the receptionist, protected behind the countertop and the laser printer.

Danush let go of Jerry and stepped toward the reception desk, firing round after round into the granite countertop. Pieces exploded across the room.

Click.

Danush was out of bullets. In less than a second, he popped the clip from his handgun and inserted another one, but not before the receptionist fired. Danush dove and her first round clipped Danush's shoulder. The next hit him in the chest, knocking him backward. She should have aimed for his head.

Danush fell. Blood oozed from his wound. Hey lay motionless on the floor, unblinking eyes facing the ceiling. The receptionist stepped out from behind her cover and strode toward Danush. It was a fatal mistake. His bulletproof vest under his shirt protected him. Jerry tried to shout a warning, but he was too late. Danush raised his hand and fired. His first round hit her in her vest, knocking her backward. The second round hit her between her eyes. Her lifeless body crashed into the wraparound counter and slumped to the floor.

Danush clambered to his feet and moved to the opposite hallway toward the conference room. He stood over the wounded agent behind the wall and fired a bullet through his head. Next, he turned to the back of the room and towered over the agent with the broken knee. For a second, Danush watched him, still trying to crawl to his weapon, and then shot him in the head.

He turned to Jerry, still standing where Danush had let go of him.

"Why did you do that?" Jerry's hands shook.

"Dead people can't dial a phone."

They both stood silently.

Danush hung his head. "I am a soldier. My job is sometimes unpleasant." He lifted his gaze; his eyes hardened. "You may be useful to me. You can come with me willingly or die here. I promise it will be painless."

Walter, waiting in the van, looked at his watch. Tabor was late. But they all knew this could not be a precision operation. The amount of time required to disable the pilot, copilot, and CDC doctor and find the blood sample could not be predicted. He started the van and drove north on Airport Road back to Oregon Avenue and turned right, now headed east toward the taxiway between rows of hangars. He drove almost out to the taxiway and stopped. Peering through his binoculars at the Locke Air building on the north side of the airport, he saw the door closing on the jet. It would not be long now.

●——————●

Jerry sat in the copilot seat next to Danush. Danush's weapon was in his lap. Still loaded. Even with Danush's shoulder oozing blood, now was not the time to try anything. But, try what? This guy just murdered eight people. Jerry fought the urge to throw up. Lord, I don't know what to do. I need your help. "Do you have a plan?"

Danush's arms flew in a million directions at once, pressing buttons and toggling switches while the engines came to life. "Our plans were thwarted." Danush took out his cell phone, tapped out a text message, and then slipped the cell phone back in his pocket.

"Um, okay, take off to the east," Jerry said.

"What?"

"Take off with the plane headed east. I've got an idea."

"Why are you helping me?"

"Two reasons. First, I want to live. Second, I want you to live. And third, I want out of this mess, and I'm on your side." Lord, if Rahab could lie to save the Israelites, I hope it's okay if I lie right now. I want to go home tonight.

"That's three reasons."

"Okay, three. Who's counting? I can come up with more if you want."

"No, this is sufficient. I will decide later whether to kill you or let you live."

The plane taxied south along the taxiway, crossed the east-west runway, and then turned right to run parallel to the runway. The plane turned right again and taxied to the runway, then one more right to start its takeoff run.

●——————●

Walter heard the engines on the plane start up. He watched the plane begin to taxi south, toward him. The handoff would be quick.

His cell phone buzzed. He pulled the phone out of his pocket, watching the plane. The one-word text message said, "Abort."

But the plane was still taxiing right toward him. The message had to be wrong.

After crossing the east-west runway, instead of continuing toward him, the plane turned left toward the west end of the east-west runway. What happened?

No matter. Walter was a trained soldier and knew how to obey orders. It was time for the fallback plan. He needed to leave. Now. Meet the rest of the team at the rendezvous point. He walked back to the van and started the engine as the plane climbed away from the airport, headed east. He took out his cell phone and did a group Reply All. "Confirmed. Rendezvous."

Jerry looked out his window and saw "27" painted on the end of the runway, retreating and shrinking underneath and behind him as the plane climbed away from the devastation below. All those people. All dead. Somehow, some way, this terrorist would pay.

Jerry fought to stay calm and bury the images burned into his brain. "Alright, here's the deal. We're supposed to be going to Atlanta. But instead, we'll go to Canada, on the north side of Lake Huron. That area is empty. We'll find an airstrip, land, and then just blend in. You find your way back to wherever you came from, and I'll disappear." Jerry looked out his window again. It was a long way down. "Do we have a deal?"

"I am considering it."

"Okay, what's your plan?"

"I kill you and parachute out of the plane over Wisconsin."

"Are you nuts? First of all, a zillion people will see that parachute in the air. You'll spend the rest of your life in a hole in Cuba. Second, that blood sample will never be deployed, so your mission will fail. And even if by some miracle you get away, do you want to tell your buddies in the Middle East how you failed?"

"I should kill you right now."

"Um, Danush, or whatever your name is, you do know that bullets are bad for airplanes in the air, right? What is your name anyway?"

"Silence!"

Jerry looked down—green fields that looked like blocks on a quilt covered the ground below. And a few clouds. Yup, now they were above the clouds. Jerry was in an airplane, alone, with an Iranian super-soldier. "Today is a good day to die." That's what Lt. Worf always said in *Star Trek* when they prepared for battle. No. Today is a lousy day to die. But you don't out-muscle Klingon super-soldier warriors. You out-think them.

"Look, Danush, I have a laptop in my backpack. Why don't I dig it out and start looking for someplace desolate to land?"

"How do you know that area of Canada is empty?"

"Because I drove through it a while ago."

Danush studied Jerry. Jerry did his best to look sincere.

"My name is Tabor."

"Okay, Tabor. Um, nice to meet you. I'm going to dig out my laptop now, okay?"

"Yes. Go ahead."

Jerry reached into his backpack and fumbled with something. "Yeah, here it is." Jerry pulled out a Taser and, in one fluid motion, fired it over the cockpit center console. Tabor screamed when the electrodes found their mark. His shriek died into a gurgle as paralysis set in.

Jerry's hands shook. He clenched and unclenched his fists, reached into his backpack again, and pulled out a syringe. "I don't remember what they said was in this stuff, just that it will put you to sleep for a while. This might sting a little." Jerry reached across the center console, jammed the needle into Tabor's left thigh, and pushed the plunger down. Next, he took the gun from Tabor's lap and set it on the floor behind the center console.

"Now, here's our situation," Jerry said. He reached into his backpack for another cartridge and snapped it into the Taser. "That Taser wears off after about thirty seconds, and the shot I gave you takes a few minutes to kick in. If you reach for anything, I'll zap you again. I'm not sure what happens after you get zapped multiple times. But if this stuff kills you, you aren't getting seventy virgins; I'll tell you that much right now. Before you go to sleep, why don't you tell me how we can find your buddies?"

Tabor stared at Jerry. Jerry stared back.

"I'm a sholjur, doing my zjob."

"Well, I'm an IT guy. And I just kicked your ass."

Tabor's eyes slowly closed. His arms went limp. Jerry waited a few more minutes and then gingerly picked up Tabor's right arm. He dropped it and the arm crashed into Tabor's lap.

"Murdering scumbag."

For the first time, Jerry noticed the maze of color displays and buttons in front, on his right, and in the center console between seats. A shaft came up from the floor between his legs and opened into what looked like a combination of bicycle handlebars and a car steering wheel. A large display behind the handlebars on a stick looked important. The pilot side of the instrument panel had some of the same displays.

The plane wasn't crashing, so maybe some sort of autopilot was flying the plane. He had time.

He looked at Tabor. Did he say his plan was to parachute out of the plane? Jerry climbed out of the copilot seat and opened Tabor's large backpack in the passenger area behind the cockpit. There it was, a parachute pack, ready to strap on.

He pulled out the packed parachute, set it on one of the passenger seats, and ruffled through the backpack. Finding nothing useful, he set it out of the way.

"I should put a hole in your head."

He picked up the gun.

Dead people don't dial phones, huh? Dead people won't wake up and attack me, either.

He put the gun barrel to Tabor's head.

Squeeze the trigger. This guy just murdered eight people.

What would that make me? Just leave him there. People land planes when pilots have heart attacks. Everything I need is probably on the copilot side. He pulled the gun away.

And what if he wakes up while we're still in the air? Then I'm dead.

So, tie him to the seat harness.

But the harness can move. And he can still reach the foot pedals.

Shoot him. He put the barrel to Tabor's head again. Jerry's hands shook. His stomach churned.

"C'mon, God, it would be self-defense."

No.

"Why not? You saw what this guy did at the airport." Jerry put his finger on the trigger. "Just one squeeze." He put both hands on the gun to steady himself.

No! He pulled the gun back. He fumbled with the bullet clip to release it and slid the gun on the floor to the back of the plane.

Can't leave him there. Can't shoot him. Then, what?

Jerry climbed into the copilot seat, reached across the center console, and found the lever to adjust the pilot seat. He slid the pilot seat as far back as it would go, in line with the edge of the center console. He pressed and turned the seatbelt mechanism to unlock Tabor from his seat belt and pulled the harnesses back. Next, he climbed out of the copilot seat and positioned himself behind the pilot seat.

He reached his arms over the center console and around the pilot's seat, under Tabor's armpits, and leaned Tabor's body over the space between seats. Hopefully, none of the buttons on top of the center console were important. But wait. Two buttons on the back-left side panel said, "AP" and "YD" and were illuminated in green. AP for autopilot? He would just have to be careful.

Jerry planted his legs and pulled as hard as he could. Tabor's limp body moved off the pilot's seat and plopped on the floor. His legs draped over the center console and onto the pilot's seat.

One more tug. Jerry planted his feet again and pulled with everything he had. Tabor's legs slid up and off his seat. His feet hit a corner of the center console, flew over the top, and fell to the floor behind the console. Jerry lost his balance moving backward and fell. Tabor's shoulders fell out of Jerry's hands and his head banged against the floor. Jerry scrambled back to his feet. Tabor was on the floor. Still unconscious.

So far, so good. Those AP and YD buttons were unchanged.

Jerry stepped around Tabor to his own backpack in the copilot seat and took out two zip ties. He rolled Tabor on his side, putting an arm behind him, and then repeated the motion with Tabor's other side. With both arms behind Tabor's back, Jerry pulled the zip ties snugly around Tabor's wrists. Jerry stood and looked at Tabor's limp body for a second. Can't be too careful. He took out two more zip ties and applied them to Tabor's wrists. Super soldier or not, he wasn't wriggling his hands free.

Still not secure enough. Jerry searched for a pocket knife or scissors or anything sharp.

He remembered Jake's pocket knife and smiled. Hopefully, somebody in the tower saw the plane take off and was on the phone right now, trying to figure out a way to get him back home alive. The grizzly scene from the airport played over and over in his mind. Jerry pushed it away. First things first.

Jerry opened Tabor's parachute and cut a few cords. He put a rope around Tabor's body and behind Tabor's arms to keep his arms tight to his body. But he had to tie it loosely enough for Tabor to breathe. So, how to keep it in place when he wakes up?

He cut another section of rope and tied it tightly around Tabor's ankles and then another one around his neck. Then he cut some more rope and tied the ankle loop to the waist loop and the waist loop to the loop around his neck. Now, no matter which way Tabor struggled, that waist loop should stay in place and not move up or down. And struggling would be bad for Tabor's neck. Just to make sure, he cut another small section of rope and tied one end to the waist loop, the other end to the loop around Tabor's hands.

Jerry stood and looked over his handiwork. "Hey, super soldier—may I offer you a beverage? How about a pillow? Oh, I'm so sorry, sir; we're fresh out."

Still not good enough. Jerry cut some more rope and tied one end to the loop around Tabor's ankles and looped the other end around the left front seat back. He did the same thing with the rope around Tabor's neck, looping it to the right rear seat back. Now, no matter which way he struggled, he would put pressure somewhere else.

Satisfied Tabor was going nowhere, Jerry climbed into the pilot's seat. He put the headset over his head.

A female voice said, "Citation two eight two delta foxtrot, Green Bay tower. What's your status?"

And then, a few seconds later, "Citation two eight two delta foxtrot, Green Bay tower. Are you receiving me?"

That had to be somebody trying to talk to this plane. "Um, can anyone hear me?"

The voice on the radio kept repeating, so apparently not. Which made the next order of business figuring out how to talk on the radio.

ESCAPE

At the Ibn Idhari Academy, Khalid's phone buzzed. It was a new group text message from Tabor. "Abort." Two minutes later, a message came in from Walter. The text Khalid dreaded. "Confirmed. Rendezvous."

Tabor must have been either unable to acquire the blood sample or unable to deliver it to Walter. But regardless, the mission was over. It was time to leave. One last task to perform first. Khalid did not look forward to it.

"Students, we need to gather in the classroom." Cypress and Lion wandered in.

"What's going on?" Cypress asked.

"Where is Owl?" Khalid asked.

Cypress and Lion glanced at each other.

The two soldiers followed Cypress and Lion into the classroom. Khalid made eye contact. The soldiers nodded wordlessly as Khalid began searching for Brian.

———•———•———

At the Anoka County Airport, Walter turned the van around and headed for the nearest exit, Gate B. Slowly, no need to arouse suspicion. Not good. A police car blocked the gate. Turn around? No, that would arouse too much suspicion. He reached into his overnight bag for his weapon and stuffed it in the back of his pants.

He stopped. One officer approached the passenger side. Another stayed back by the police car. Standard operational procedure. It would be difficult to get them both.

The officer signaled for him to roll down the passenger window. Walter reached for the handle but then realized the van had power windows. Which triggered an idea. He opened the driver's door and stepped out.

"Get back in the van and roll down your passenger window."

"I am sorry, but the power window isn't functional. Is something wrong?"

"I need to see your driver's license and registration."

"Ah, yes, let me find them."

The officer by the police car looked nervous.

Walter fumbled in his pocket, pretending to look for his driver's license.

The officer by the police car spoke into his radio. Moment of truth. Engage or dialogue?

"The registration should be right here in the glove box." He reached inside the van, now below the window where they wouldn't see his arms.

"Stop right there! Let me see your hands!"

Both officers reached for something. No choice but to engage.

Walter reached behind his back, drew his weapon, and fired two rounds. The first shattered the passenger-side window. The officer staggered. The second round found its mark. The officer went down. Walter dove away from the van and fired at the other officer, just as he fired at Walter's position behind the van door. Walter's round hit the officer in the shoulder. The officer dove for cover behind the police car.

"Shots fired! Officer down, shots fired!"

Walter fired three more rounds and ran toward the police car. When Walter's weapon went silent, the officer lifted his head to fire. He never got a chance to pull the trigger. Walter put a bullet between his eyes from point-blank range.

Both officers were dead.

He turned to the police car and checked the dash camera. No cables; all the storage must be internal. He put a round through it. The engine was still idling. Walter pressed the brake pedal and shifted the gear selector to drive. He turned the steering wheel a quarter turn, took his foot off the brake pedal, and jumped away as the car rolled off the asphalt and out of the way. He dragged the dead officer's body into the grass, away from the gate. No need to desecrate the dead. He fought well. He grabbed the officer's body camera and weapon.

He jogged back to the other dead officer and grabbed his body camera and weapon. He dropped it all into the overnight bag, jumped into the van, and floored the accelerator pedal. The van rocketed forward and crashed through the gate. Now outside the gate, he backed up and scraped the passenger side panels against the fence, blocking the gate opening, and turned the van off.

He locked the doors and climbed out. He grabbed his overnight bag and dropped the van keys in it. Sirens wailed. He jogged into the trees on the other side of the street.

A chain-link fence topped with barbed wire blocked the way. But a grass clearing only a few feet beyond the fence and bordering an asphalt parking lot offered an escape. Sirens were louder.

He took off his jacket and placed it over the barbed wires. He threw the overnight bag over the fence and then climbed up and over. The sharp barbs poked through the heavy fabric and scratched his palms. He dropped into the mud on the other side. No time to retrieve the jacket.

He jogged across the parking lot to a small street and stopped. 93rd Lane to the north? No good. Police cars would be coming down that road any second. South? A mystery. A wooded area behind the light industrial buildings across the street beckoned. He ran across the street and followed a tree-lined driveway into a parking lot behind one building and into the woods.

Safe for the moment, he took out his cell phone and brought up Google Maps. A car dealership was only two miles away.

The sirens were deafening as the first of dozens of police cars arrived at the airport gate. He turned into the trees and disappeared into the shadows.

FLIGHT

"Citation two eight two delta foxtrot, Green Bay tower. Be advised, we have two jets scrambling from Madison to assess your status and escort you. If you can hear this but are unable to transmit, please signal the approaching aircraft by waving your wings."

"I'd love to if I knew how to do that," Jerry said into the headset. "How do I talk to you?" He looked again at the bewildering sea of buttons surrounding him. "Which button do I press?"

But maybe . . .

Two small military jets appeared a few minutes later. They flanked him on the left and right, close enough to look him over.

Jerry made eye contact with the pilot on the left side and then waved his arms and pointed to the headset over his head. He moved his thumb and fingers together with his right hand, near his mouth, symbolizing trying to talk, and gave an exaggerated shoulder shrug. "Oh, this is great. Charades in the air."

A few seconds later, "Citation two eight two delta foxtrot, Green Bay tower, is your radio transmitter malfunctioning?"

Jerry looked at the pilot to his left and shrugged his shoulders. He mouthed, "How?" holding the palms of his hands up and shaking them.

"Citation two eight two delta foxtrot, Green Bay tower, are you an experienced pilot?"

Jerry looked at the pilot next to him and shook his head, no. Then he did the best gesture he could come up with for "How do I use the radio?"

"Citation two eight two delta foxtrot, Green Bay tower, we understand you want to know how to talk to us. Look for a small button on your yoke. Not the big red button, that's the wrong one. You want the smaller one. This should be the radio push-to-talk button. If you can hear me, please acknowledge."

A big red button. There's always a big red button. Where was the other button? There it was! Sitting on the left side of that handlebar on a stick, opposite the big red button he wasn't supposed to press. So, it was called a yoke. He pressed the button. "Can you guys hear me?"

"Citation two eight two delta foxtrot, Green Bay tower, was that you asking if we can hear you?"

Jerry pressed the button again. "Yes!" He gave a thumbs-up to the pilot on his left. "Yes! I need your help."

"Citation two eight two delta foxtrot, Green Bay tower, are you declaring an emergency?"

"Um, yeah. Yes, I am. I'm not a pilot, and I need to get this plane on the ground. And I have an unconscious terrorist onboard who was part of the group that bombed the Mall of America."

A few seconds passed.

"Am I pushing the right button? Can you guys still hear me?"

"Citation two eight two delta foxtrot, did you say you're carrying a terrorist onboard?"

"Yeah, but he's unconscious. And I'd like to be on the ground before he wakes up."

"Do you have any flying experience?"

"This is the first time in my life I've ever been in a cockpit."

"Roger that. The pilots next to you report you're in a small, corporate jet. And from your tail number, we know it's a Cessna Citation. Would you know the specific model?"

Jerry looked around the cabin. "Your guess is as good as mine. I see on this, um, yoke, a logo that says 'Citation' in small letters and 'XLS' superimposed in large letters. Does that mean anything?"

"Indeed, it does. You're on a Cessna Citation XLS."

"Great. How do I turn around and head west again, toward Minneapolis? This plane took off from the Anoka County Airport."

"First things first. I'm transmitting on all frequencies and clogging up radios across the region, so let's get you on the emergency frequency of one-two-one-point-five. And you'll just stay on that frequency all the way in."

"Great, how do I do that?"

"We're looking up the manual for that aircraft now. Give me a minute."

"I'm not going anywhere."

A few seconds later, "Okay, look for a display on your instrument panel about five inches high by four inches wide. It should be broken up into six display sections, two across and three down. You'll see buttons along the sides and across the bottom, with a tuning knob on the lower right corner. Do you see it?"

"Found it. Right next to this big center display."

"That sounds right. Here's what you do. In the top-left section of that display, do you see two frequencies, one above the other?"

"Yes."

"Good. Does the top number say one-three-two-point-four?"

"How'd you know that?"

"That's the frequency you're answering on right now. It's also the KANE tower frequency. Your radio is tuned to it right now."

"What's KANE?"

"The call letters for the Anoka County Airport where you took off. Now, that section of the display has two frequencies, one right above the other."

"The bottom one is one-twenty-six-point-five."

"Makes sense. That's the Minneapolis departure frequency."

"Okay, so the top number is the frequency I'm on, and the bottom number is the next frequency I want to use, right?" Jerry asked.

"That's right. And that's where those two buttons to the left come in."

"There are six buttons down the left side," Jerry said.

"Yes, but you only care about the top two, next to that display section. Hit the bottom of those two, and a yellow box should highlight that one-two-six-point-five number."

"Okay, pressing it. Yup, now it's highlighted."

"Great. Now you need to change it to one-two-one-point-five. Do that with your tuning knob on the lower right of that panel. It has an inner and outer piece. Turn the inner part until the frequency says one-two-one; then tune the decimal point on the outer one until the whole thing says one-two-one-point-five."

"Okay, turning the knob. Got it. Now the highlighted number says one-twenty-one-point-five."

"Good. Now, here is where we switch frequencies. Press that top-left button to change to it."

"And if I mess this up, what happens?"

"I'll find you, and we'll try it again."

"Okay. Here goes."

Jerry pressed the button. "Can you guys still hear me?"

"Yes, great job. I hear you on one-two-one-point-five now. So, what happened to the pilot?"

"I tasered him and then gave him a shot of some stuff the hospital made for me that hopefully put him to sleep until after we get this plane on the ground."

"Please confirm, you tasered the pilot?"

"Yes, I did. And then I tied him up with his parachute cords and some tie wraps. He's sprawled out on the floor behind me."

"The pilot had a parachute?"

"Yes. I told you. This guy is one of the terrorists who blew up those Mall of America hotels. He stole the plane and grabbed me as a hostage. He told me his plan was to parachute over Wisconsin. And I tasered him."

"What made you carry a Taser onboard an aircraft?"

"A forward-thinking FBI agent."

"Okay. Stand by while we put together a plan."

Jerry waited a few minutes.

"Okay, right now, I show you headed northeast at zero-six-six toward Sault Ste. Marie. We're looking for somewhere close that has a long runway where you won't have to deal with any traffic, preferably landing into the wind. Does that work for you?"

"Yeah, that works. Make sure they have plenty of police on hand. This guy murdered eight FBI agents back in Minneapolis."

"Roger that."

"And now I need a quick lesson."

"We're on the phone, looking for a pilot experienced with this aircraft. Stand by."

"It's not like I'm going anywhere. By the way, what's your name?"

"Carolyn."

"Well, nice to meet you, Carolyn. I've had a tough day. But while you're looking for that pilot, I just thought of a way you can help me make it better."

"Sir, we really need to keep this on a professional level."

"Huh? Um, no, wait a minute; that came out wrong. It really has been a long day. I was rousted out of my house before dawn, recruited to help catch a terrorist, and kidnapped at gunpoint. I watched eight good people die, and now I have to land an airplane or I'm dead."

"I understand, sir. And we need to focus on making sure your day only gets better from here."

"Yes, we do. Do me a favor and call me Jerry. 'Sir' makes me nervous."

"Okay, s—um, Jerry."

"That's better. Thanks. Listen, this is how you can help make this all worth it. Did I phrase that better?"

"I'm not sure where you're going with this."

"Okay, sorry. Here's the deal. This guy wasn't planning to just disappear after jumping out of the plane. He was planning to rendezvous with his buddies."

"Okay . . ."

"This plane was supposed to fly from Minneapolis to Atlanta. And this guy said he was going to parachute out somewhere over Wisconsin. Chicago is in-between Minneapolis and Atlanta, right?"

"Yes."

"So, he was probably planning to parachute out along that route somewhere. And I'll bet they're catching a flight at O'Hare back to where they came from."

"Maybe. But maybe not. He could turn the plane. You're headed toward Sault Ste. Marie, not Atlanta."

"True. I told him to do that. And if the plane crashes, nobody would know why."

"Exactly."

"But what if we can influence that rendezvous point?"

"How?"

"This guy sent a text message to his buddies right before we took off."

"Okay . . ."

"So, no way does he know exactly where he's jumping out of the plane. They probably don't have the exact rendezvous point preset. I'll bet their plan was for him to send a text message with the rendezvous point after he's back on the ground."

"Okay, now I see where you're going with this. But let's focus on those things after we get you on the ground."

"Not to be overly dramatic, but we need to do this first. Just in case."

"There's no 'just in case.' We're getting you down."

"Thanks. But things can go wrong. And these guys murdered a lot of people today. So, while we're waiting for your pilot, if you can bring up a map of Wisconsin and look for a likely rendezvous point, I can send the text message from the plane. They'll think he's already bailed out. And I need you to call Special Agent Jake Channing with the FBI and tell him about our plan. Also, tell him I still plan to return his pocket knife, but I'll be a little bit late."

Jerry waited for an answer. "Carolyn, can you still hear me?"

"Yes. We've talked it over here. You're up too high. There's no cell service at that altitude."

"So, I'll drop down to an altitude where there is service. I'll send the text message, and then we land the plane.

"Okay."

"Okay. So, hang on a second while I get his cell phone. I'll be right back."

Jerry climbed out of the pilot's seat back to the passenger cabin. He rolled Tabor's limp body to the side, picked the cell phone out of his pocket, and turned it on as he climbed back into the pilot's seat.

"Carolyn, still there?"

"Yes."

"Groovy. And no phone password, even better. It looks like he sent one last message to a group of phone numbers. It's one word, 'Abort.' And then one of his buddies sent another message, 'Confirmed. Rendezvous.' That was probably the guy on the tarmac he was supposed to meet. So, let's find a rendezvous point where the police can nail these guys. You get me down to an altitude with cell service; I'll reply all to this group text message; and then you and I land this plane, and I'll go home to my wife tonight."

"Sounds like a plan."

●————●

"Jerry, I have good news," Carolyn said a few minutes later. We have a radio hookup with the charter pilot for your plane back at your departing airport. His name is Jon."

"Hi, Jon. Show me what I need to know."

"Hi, Jerry. Nice to meet you. We'll shake hands later."

"Sounds good to me."

"Okay, the basics. Everything you need to know is on the display in front of your yoke. It's called the primary flight display or PFD."

"PFD. Got it. I see a top section with a graphic in the middle, showing wings against a horizontal line. Top half is blue; bottom half is brown. And there's a scale on the top and bottom going from zero to twenty."

"Yes, that's your pitch and roll."

"Roll, meaning when I turn, right?"

"Yes. And you'll need to turn as soon as I show you how."

"I just turn these, um, handlebars, right?"

"It's called a yoke. And not yet. Look on the top of that display for letters in a green block that say, 'AP ENG.'"

"Got it."

"That means the autopilot is engaged. For now, just leave it while I show you the rest of that PFD. On the bottom, you should see a round scale that looks kind of like a clock, except the numbers go from zero to three-sixty."

"Yes, I see it."

"That's your heading. Look for N in that display. It should be on the top, a little left of center."

"Carolyn said I was on a heading of zero-six-six. And, it says zero-six-six in green right on the top. So, three-sixty must be due north, ninety is due east, and so on, right?"

"Yes."

"Okay, now I know which direction and how level I am. How do I know how fast I'm going?"

"That's the display on the top left of your PFD. It shows a readout in the middle and a tape scale above and below the readout."

"Okay, yes, I see the readout. Looks kind of like a tape measure, and I'm at three-hundred. Are those knots?"

"That sounds about right. Yes, knots. Now, do you see a green arrow, probably pointing right at the three-hundred readout?"

"Yeah."

"You're at a steady speed right now. But when you speed up or slow down, the computer calculates what it thinks your speed will be in ten seconds and points that green arrow at it."

"Cool. So, if the computer is so smart, can it land this thing by itself?"

"Not as well as a pilot."

"I'm not a pilot. I've never done this before. Could the computer land this thing?"

"Maybe. But you'll do it better. And that should tell you how much I trust a computer to land my jet."

"Okay, fair enough. So, I'm guessing the dial on the right side is altitude?"

"Yes. And with a needle display showing your rate of climb or descent just to the right of that."

"Okay, got it. So, that's how I look up what I need to know, but how do I do stuff?"

"Hang on. A couple more things and then we practice so you get the feel of it."

"Okay."

"You're in the pilot's seat on the left, right?"

"On the left."

"Right. Um, okay."

"Who's on first?"

Jon laughed. "That's a good sign; you still have humor."

"I use it to cover up my panic."

"Okay. Deal with it by focusing. Fall apart tomorrow when your PTSD kicks in."

"Can I say 'LOL' on the radio?" Jerry laughed. And then stopped. "Listen, Jon, I stood there with my thumb up my butt while this guy murdered eight people. It keeps playing back, over and over in my head."

"After this is all over, talk to somebody. But for now, you gotta focus."

"I know. If I grab this yoke tight enough, it helps my shaking hands."

"Just concentrate on the task. Nothing else matters for the next few minutes."

Jerry laughed. "That sounds like me talking to my grandson about his homework."

"Well, you'll have a good story to tell him tonight. Look at the top of your PFD. There should be a green arrow pointing left. That means the flight director is coupled to your PFD."

"I see it—yes, pointing left."

"Okay, good. There are a series of buttons on top of your PFD. Those control the flight director."

"Yes, I see 'em."

"Good. Now we need a plan. I'm in Minneapolis; you're over north-central Wisconsin, headed away from me. That means I won't be able to see you when you touch down."

"So, come meet me. Or why don't I turn around and come back to you?"

"Let's see where ATC wants you to land. Carolyn, what do you think?"

"I've been checking," Carolyn said. "We have wind out of the north in Marquette, Michigan. And we have a twelve-thousand-foot runway at KSAW. That's where we want to go. Piece o' cake."

"Sawyer International?" Jon asked.

"Yes," Carolyn said. "Jerry, stay on your present heading of zero-six-six and start your descent. I'll turn you left and hand you off to Sawyer when you're at five thousand. You should be about twenty miles out. They'll line you up on their runway. That should give you a few minutes to familiarize yourself with the controls and should put you on the ground before rush hour. And it gives Sawyer a few minutes to get ready."

"Jerry, this is Majors Jack Taylor and Kevin Brown in the fighters. Great hand signals, by the way. I just wanted to say, you're doing great. We'll follow you right in and give you guidance."

"You're trying to make me feel better, aren't you?"

"Is it working?"

"Yeah. Well, sort-of. Thanks, everyone. I can't tell you how much I appreciate all this."

"You can thank us after you land," Carolyn said. "By the way, I spoke with Agent Channing. He says he wants his pocket knife back, but you can keep it until tomorrow. He also found a spot for your terrorist rendezvous."

"Oh, good. Where?"

"It's the parking lot for a place called the Olympus Water Theme Park in the Wisconsin Dells area. It's on the west side of Highway 12, right on the border between Wisconsin Dells and Lake Delton. Google Maps shows plenty of trees on the east side for your guy to hide and watch for his ride to show up. And the parking lot has plenty of room for law enforcement to operate."

"Thanks. That sounds good. The next question is, how would he send it?"

"When I click on that parking lot, Google Maps shows me GPS coordinates," Jon said. "Think about it—that's probably what he'd do. He'd probably look at Google Maps and find a spot the way I just did, tap it, and get coordinates. That's what he'd send. And then his friends would get directions to those coordinates and pick him up."

"Makes sense," Jerry said.

"Let me give them to you now. Put them in the phone while you're still at altitude and things are leisurely. As soon as you see cell service, send them, and then forget about that phone and focus on landing. Things move considerably faster at five thousand than thirty thousand."

"Sounds good."

"Okay. The numbers are 43.617971 by negative 89.786852. Google Maps shows those two numbers separated by a comma."

"I'm setting it up now," Jerry said. "Give me those numbers again, slowly."

Jon repeated the numbers back slowly, and Jerry tapped them into the phone.

"Send it as soon as you have service," Carolyn said.

"Okay, thanks," Jerry said.

"All right—Jerry, you ready?" Jon asked.

"Yup."

"Okay," Jon said. "Carolyn, you have the best eyes on Jerry's current position and his left turn coming up. What's a good rate of descent?"

"Let's do fifteen hundred feet per minute," Carolyn said.

"Okay, Jerry, here's how to do that," Jon said. "We're going to turn off the autopilot. There's a panel on the pedestal between the two seats toward the back. Look for two buttons illuminated in green, labeled AP and YD. Press the AP button to disengage the autopilot. Leave YD engaged to keep the yaw damper turned on."

"Yeah, I saw those before," Jerry said. "AP off."

"Now you're controlling the airplane," Jon said. "Move the engine throttle levers backward a little bit to reduce your engine power slightly. That should start your descent. Watch your descent rate on the right side of your PFD. Keep your pitch pointed slightly down."

"Those levers in between the seats, right?"

"Yes."

Jerry pulled the levers backward. "Whoops, that was probably too much." The nose dipped to about ten degrees. "Oh, crap." He pulled back on the yoke, which brought the nose up. The rate of descent slowed for a second and then the plane started dropping again. "Aw, nuts! Crap, crap, crap, CRAP!"

Tabor stirred in the passenger cabin.

HOMECOMING

Brian Cox had nowhere to go. And no way to get there. He didn't even know where he was. After running away from the academy until his legs refused to run anymore and his lungs felt on fire, he found himself at a stoplight in front of a shopping mall. A median with grass and shade trees separated the street and sidewalk from the parking lots. Out of breath, exhausted, sweating, and thirsty, he staggered under a tree and collapsed in the cool grass, bawling.

"Why, Allah, why? Why did you let me get involved with those monsters? Why did I come here? And what do I do now?"

He sat up and leaned against the tree, watching cars pass through the intersection. He made eye contact with one driver turning into the parking lot and followed the car with his eyes as it drove to a parking space. The car door opened and an adult stepped toward him.

Brian felt the salty tears on his face and noticed his grass stained pants. He probably looked similar to that awful afternoon at school. Another freak show for kuffar to gawk at. He couldn't stay here.

He forced himself to his feet and ran, off the grass, over the median, and into the street. Car brakes screeched. His right arm smacked a car bumper. The driver had a look of horror and relief on her face. A voice behind him shouted, "Hey, kid, are you okay?"

He kept running past driveways, houses, and fenced-in yards. Nowhere to stop without gawkers in passing cars mocking him. He slowed to a trot, then a walk. He stopped and put his hands to his knees. His chest heaved as he gasped for air between sobs.

No! He could not be seen like this. He continued walking. One block. Another block. He saw a larger building on his left, in a neighborhood off the busy street. He headed toward it. It had a large, empty parking lot with a Christian cross above the roof. A quiet lawn beckoned on the back side of the building, bordered on the far side with trees. And privacy.

He walked through the lawn and collapsed again near the trees, this time out of sight from gawking drivers. "What have I done? What do I do now? Where do I go? Allah, please help me."

He had to get home, but the only way home was with his car. And his car was back at the school, along with his wallet, keys, and cell phone with Google Maps. He had to go back inside one more time. Maybe he could warn Cypress and Lion. He got up and walked back in the direction of the school.

The academy office building looked like a gateway to hell in the late afternoon sunlight. Brian trudged through the empty parking lot and peered through the office building front window. Nobody was inside. The glass doors at the front were locked.

He walked around to the back. The overhead door was wide open. He peeked inside. His car was right where they had left it when he arrived. But all the vans were gone. He poked his head in and looked around—nobody was in back. He walked inside and up to the back hallway door. He slowly turned the handle and pushed the door open a crack. He peeked through the crack. The hallway was still empty.

He pushed the door open and crept down the hallway, looking in the dining room and classrooms. The desks were disturbed in the middle classroom on his left. He entered and found Cypress and Lion lying dead on the floor in the front of the room. Their necks were discolored and crushed. Their lifeless eyes still registered fear and shock.

Brian stumbled backward against a desk and hit the floor. He scrambled back to his feet and ran back down the hallway, through the hallway door, and outside through the overhead door. His shoulders quaked. He leaned against the concrete-block wall and collapsed on the asphalt. Sobs and wails poured from his mouth. Those dead eyes seared into every corner of his mind.

Brian wiped his eyes. He had to go back inside. He had to find his keys, wallet, and cell phone and get away. He steeled himself and walked back in. He found his things in a cubbyhole in Khalid's office. He marched to the back and drove his car out through the overhead door. Now outside the building, he stopped, got out of his car, and walked back inside. He took one last look around, shivered, and then pushed the red button to close the overhead door and the memory of this place one last time. He walked through the small door next to the now-closed overhead door, got back in his car, and drove away. He would purge this place from his mind.

Two hours later, somewhere on Interstate 90, he saw Lion and Cypress's eyes again. If he hadn't left, his dead body would be on the floor in that classroom next to them. His hands shook. He exited and parked near the grass at the back of a truck stop. He needed fresh air. He climbed out of his car, staggered into the grass, and threw up.

How would he face father?

LANDING

"I don't like to hear, 'Oh, crap.' Talk to me, Jerry," Jon said.

Jerry looked over his shoulder. Tabor's eyes were open.

"He's awake."

"Who's awake?"

"The terrorist I told you about."

"Oh, crap."

"One problem at a time. I know what I did wrong with the levers. Giving it more power." Jerry pushed the levers forward, almost to their original position. The rate of descent slowed. "Okay, that's better. Sorry. I'm getting the feel for it now. It's smoothing out."

"You're doing great," Carolyn said.

"Thanks for the encouragement." Jerry looked over his shoulder again. "His eyes are open, but maybe he's not awake yet. Jon, before we get too low, how can we practice what I need to do while there's room to make mistakes?"

"We can't do some of it until the right time," Jon said. "But, if you're not approaching the runway properly, you can always go around for another pass. Our guys in the fighters will make sure you're lined up properly. We can practice a few turns, though. Why don't you turn right bearing, say, zero-nine-zero, and then turn left again back to zero-six-six."

"Okay, sounds good."

"And nice and easy. It's not a car. Just a slight turn on the yoke will do the trick."

"Okay, turning right. Zero-seven-five, zero-eight-zero, zero-nine-zero."

Jerry glanced over his shoulder again. "Oh, crap, he's trying to move his legs to stop his body from rolling. He must be awake. We're still turning. Now at zero-nine-five."

"Turn it left."

"One hundred."

"Turn left. Bring it back."

"One-zero-five. Oh—right. Bringing it back. Now at zero-nine-zero. Zero-eight-zero. Zero-seven-zero. Zero-six-five. Noodling back right. Okay, I'm holding at zero-six-five. Giving a touch to the right and back left. Now back at zero-six-six."

"And now I show you at zero-six-six," Carolyn said.

Jon asked, "What's your altitude and rate of descent?"

A thud from the back vibrated the pilot seat. Jerry jumped. He turned. Tabor's legs were in the air, trying to lift the rope over the left front seat. His legs fell to the floor again. Another thud.

Jerry exhaled. "I'm at twenty thousand, descending at fifteen hundred. So, when you turn, you have to turn back to straighten out again?"

"Yes. It's not like a car. What's your speed?"

"Be still back there, or I'll turn this plane upside down, and you can choke on that rope around your neck."

Jon asked, "I take it he's awake?"

"Yeah. He probably wants me dead. Speed is two-forty."

"Stay focused on getting on the ground."

"I should have left that gun up here. I could shoot him if he gets loose."

"How secure is he?"

Jerry surveyed the passenger cabin. Tabor tilted his head and made eye contact.

"You are a dead man."

"Not if I can help it." Jerry pressed the talk button. "Hopefully I tied him up good enough."

"Good. Then focus on your landing."

Tabor howled and kicked in the passenger cabin. The ropes held.

"I have to do flaps in a minute, right?"

"Yes. Control the flaps with a black lever on the copilot side of the engine levers. You'll bring it out to the fifteen-degree setting first and then go in stages to full flaps at thirty-five degrees to land. The flaps give you lift at slower speeds. When the flaps extend, your yoke will be tougher to push and pull. There's a black wheel on your side of the center pedestal to adjust that feel. The other thing you need to know is the landing gear. The landing gear switch is on the bottom of the copilot side of the instrument panel. When all three lights are green, you know the landing gear are locked. You'll put those down on your final approach."

"When I'm in commercial flights, as soon as the plane is on the ground, I feel it slow down so fast, I almost fly out of my seat belt. How do I do that here?"

"Thrust reversers mostly and spoilers. Don't worry about thrust reversers; let's just keep it simple. First, look on the left side of the center console, just behind the engine handles. You'll see a switch that says, 'Speed brake.' It has a little protective bar covering it. See it?"

"No. Nothing like that on the left side."

"Look on the side—not on top, but on the side."

Jerry turned his head. Tabor was still struggling in back.

"Maybe he'll wear himself out. Oh, okay, there it is."

When your wheels are on the ground, flip that switch. That turns up vertical flaps on the wings and pushes the airplane down. It will also help you slow down initially."

"What about the spoilers?"

"They're called spoilers when you're on the ground and speed brakes in the air. Same thing."

"Okay, got it."

"Good. Do you see the foot pedals?"

"Yeah, one for each foot."

"Yup. Foot pressure on the pedals controls both the rudder and the nose wheel when the airplane is on the ground. That's how you turn on the ground. While you're slowing down, use your rudder to stay centered in the runway. Press with your right foot to go right, left foot to go left. But just a little bit. Nice and easy. As the airplane slows down, the rudder means less and less. But take it easy on the rudder pressure. Turning too sharply could get you in lots of trouble. Hopefully you don't even need your rudder, especially with those spoilers slowing you down. Toe pressure controls the wheel brakes. You have twelve thousand feet of runway, so just coast until you slow down to about sixty knots. Then lift your heels up and press with your toes to activate the brakes. But don't slam on the brakes. Nice and easy, maybe tap and release at first to get the feel for them. And press the brakes equally so you don't veer off into a ditch."

"What about the thrust reversers?"

"Don't worry about them. Let's keep it simple."

"Okay. Speed 220, altitude fifteen thousand."

"Good. Carolyn, what's his position?" Jon asked.

"I show about sixty miles before your left turn. I'm going to lose you in a few minutes. We're on the phone with Sawyer tower, and they're picking you up."

"Jerry, this is Rich Darby in the Sawyer tower. We've got you the rest of the way in."

He sounded like Lloyd Bridges, pacing back and forth in that airplane spoof movie. Was it named *Airplane!*? Rich was probably pacing in the control tower right now, telling everyone, looks like I picked the wrong week to quit smoking.

"Sawyer says they've got you," Carolyn said, "so we're handing you off to them. They'll be able to see you from their tower."

"Thanks, Carolyn, for everything. I don't believe I'm saying this, but go Packers!"

"You're welcome, Jerry. Be safe."

"Jerry, we're calling Jon back from our phones here," Rich said. "For now, just keep descending and stay on the heading you're on."

"Okay. You're not a smoker, are you?"

"If I were, this would be the wrong week to quit."

Jerry laughed. "Was the name of that movie, *Airplane!*?"

"Yeah, one of my favorites."

"Do you look like Lloyd Bridges?"

"You'll find out when we shake hands in a few minutes."

"Works for me."

Jerry looked at Tabor's cell phone. "And I'm watching Tabor's phone for cell service."

Two minutes later, Jon was back in the headset. "Okay, Jerry, what's your altitude and speed?"

"Looks like I'm going through ten thousand. Speed is two hundred."

"Perfect."

"Jerry," Rich said, "in about three minutes, we'll want you to turn left and come to heading zero-five-zero. By then, you should be at five thousand feet and twenty knots out. If that all works out, we'll slow you to one fifty and flatten your descent to 625 feet per minute."

"Okay. When do I lower the landing gear?"

"That's a couple steps away," Jon said. "First, make your turn and then put your flaps to fifteen degrees. That will slow you down, and it will feel bumpier. And you may need to goose the power just a touch to keep it at one fifty."

"Okay," Jerry said. "And my altitude is a little above nine thousand right now."

"Looking good," Rich said.

"I see some bars on the cell phone. Sending that text message now," Jerry said. Thirty seconds later, "Okay, good, the phone says it was delivered. Jon, make sure the FBI guys know where they need to meet those scumbags."

Tabor howled and thrashed.

Jerry looked over his shoulder. "Whether we live or not, your buddies are gonna fry."

Tabor thrashed even harder.

"Done," Jon said. "Now, forget about that cell phone and the rest of the world for a few minutes. From here on out, things will happen fast, and you need to focus on the tasks at hand."

"I think my passenger just figured out what I did with his phone."

"Jerry, this is Major Taylor on your left side. Looks like you're bouncing around a little."

"I wish you could beam you guys in here. They only gave me one shot of knockout juice at the hospital."

"You could do a near-vertical climb. The G forces might put him back to sleep."

Jerry laughed. "Yeah, 'cause now I'm a fighter pilot."

"Well, an honorary one anyway."

"Thanks."

"Jerry, your altitude shows feet above sea level," Rich said. "The elevation here is twelve twenty. So, just remember, when your altitude says seventy-five hundred, it really means sixty-two eighty above us. When you're at twelve twenty, you're on the ground."

"Oh, wow, thanks for that!" Jerry said. "Good to know."

"I figured now was as good a time as any to tell you."

Jerry rotated his shoulders, but it didn't help the tension in his neck.

"Jerry, your pitch looks good," Major Taylor said a minute later. "Nose about one degree down."

"Thanks," Jerry said. "And I'm at, um, six thousand."

"Okay," Rich said. "Turn left."

"I thought that was at five thousand," Jerry said.

"It is," Rich said. "Remember, ground level. And come to heading zero-one-zero for now."

"Okay, turning," Jerry said.

"Jerry, I'm above you and watching," Major Taylor said. "A little too much bank. Ease it back a little bit. A little bit more. There, that's better. Now, straighten it up."

"I show you at three-six-zero, and your altitude is forty-five hundred," Rich said. "You're a little too low. Adjust it right just a touch to zero-one-five and slow to one fifty."

"Sorry, guys, still getting the feel for this. Do you want me to do the flaps?"

"Yes. Fifteen degrees, position one," Jon said.

"Okay, flaps at fifteen degrees," Jerry said.

"What's your speed?" Jon asked.

"Um, I'm showing one sixty. But that ten second predictor says one forty," Jerry said.

"Goose the power just a bit," Jon said.

"Yeah, okay, now we're steady at one fifty."

"And you're at about four thousand," Major Taylor said.

"Put your landing gear down," Jon said. "You'll feel the drag."

"Okay," Jerry said. He pressed the landing gear switch. All lights showed green a few seconds later. "All green. I'm at thirty-five hundred feet."

"Give it a little more power," Jon said. "How far out?"

"About fifteen miles," Rich said. "Jerry, I want you at twenty-two hundred feet when you're ten miles out. At a hundred fifty knots, you need to descend at six-fifty per minute. You should be able to see the airport now."

"I see it, in front and a little left."

"Good. Nudge it left so you line up right on that runway."

"Okay. Turning slight left. And recovering. Crap. I went too far."

"Not a problem. You have time. Just straighten it out. Nice and easy."

"I'm learning you have to kind of anticipate the recovery. The response isn't instant; it takes about half a second."

"Jerry, you're wobbling back and forth," Major Taylor said. "You're right, work on anticipating that recovery move to finish off your turns."

"Okay," Jerry said, "I'm lining up right down the middle of that runway."

"Alignment looks better now," Major Taylor said.

"I'm at twenty-two hundred feet," Jerry said.

"And I show you ten miles out," Rich said.

"Full flaps then, thirty-five degrees," Jon said.

"Right," Jerry said. "Moving that flap lever all the way down."

Beads of sweat rolled down Jerry's face. He took off the wig and tossed it onto the copilot seat. He tried to wipe the sweat from his eyes, but it only smeared the makeup on his face.

"What's your speed?" Rich asked.

"Um, I show one twenty," Jerry said.

"Drop your power a little bit. Bring your speed down to one fifteen," Rich said.

"Jerry," Major Taylor said, "when you're over the runway and maybe five feet off the ground, bring your engines to idle and pull the nose up about three degrees. That's called a flare maneuver and should set you down gently on your two tires under the wings. And then the nose will follow down to the ground. And then put up your spoilers and just coast to a stop. You'll have plenty of runway."

Jerry looked back to the passenger cabin. The front seat jerked as Tabor yanked his heels in, trying to break the rope and free himself.

"Um, Okay."

"Jerry, you're drifting a little to the right. Bring it back," Major Taylor said.

"What? Oh, yeah, right. Okay. Bringing it back. Crap! Too far again. Hang on; I can fix it."

"What's your altitude?"

"Seventeen eighty. Hang on, getting it lined up again. Just have to anticipate that recovery."

"You're a little too low," Rich said. "Level off for a minute."

"Jerry, turn up your power a little bit," Major Taylor said.

"That's better," Rich said a few seconds later.

"Five miles out. Jerry, what's your elevation?" Rich asked.

"Fifteen thirty."

"Two hundred fifty feet to go. Just keep easing her down," Rich said.

Jerry willed his heart to slow down before it pounded out of his chest. Unlike this morning in the holding cell, it only pounded harder this time. Was that this morning? It seemed like a lifetime ago. A chill ran up his spine. His armpits were sticky. C'mon Jerry, we eat pressure for breakfast. Isn't that what you tell your grandsons? Time to demonstrate it. What kind of example do you set if you crash the plane? Here lies Jerry Barkley, dead because he screwed up. Lynn, Ann, Aaron, Alex—I love you guys. I'm not missing dinner tonight. He wiped the sweat from his hands onto his shirt and flexed his fingers.

About two minutes later, "One mile out. I show you at twelve seventy. Fifty feet up."

Something vibrated in the cabin. Jerry looked back. Tabor thrashed and flexed his arms, trying to loosen his legs and pop the tie wraps around his wrists.

"I will free myself, and then I will kill you."

"You're going to prison, buckwheat."

"I will die first. And take you with me," Tabor said.

"I don't think so."

"Jerry, you're drifting again," Major Taylor said.

"Nuts!" Jerry said.

"Jerry, pull up. You're off the runway," Major Taylor said. "Jerry, full power and pull up. All the way back on that yoke. Pull up. Pull up. Now!"

Jerry pulled back on the yoke and pushed the engine levers all the way forward. The plane nosed up and climbed. The top of the tower whizzed below the plane, looking close enough to touch. Engine noise echoed off the building and roared through the cabin.

Jerry's heart jumped into his throat. "Sorry about that."

"What happened?" Major Taylor asked.

"My fault for being stupid," Jerry said. "I got distracted. Hey, terrorist, I'm spending tonight with my wife. You're spending the rest of your life in prison."

"I am no terrorist. I am a soldier, doing my job, just as your soldiers do their jobs."

"That's what you call murdering all those people?"

Tabor laughed. "You almost killed a few people yourself. You are a pathetic excuse for a man."

Rich said, "Stop talking to that guy and let's land this airplane."

"Guys, you're right. I'm sorry. He's kicking and thrashing like mad, and now he's playing mind games. If he gets loose, he'll crash this plane right into that tower, and we're all dead. Make sure you have plenty of people when we land. I'll do better next time," Jerry said.

"No harm done. I guess we're all a little jumpy. Let's come around and try it again."

Five minutes later, it was time to try again.

"Jerry, you're lined up nicely this time. Now that you're lined up, keep your heading at zero-zero-one. I should have told you that last time instead of just eyeballing it."

"Yes, thanks, that helps," Jerry said. "Wasn't your fault last time."

Thoughts about Bahir Mustafa and Tabor and terrorism and world politics and family and horrible diseases flooded Jerry's mind. And dead bodies. And an Iranian super soldier thrashing behind him. He willed all of it away. At least for now, only one task mattered—getting on the ground alive. Everything else would wait. The analytical portion of his brain bubbled up another thought. Was landing this plane a critical path item or a dependency? Not now! Shut up and focus.

"Looking good coming in," Major Taylor said. "A little bit steep. Flare it out a little bit."

Jerry pulled back on the yoke.

"No, too much," Major Taylor said. "Pull up. Full power. Let's try it again."

"Crap." Jerry pulled up on the yoke, pushed the engine levers forward again, and started another pass. As the plane came around for the next pass, he took his hands off the yoke, flexed his fingers, and then gripped it again. He took a deep breath. Enough messing around. Get it right this time. Tabor continued thrashing in back.

"Looking good, Jerry." Red and blue flashing lights on top of emergency vehicles whizzed by next to the runway. "Ten feet . . . five feet. Okay, bring engines to idle and flare. Nose up three degrees."

The tires under the wings hit the ground with a thud, followed by the front landing gear a few seconds later.

"Beautiful, Jerry, just beautiful. Engage your spoilers."

"Oh—right." Jerry flipped the speed brake switch. "I can feel it. Definitely makes a difference."

"Yup. It sets up wind resistance as you slow down. Now just coast to a stop. Use your rudders to keep it straight down the middle and use your brakes to ease it to a stop once you slow down to around sixty knots. You have twelve thousand feet of runway," Major Taylor said. "We're coming around, and we'll land as soon as they move you off the runway."

The plane came to a full stop with one thousand feet of runway left, engines still idling. Jerry flexed his fingers and shrugged the tension from his shoulders. He tried in vain to blink away the tears forming salty waterfalls of makeup down his cheeks. "Thanks, God, for letting me stay alive today. And for not letting me commit murder." He turned toward Tabor. "And help out the families of all those people this guy and his buddies murdered."

Now, to Tabor, "Why?"

"I told you, dead people can't dial a phone."

"No. Why the whole operation? Why blow up that mine and those hotels? Why try to spread Ebola across the country?"

"I am a soldier, doing my job."

"That's a load of crap. You're a murdering terrorist, and I should have blown your brains out when you were asleep."

"And I should have killed you before we took off. You're not an FBI agent. Who are you?"

"I'm an American. And a Christian. God wouldn't let me pull the trigger, and that's why you're still alive."

"And I'm an Iranian soldier. I swore a duty before Allah to serve my country."

"How does murdering innocent people serve your country?"

"Ask your own CIA that question. How much blood is on your hands, keeping the Shah in power?"

"What?"

"In 1953. Your CIA engineered a coup in my country and brought the Shah to power. You talk about freedom and democracy, but you prop up dictators who murder their own people."

"Wait a minute. You guys got rid of the Shah a long time ago. And I wasn't even born in 1953. The ayatollah running your country today is a dictator, and his buddies are a bunch of nutcases."

"I would kill you if you said that in my country."

"Well, we're not in your country. We're in my country. I hope I get to testify at your trial."

The door flew open. Bright light flooded the inside. A man looked in, wearing a police vest and holding a weapon.

Jerry ducked. "Holy crap, I'm the good guy. Put that thing away."

"What's your wife's name?" the man shouted over the engine noise.

"Lynn. Does your wife know my wife?"

"When did you get married?"

"A long time ago. What is this, twenty questions?"

"Where did you go on your honeymoon?"

"Lynn's uncle's cabin on the White River in Indiana. Why?"

"You and your half-brother. What's your mom's name?"

Jerry nodded and smiled. "We don't have the same mom; we have the same dad and his name was Doug."

The man smiled and lowered his weapon. "Detective Mike Stanley, with the Marquette PD. Nice to meet you, Jerry. I needed to make sure you're you." He poked his head in and looked at Tabor. "Not a bad packaging job."

"Didn't anyone send you a picture of me? How do I turn off the engines?"

Mike laughed. "Don't worry about it; we'll take care of the rest. And you don't exactly look like you right now."

Jerry lifted his makeup-smeared hand. "Oh, yeah. I see what you mean. Be careful stepping over this guy. He bites. And do me a favor. Nobody needs to know I'm bawling my eyes out, okay?" Jerry wiped the tears with his shirt, smearing the makeup even more.

Mike nodded. "You did good, man."

"Is it okay if I take some pictures? My wife is not going to believe this."

"She's on her way here. The charter company said Uncle Sam is treating you and your wife to a night in a hotel. Oh, and they want you to bring their plane back tomorrow."

Jerry bowed his head and smiled. He chuckled. And then more tears flowed as images from the Airport terminal flooded his mind. "I might need help getting down. My legs are a little shaky."

AFTERMATH

"Jerry, it's good to hear your voice," Jake Channing said over Jerry's cell phone. Lynn sat next to Jerry in the back of a police squad car.

"Jake, I'm sorry. I know Agent Blackwell was your partner. And everyone in that airport had families."

"Ron's still fighting. I need to apologize to you for putting you in harm's way. We took an oath. You didn't."

"Agent Blackwell's still alive?"

"It's touch and go. We'll know more in the morning."

"I should have done more to stop him."

"You'd be dead right now. These guys were professionals."

"I want to meet their families."

"That's not a good idea."

"I was there when they died. Trying to protect *me*."

"They died doing their jobs."

"Jake, I was there. Pull whatever strings you have to so I can meet their families. And I want to visit Agent Blackwell."

"It's not that simple. You weren't at that airport on FBI business. Not officially, anyway."

"What?"

"You were there to do some IT work. You happened to be in the terminal on one of their computers and a terrorist trying to steal a plane took you as a hostage. That's the official story."

"So, you guys sweep this whole thing under the rug as if it didn't happen? Seven people died in that terminal, Jake. And maybe one more. I was there. I was part of it."

"And every news station across Wisconsin and Michigan heard you on the emergency frequency. You're a hero. But the official details are different."

"Why?"

"Because we don't want to give information to Iran."

Jerry paused. The reasoning made sense. "What about all the other people who know?"

"We're reaching out to them right now. Enjoy a night in the hotel with your wife, courtesy of a grateful country."

"And that's it? We stay in a hotel tonight and fly back home tomorrow and life goes on like nothing happened?"

"No. You and I are going into an intensive debriefing session with my supervisor's boss's boss in the morning as soon as you land, and after that, we're having a press conference where you'll say what we tell you to say."

"Did you get the rest of those scumbags?"

"Not yet. But we have agents and police waiting."

"I guess I'll give your knife back in the morning then."

"Keep it. You've earned a souvenir."

Shortly before sundown, while Jerry showered off his makeup in a hotel in Marquette, Michigan, Walter—aka, Hamza El-Sayed—arrived at the Wisconsin Dells Olympus Water Theme Park rendezvous point in his four thousand dollar used car, for which he had paid five thousand in cash to ensure no questions were asked. He parked a few hundred yards away from the rendezvous point and walked toward the coordinates. He stopped when he saw a sea of distant red and blue flashing lights surrounding the edge of the parking lot. He crossed the street, blending in with the crowd for a better view, and worked his way closer. He spotted a tow truck attaching to Khalid's van.

"What happened?" he asked someone in the crowd.

"Not sure. But there sure are a lot of cops just to tow one van."

Just then, three of the police cars left the sea of lights and started up the street, heading straight toward Hamza. He resisted the urge to run and watched as they moved closer. As the cars zoomed past, he made eye contact with Khalid and the two soldiers in the back seat of the second car. The caravan turned on sirens and disappeared down the road, screaming into the night.

Hamza made his way back to his vehicle and drove away. He stopped at a Wal-Mart, dropped his cell phone in a dumpster, and went inside and bought another one. And a change of clothes. He would need to make contact for instructions. Trying to fly home from O'Hare was out of the question now. He had one advantage: none of the Americans would know he was here.

———•———

A few days passed.

"I'm still having trouble keeping all this straight," Dan Standish said. Dan, Jerry, Farah Aziz, and her girls were together in Farah's living room in St. Paul.

"How did they steal the material without Aamir knowing it?" Farah asked.

"I had the same question," Jerry said. "I was talking to Jake about that. Apparently, one of the guys they arrested in Wisconsin Dells was named Khalid Farooq. He ran a Muslim school here. The FBI went to UPS, Fed Ex, and the USPS to find any shipments to that school, and they found a shipment from overseas of some stuff called ketamine. It's an anesthetic, and it causes amnesia."

"Amnesia?" Farah asked.

"The theory is, they persuaded Izy to pull over in his truck and injected this stuff into him," Jerry said. "That would have put him to sleep. While he was asleep, they offloaded half his load into their vans for the Mall of America bombing. Izy woke up later with no memory of what happened and finished his delivery to the mine. That's why he was so late for the delivery."

"I cannot thank you enough for all your help," Farah said. "You are a hero to me and my family."

"I'm just an IT guy," Jerry said.

———•———•———

"You're quite the celebrity, Jerry," Sally Brock said back in her office in Burnsville, Minnesota. "If you need a PR firm to represent you, think about us."

"Funny you should bring that up," Jerry said. "You guys are the reason I'm in the news. That's why I wanted to come see you."

"Is that why the FBI was snooping around here?" Sally asked.

"I figured they'd want to talk to you. Remember when I cloned your owner's nephew's computer?"

"I know you said something in his computer slowed us down."

"Right. And you read the stories about the Mall of America bombing and the mine explosion, right?"

"And a terrorist stealing a charter plane. You've been busy. I didn't realize you had customers as far away as Blaine."

"Well, that's the official story. The real story is, the whole thing started right here. That computer in Andrew's office was a control node in the botnet gathering data from companies across the country."

"I have no idea what you just said," Sally said.

"Okay, let's try it this way. Thousands of computers across the country were infected with malicious software and sending shipping schedules and other data back to their masters. Your owner's nephew's computer, right here in this office, relayed instructions from its mother ship to drone computers across the internet."

"Now you sound like bad science-fiction. I keep trying to tell you, we're a PR firm, not the NSA. We don't keep information any terrorist would care about."

"And they didn't care about your information. They used your computer to steal information from other people."

"I still find that hard to believe."

"So do lots of people. But we all lived through the past few days. And I'm telling you, it started right here."

"Does that make us liable for anything?"

"I'm not an attorney."

"What do you suggest we do about it?"

"I already told you. Clean that computer for starters and then implement good security practices here."

"And what will all that cost? What's our ROI?"

"I've given you proposals. As for ROI, how much will the negative publicity cost when the world finds out it all started here?"

"Are you threatening us?"

"Huh? No! I'm telling you what happened."

"For your information, after your friends in the FBI talked to me, we spent hundreds of dollars to make sure we weren't doing anything bad. And our IT support company said we were fine."

"What did they scan?"

"I'm not a technology expert. They said we were fine."

"What are you gonna do, so there's no next time?"

The top of Sally's ears turned red. "You're trying to blame me for what happened and I've told you repeatedly, we're just a marketing company. None of this is our responsibility. Where were your FBI friends during all this? What about the CIA and the NSA and all the other government agencies my taxes pay for? Thanks for the courtesy call and for letting us know how this turned out. You can see your way out?"

"You're blowing me off again?"

"Threats and science fiction stories don't help your cause."

"It's not my cause. Drive by the Mall of America and look at the rubble. It started right here in this office."

"We're not spending money on tech toys."

"Ya know, lots of people died because you were sloppy."

Sally's face turned red. "Get out. And stop interfering with our business."

Jerry shook his head. Enough was enough. "Have a nice day, Sally."

●———●

"You sure you're ready for this?" Jake asked Jerry.

"Yeah. I need to see him."

"And he wants to see you."

Jake knocked on the ICU glass door and entered. Jerry followed.

IV tubes and monitors were everywhere. But underneath all the medical technology and the bandage wrapping his head, FBI Agent Ronald Blackwell was awake and alert.

Jerry pulled up a chair next to the bed. "I wanted to tell you I'm sorry. It all happened so fast, I didn't know what to do."

Blackwell looked up. "G—gl—glad . . . okay."

Jerry bowed his head and closed his eyes.

"You . . . good . . . in— instincts."

Jerry smiled. "I'm not so sure."

"You . . . t—t—tr . . ."

"I tried?

Blackwell nodded.

Jerry shook his head. "I couldn't stop it."

"I know. Who . . . G—George Ba—Baker?"

Jerry laughed through tears. "The best name I could come up with on short notice."

Blackwell's lips turned up. And then he grimaced. "Hurts."

"It hurts to laugh?"

"Yeah." Blackwell closed his eyes and took a few breaths. "You . . . did good."

Jerry wiped his eyes. "Thanks."

"Shake." Blackwell lifted the fingers of his right hand.

Jerry took Blackwell's hand in both of his. "Get better, okay?"

SMALL WORLD

Two weeks later, Jerry found himself driving to Sioux Falls, South Dakota, to meet an online friend and his parents. Another face to face with a potential terrorist. It was Jake's idea. But, Jerry had to admit, Jake's reasoning made sense. Two FBI vehicles followed, and Jerry was wired up like a Christmas tree with hidden microphones and cameras. This latest meeting started with another online chat.

Jerrybarkley: Hey, Bcoxsf, it's been a while.

```
I missed you. How is your NAT gateway we
talked about a few weeks ago?
Bcoxsf: I was away for a while and haven't
had time to look at it until now.
Jerrybarkley: So, what great vacation spot
did you visit? And do you have pictures?
Bcoxsf: PM
Jerrybarkley: OK
```

Wow, why does he want to talk privately? Jerry opened a private chat with his online friend.

```
Bcoxsf: You know I am Muslim, right?
Jerrybarkley: Yeah, we talked about it.
Bcoxsf: I graduated from Sioux Falls Jeffer-
son High School this spring and found a sum-
mer job in Minneapolis. But it didn't work
out.
Jerrybarkley: What was the job?
Bcoxsf: They wanted me to help get some
things ready at a Muslim school. But they
lied.
```

Jerry's heart beat faster. No way . . .

```
Jerrybarkley: How did they lie?
Bcoxsf: They lied about who they were.
Jerrybarkley: Who did they say they were?
Bcoxsf: They said they were true Muslims.
They even quoted the holy Quran.
Jerrybarkley: I'm Christian and lots of peo-
ple who aren't Christian quote my holy Bible.
So, who were they really?
Bcoxsf: They were imposters.
```

No way is this happening. No way. Not possible. But maybe . . . Only one way to find out.

> **Jerrybarkley**: Did you ever meet a guy named Yazid Kalil?

The reply took a few minutes to come back. The one-word response was chilling.

> **Bcoxsf**: Yes.
> **Jerrybarkley**: What do you think of him?
> **Bcoxsf**: He is a liar. And you are kuffar.
> **Jerrybarkley**: I've been called lots of names. What's a kuffar?
> **Bcoxsf**: Someone who does not believe in Allah.
> **Jerrybarkley**: OK, I'm a kuffar.
> **Bcoxsf**: All kuffar will die.
> **Jerrybarkley**: Well, pretty much everyone will die sooner or later. Maybe we can get together in the real world and talk about this sometime. Meantime, how did you meet Yazid Kalil?
> **Bcoxsf**: Online.
> **Jerrybarkley**: Did you ever meet him face to face?
> **Bcoxsf**: No. Only online.
> **Jerrybarkley**: You know he's not a real person, right?
> **Bcoxsf**: Yes. But I did meet many of his friends face to face.
> **Jerrybarkley**: Seriously?
> **Bcoxsf**: Yes. We met at a school in an office

building in Blaine, on the north side of the
Twin Cities.

Jerry's hands shook. Chills ran up and down his spine. Was he actually
chatting online with one of the terrorist recruits? Law enforcement caught three
of the Iranians, right at the GPS coordinates Jerry sent from Tabor's phone.
Once the FBI found out one of them was Khalid Farooq, director of the Ibn
Idhari Academy of Muslim History, they searched the school and found two
dead recruits. And now, apparently, here was a third recruit, very much alive.
How many more were there?

Jerrybarkley: How did you get hooked up with
these guys?
Bcoxsf: Yazid Kalil contacted me, and we arranged to meet.
Jerrybarkley: You know more than six hundred
innocent people died because of Yazid Kalil and his buddies, right? And it could have
been lots worse.
Bcoxsf: Yes. That's why I left. They murdered
my other teammates, Cypress and Lion. I was
Owl.
Jerrybarkley: How do you know they murdered
your teammates?
Bcoxsf: Because I went back, and they were
dead. The overhead door was open, and the
vans were gone. I found my car keys and left.
I shut the overhead door behind me to shut it
out of my life. But it does not go away.
Jerrybarkley: Who else knows about this?
Bcoxsf: You.
Jerrybarkley: I'm it?
Bcoxsf: Yes.
Jerrybarkley: Why are you telling me this?

```
Bcoxsf: I don't know.
Jerrybarkley: Are you willing to meet in the
real world?
Bcoxsf: Yes.
```

And that was why Jerry found himself on his way to meet Brian Cox and his parents. Because Jerry had the relationship and Jake thought a fellow techie would be better to approach Brian than a group of intimidating FBI agents. "We'll try the soft approach first. He's just a kid who got in over his head." That's what Jake said.

A security fence with a gate and intercom stood in front of a long driveway leading to the house. Jerry drove up and pushed the button as the FBI vehicles took up stations down the road.

"Hello?"

"Hi, yes, um, I'm Jerry Barkley. We had an appointment?"

The gate slowly opened. Trees behind the fence hid the house from view until Jerry drove farther up the driveway. The driveway split near the house. The right side went into a circle in front with a fountain in the middle, probably a place to drop off cocktail party guests dressed in nice suits. The left side widened into a large turnaround area in front of a massive garage.

Jerry chuckled; his 2009 silver Toyota Corolla was probably not at home here in the land of Jaguars and Mercedes.

He climbed out of the car, walked up to an imposing front door, and rang the doorbell.

The house had a concrete front porch, supported by decorative concrete columns. The front was brick halfway up, with weathered wood siding up to the roof. Next to the imposing front door was a massive, cantilevered front window. The upstairs windows overlooked the front porch roof and were accented with white decorative shutters.

An olive-skinned man with black hair answered the door, with a woman behind him. He was dressed in a suit. She wore a business blazer with high heels. Jerry tugged on his pants to cover his white socks. Maybe Lynn was right.

"Hi. I'm Jerry Barkley. We talked on the phone the other day?" He extended his right hand.

The man at the door shook Jerry's hand. After shaking hands with the man, Jerry extended his hand to the woman. She looked at the man, probably her husband, and took a step back. Jerry, feeling sheepish, pulled his hand back.

"I am Gohar Quasim. This is my wife, Hana," the man said. "Come this way." He led Jerry down a hallway and into a sitting room on the left. The room looked immaculate, with a plush carpet and tapestries decorating the walls. A low glass table sat in the middle of the room surrounded by chairs and a couch on the other side. A young man, hands folded in his lap, sat attentively on the couch and watched the group enter.

Jerry walked across the room, extending his right hand for a handshake. "You must be Brian."

Brian stood and weakly extended his hand, looking down and avoiding eye contact with Jerry.

Gohar gestured for Jerry to sit in the chair opposite Brian's couch. Jerry followed Gohar's lead and passed behind Hana. He caught a faint whiff of alcohol. Gohar took a seat in the chair to Jerry's left, between Jerry and Brian.

"May I offer you a drink?" Hana asked.

"Sure. I'll have some ice water," Jerry said.

Hana gave Jerry a curious look and disappeared out the door.

"I couldn't help but notice, your last names are different," Jerry said.

"My American name is Gary Cox," Gohar said. "We try to fit into American culture, but it is sometimes difficult for our son."

Hana returned, carrying a tray of drinks. She set the tray down and handed them to Brian, Gohar, and Jerry. Gohar took a sip from his. Hana sat in the chair opposite Gohar and took a sip from hers. It had a yellow tinge and Jerry smelled alcohol. Jerry sipped his and his throat burned. His eyes watered, and he set the drink down. He coughed and wiped his eyes.

"I thought you might enjoy one of our drinks from our homeland," Hana said.

"Thanks," Jerry said, still coughing as he wiped more water from his eyes. He noticed a faint smile cross Gohar's lips.

"You guys, I want to apologize in advance if I do something against your culture," Jerry said, still sputtering. "I'm a dumb, bald-headed American, born and raised in the USA, and I'm not as familiar with other cultures as I should be."

"You're doing fine," Gohar said. "I understand you are a computer expert and you've developed a friendship with our son."

"Well, 'expert' is a strong word, but, yes, we've had a few conversations. And I've built some of the things Brian is trying to build now. So, we have some common ground."

"Very well," Gohar said. "Perhaps you can start by telling us why you drove all the way across Minnesota to visit our home."

"Okay. You know Brian took a job with that Muslim school, right?"

"Yes. His mother and I discussed it after he left."

Hana looked away.

"And you no doubt heard about the Mall of America terrorist bombings?"

Gohar and Hana exchanged glances. Brian looked down. "Yes."

"Well, I think—and the FBI agrees with me—that the people in that school planned and executed those bombings. And Brian was there while they planned it."

"Yes, Brian shared that you feared he may have played some role. Which cannot be true. But why are you here and not the FBI?"

"Because my friends at the FBI thought it would be best if I approached you first. But FBI agents are nearby, and they want you to invite them in."

"Perhaps later."

"I'm also here because I helped track down the terrorists, and I know they had more in mind than just to bomb those hotels. They wanted to use Brian and some other recruits to start an Ebola epidemic."

"That is preposterous," Gohar said.

"Well, no, it's not," Jerry said. Turning to Brian, "Do you know a guy named Tabor?"

"Yes," Brian said. "He was one of the assistants at the school."

A thought entered Jerry's mind. "How many assistants were there?"

"Four."

"Wait," Jerry said. "There was Khalid Farooq plus four assistants?"

"That's right. Tabor, Walter, and two others. I never learned the names of the others."

No doubt the FBI guys were madly taking notes. This Walter was one more they didn't know about. That must have been the guy at the airport gate who killed the police officers. He must have traveled to the rendezvous point separately and left when he sensed trouble.

"Well, Tabor was more than an assistant. You heard about the hostage situation at the Anoka County Airport a couple weeks ago? It was on the national news."

"Yes. I saw the stories. That's why your face is familiar. You were the one who landed the plane," Gohar said.

"That's right. I was Tabor's hostage. He gunned down eight FBI agents before I got on that plane with him. What was not on the news was, he was trying to steal an Ebola-tainted blood sample."

Jerry turned to Brian. "The plan was to inject you guys with it and send you out to infect people. They were going to turn you guys into biological weapons."

Hana's eyes registered shock.

"My God," Gohar said. "Are you telling me my son tried to join that terrorist organization?"

"Yes," Jerry said. "He thought he was joining ISIS. But it was the Iranians impersonating ISIS. The goal was to hit our country and blame it on ISIS. We would go to war and destroy ISIS, leaving Iran the last man standing."

"Is this true?" Gohar asked.

"No, father, it is not true!" Brian said. "I thought I took a job helping at a Muslim school. But they lied and when I found out it was not a school at all, I left."

"Brian, the FBI doesn't want to prosecute you," Jerry said. "But you need to come clean. Why were you really in that school, and who else was there with you? And what did you see?" Turning to Gohar, "And if Brian does come clean and helps the FBI, they promise they can arrange for counseling or anything else that makes sense to deal with the situation he's in."

"You are all kuffar! Why should I trust any of you?" Brian asked.

"Brian!" Gohar said.

"It's okay," Jerry said. "I'm guessing 'kuffar' is a derogatory word for non-Muslims?"

"Yes, and please accept my deepest apologies," Gohar said.

"Don't worry about it." Now turning to Brian. "So, Brian, what did I do to deserve your wrath?"

"You are like all other kuffar. You persecute us at every turn."

"Have I ever persecuted you?" Jerry asked.

"You will. Sooner or later. All kuffar persecute us."

"I apologize," Gohar said. "Our time here in Sioux Falls has been difficult."

"How so?" Jerry asked.

"The kuffar at school have tormented me since the day we arrived," Brian said.

"He had an incident this spring where he got in a fight with some boys," Gohar said. "We protested but the school did nothing to remedy the situation."

"Let me guess. A bunch of idiots picking on somebody who's different?"

"They were kuffar persecuting me and my family for my religion!" Brian said.

Jerry paused for a few seconds, remembering. Events and places. Words exchanged. Punches thrown. Painful memories he kept locked away. Except for when he needed them. The others looked at Jerry expectantly.

"Do you guys read the newspaper?"

"We get most of our news from the internet," Gohar said.

Jerry leaned forward and faced Gohar. "Back when I was eleven, there was no internet. Everyone read newspapers. And I delivered them. Every morning, rain or sun. I got up out of bed before dawn, seven days a week, and rode my bicycle to the paper pickup station in front of a convenience store, loaded fifty or so newspapers on my bike, and delivered the morning paper to people's houses."

Jerry turned to Brian. "I was the youngest and skinniest kid at that paper station, and the older kids made my life a living hell every morning. I tried to fight back one day. I lost. I came home scratched and bloody and crying. My mom called me a wimp."

"What did you do?" Brian asked.

"I got up earlier in the morning so I wouldn't need to put up with those jerks," Jerry said. "I wish that story had a better hero ending. But it doesn't. My family moved to Minnesota when I was in seventh grade, and it got worse. In high school, some of the girls called me Bumpkin. That was my name to them. I hated it."

Jerry stood. "I remember one time when one kid and a couple of his friends stood in the hallway and told me if I wanted to go to class, I had to go through them first."

"Did you fight them?"

"No. A teacher happened to show up right before the fists started flying. And I went to class peacefully. But I was mad for a long time. I played out all kinds of scenarios in my mind about what I would do to Roger Farnsworth. But in the real world, I probably would have gotten the worst of it."

Jerry returned to his chair. "Brian, you're not the first and you won't be the last to be picked on because you're different. You call it religious persecution; I call it idiots in high school. You want revenge? Make something of yourself. Joining groups like ISIS and trying to blow up the world will just get you killed. And don't believe that crap about how it will be paradise after you murder a bunch of innocent people."

"I did not join ISIS!" Brian said.

"Jerry, I think you need to leave now," Gohar said.

"Mr. Quasim, I helped the FBI uncover Yazid Kalil. The FBI has records of all social media correspondence with him. Brian, I have printed copies of what you said right here."

Jerry dug into his pocket, pulled out some papers, and unfolded them. He handed them to Gohar. Gohar took the papers and started reading. His face gradually reddened the more he read.

"Brian, some FBI agents are parked outside. They're listening to everything we say in here. You're eighteen years old now, and that makes you an adult. And right now, you need to make an adult choice. You can either get up right now and go invite the FBI agents in and fully cooperate with them, or they'll come here with a warrant and put you on trial. You were involved in an operation that killed over six hundred people and could have killed millions more. No defense attorney will be able to keep you out of prison.

"Mrs. Quasim, thanks for the drink. Mr. Quasim, I'll see myself out."

"Wait," Gohar said. "Brian, please invite them in."

YOUTUBE

Six months later, snowbanks lined the winter streets near Jerry Barkley's Minnesota home. But for the next three days and two nights, Jerry and Lynn wouldn't care because Jerry was invited to participate in a keynote panel at the annual Grey Hat computer security conference in Las Vegas. The topic was "When Bio-Viruses Meet Cyber-Viruses: How CDC Inoculated Itself." And when the event organizers offered to pay for Jerry and a guest to attend the conference, it was an easy decision.

The main ballroom and balconies were packed, and Jerry and the other panelists sat in chairs on a raised stage. Video projectors displayed giant images of the panelists onto screens above stage right and left, giving the audience of eleven thousand security practitioners a close-up view of the action. A few floor mics were in the aisles around the room for audience questions.

Jerry had seen panel moderator, Richelle McFate, in other forums. She had a reputation for a sharp wit and a knack for asking pertinent questions and drawing out insightful answers. This should be a good discussion. Maybe they could make a difference or, as a friend taught him a few years ago during the Bullseye breach incident, turn lemons into lemonade.

Richelle made introductions and summarized the public version of what had come to be called the MOA incident. Then she asked Dr. Ben Donovan the first question, exactly as they had discussed earlier: "Dr. Donovan, you're an epidemiologist. Why are you on a panel at a computer security conference?"

"Because," Ben paused. He looked at Jerry and smiled. "Because you invited me?" Now he was grinning ear to ear. Jerry lifted his right hand and looked back at Ben. Ben lifted his hand. They high fived.

"Good to know I've had an influence on you," Jerry said.

The room erupted in laughter. Richelle smiled.

After the laughter died down, Ben's smile faded. "I'm here because I'm a victim." He looked at Jerry and smiled again. "And I'll take another page out of your playbook, Jerry. I'm a doctor, not an IT guy." The audience laughed politely. "I chase biological viruses for a living, not computer viruses. But somebody got into my email and found out when, where, and why I was taking a charter flight to bring a very dangerous blood sample back to CDC. And if not for some heroic work from this quirky guy sitting next to me, we would probably be convening a different panel today about limiting the death toll of a biological epidemic. Except I wouldn't be on that panel; I'd be dead from a mysterious plane crash. And I don't like to even think about the global what-ifs."

Now the room was silent. Ben continued, "So, I need your help. I need to know my email is safe and the information I need to do my job is protected. I'll never be an IT expert, but teach me what I need to know so I can use this stuff safely. Metaphorically, teach me how to use the accelerator pedal and the turn signals and the shift knob and when to bring in a professional for tune-ups and repair. Use me as your Guinea-pig, and I'll help spread the word. Because what almost happened last summer in Minneapolis must never happen again."

"Thanks, Dr. Donovan," Richelle said. Now turning to CDC Chief Information Security Officer Christine Garland, sitting on Jerry's right, she asked, "Christine, from your perspective, what happened, and what can we learn?"

"Thanks, Richelle. First, CDC would like to publicly acknowledge Jerry Barkley and Saphas Antivirus again for their work uncovering the malicious software installed on many of our doctors' traveling laptop systems. The attackers exploited a previously unknown software defect in Microsoft web mail that has since been patched. The defect appears to have been a debugging legacy from the product developers. When composing an email message, if the 'bcc' field had a certain key sequence of nonprintable characters, the webmail client executed a script on the user's workstation. That script could perform any arbitrary function, restricted only by the permissions assigned to that user. The malware included two components. First was a patch to the users' browsers to fill that key sequence into the bcc field for all outgoing email messages, and second was the script itself, that copied the just-sent email and the user's calendar to one of many botnet command and control systems."

People in the audience were already lining up at the microphones.

"Let's take an audience question," Richelle said. She gestured to a questioner wearing a suit and tie at a mic on the left side of the room.

"So, what you're saying is, every time someone sent an email message, that malware sent a copy of the email and their calendar to the attackers?"

"That was the end result," Christine said. "They ended up with calendar details for every CDC employee who used a compromised system."

Next up was a questioner on the right side with a Mohawk haircut and wearing sandals. "Thanks. I read everything I could find about the zero-day you found and the mitigation. But my question is, how did that malware get onto so many traveling laptops?"

Dr. Donovan and Jerry looked at each other. Jerry nodded for Dr. Donovan to take this one.

"Now that I know more than I did a few months ago, this is embarrassing," Dr. Donovan said. "And it would be funny if the stakes weren't so high. But as a public health agency, we decided to be forthcoming and transparent about all this. So, at the risk of my ego in front of a group of technologists, the simple answer is, I received an email I thought was from a colleague. The email convinced me to open an attached document, and the rest is history. Since that time, Jerry and Christine have educated me about spear phishing, and now I know how to look at email headers to find out where an email really came from, instead of just blindly trusting where it claimed to come from."

Christine continued. "We found at least three dozen laptops similarly compromised. When we interviewed the end users, most of them remembered a strange email with an attachment, claiming to come from a colleague. The emails usually referred to an attached agenda or a report that would be of interest to the recipients, and since the recipients had no reason to doubt the colleague, they opened the attachment. And that loaded the exploit onto their laptops."

Christine and Ben both looked at Jerry. "I'm just an IT guy."

Dr. Donovan laughed with the audience.

Jerry picked up the narrative. "Christine explained how the malware worked once it was deployed. Here's the scary part—every single one of those three dozen or so spear phishing emails was unique. The other question you should be asking—and we've been asking ourselves—is, how did the attackers know enough about CDC personnel to craft these specific, targeted emails? How did they even know Ben and his colleagues existed? And how did they know enough about Ben to craft a fake email, designed to get his attention? The best explanation we came up with is just a theory. They had to have an employee roster, and that would most likely have come from the 2015 US Office of Personnel Management breach attributed to the Chinese. So, maybe the attackers collaborated with the Chinese to pull this off."

Another audience member asked, "How does landing that plane fit in with all this?" All eyes were on Jerry.

"And I'm sure everyone in this room wants to know, what was it like landing that plane with a known assassin onboard?" Richelle asked.

"Scary," Jerry said. "But the press conferences later where the press tried to make me into a superhero were worse. I'm not any kind of hero. I'm a pretty good IT contractor, but that's it. Heather Magnussen, who worked in that Ebola clinic in Africa, is the real hero. She volunteered to risk her life to save other people. I was drafted."

Jerry paused for a few seconds. The audience still wanted more. "But since everyone thinks I'm a hero, I may as well milk it for all it's worth. If you need a contractor to set up your servers the right way, call me: the superhero. Whoops—was that okay to put in my Barkley IT Services plug?"

"Sure." Richelle laughed along with the audience.

"Jerry," she went on, "we're in a room full of security professionals, and you've all been exposed to lots of different tactics. Is there a framework that audience members could bring back home?"

"Sure. Or as we say in Minnesota, you betcha. It has four components. Care, which leads to vigilance, which leads to topology, which leads to sharing. And then rinse and repeat.

"Care, starting at the top. Do whatever it takes to make your CEOs care about what you do. Make them care enough to pay attention to the data you give them. Make them care enough to ask you the right probing questions until they understand what you're telling them. You know you've won that battle when they start asking you good questions instead of throwing it over the wall.

"Next is vigilance. This audience already knows that people are the last and best defense. Teach your people how to spot con jobs like phishing schemes, fraudulent websites, tech support scams, and others. Do practice drills to keep it top of mind. Vigilance also plays a role in evaluating vendor products, such as POS systems and software packages. You need to earn a seat at the decision-making table because we all know it turns out badly when you force fit junk into your network. So, ask the right what-if questions and don't let anyone in your organization be satisfied with wimpy answers. That's how you earn your seat at the table. And keep your patches and antivirus subscriptions up-to-date. Good backups belong here, too. Especially in today's era of rampant ransomware, good backups are the only recovery other than paying the ransom and making the crooks stronger.

"Topology counts. Of course, you put your critical systems behind a firewall and your most critical systems behind another firewall when warranted. Consider retailers with POS systems. Given recent history, you must assume all vendor-supplied systems are insecure. So, put them behind another gateway with a whitelist to regulate their interactions with the world.

"Sharing is huge. It took me a while to realize how important this is. Just like CDC is doing right here, share how you do security and why you do it that way. And share your mistakes. Present it at conferences like this one; discuss it with peers; and put it all through a gauntlet of peer review. And then use the feedback you get to rebuild it, better and stronger. Level the playing field because bad guys have been sharing with each other for a long time, and they already know more about your weaknesses than you do.

"Do those four things and convince your bosses that security is a process, not an event and you'll go a long way toward protecting your organizations. Who knows? Maybe somebody will notice and give you a promotion.

"I'm not telling you anything you don't already know. Except for stop accepting no as an answer because doing it wrong really does have consequences. Use the MOA incident as a case study. When you go back home and your end users don't want to pay attention to you, ask them how they think the attackers knew so much. The whole reason I had to stumble through all the hero stuff was poor IT security. Think about that—the attackers penetrated an entire industry, in addition to CDC, to plan this whole attack. How did they know when and where to get the explosives? How did they know Ben would pick up the blood sample, and how did they know the exact charter flight he was scheduled on? So, don't make this about me being a hero because I'm not. I was in an extraordinary situation and did what I needed to do to live. But the whole reason I was in that situation in the first place was a lot of IT security failures. This stuff is real, with real consequences."

"That's why we wanted to share our experience," Christine said. "So people can learn from us. And maybe a few more organizations will share what happened in some of their data breaches."

"I want to ask you one last question," Richelle said to Jerry. "And that is, why? Why do all this?"

Jerry looked at Richelle, trying to come up with a good answer. Finally, "I don't know! Everyone needs a job. Mine happens to be high-tech. I don't want to be an airline pilot."

But Richelle wasn't done. "No, not why are you a computer nerd. Why run toward danger, chasing terrorists who just blew up a shopping mall? Why not let law enforcement and the military handle it?"

"Wait, who said I ran toward danger? I happened to be at that airport, doing some IT work, and that guy tried to kidnap me."

Richelle interrupted. "Show of hands; does anyone believe that cover story?" Not a single hand went up. "Jerry, the ATC recordings have you setting up a rendezvous point for law enforcement to catch the attackers. You knew who they were and what they were planning. I listened to the recording myself. It was front-page national news. There's no way you just happened to be there."

Jerry squirmed. "You really want to know, huh?"

Richelle nodded. "Yes. And so does everyone else in this room."

Jerry paused and closed his eyes for several seconds. He took a deep breath. "Well, okay. It's not anything dramatic. I'm an American, and when they attacked my country, they attacked me. A lot of people fought and died so I could sleep in my comfortable bed every night with my wife. We have a good thing in our country, and it's worth fighting for. I was in a position to do something about it, and so I did. And, I guess there's also something else, a little closer to home."

"What's that?"

"Izy's family."

"Izy?"

"That was his nickname. He was the driver of the truck that blew up the mine in Ely, Minnesota. A friend brought me to meet his family after it happened, and I heard their story. It tore me up inside. He left a wife and two beautiful girls. He was a truck driver, just trying to take care of his family, and these guys murdered him because he was in the wrong place at the wrong time. Some scumbags wanted to own the world, so they murdered an innocent truck driver."

Jerry paused. "Sorry." He wiped his eyes with a shirt sleeve.

"That's okay."

The room was silent.

Jerry composed himself. "Richelle, I'm not a hero. I wish the press wouldn't make me out to look like one."

Richelle paused, fighting tears herself. "Just one more question. Would you do it again?"

Jerry took a deep breath. He closed his eyes and bowed his head. The video loop that never stopped after that day surged to the foreground again. Images that would stay in his mind the rest of his life. The counselor, paid for by a grateful Uncle Sam, had said to expect PTSD reactions. Another tear formed in his eye. He wiped it with a sleeve. I'm an IT guy, not a war veteran. He lifted his head and looked out at the audience. "I hope I never have to do it again."

In the third row, Billy Edwards tapped the pause button on his cell phone. This would be a great YouTube video. Who knows? Maybe it could generate a few thousand hits and earn some ad money. Six hours later, it was live on YouTube.

A few days later, Atesh Zare searched for Grey Hat conference videos and found one titled, "Panel Discussion; How CDC Inoculated Itself." He paused at "What was it like landing that plane with a known assassin onboard?"

He finished the video and then replayed it from the beginning.

The video ended. "I hope I never have to do it again."

Atesh picked up a pencil, stared at it for a few seconds, and then played the end of the video one more time. He snapped the pencil in two.

Who was this American, this Jerry Barkley, who not only ruined his plan to introduce Ebola to the Great Satan but also captured his mission team leader? No doubt, he played a role in moving Bahir Mustafa out of his grasp, too.

This Jerry would pay for his crimes.

ACKNOWLEDGEMENTS

As of this writing, and just like Jerry Barkley, I have also never been in the cockpit of an airplane. So, Jerry and I shared the same challenge—how to land a corporate jet with no background in aviation. Fortunately for Jerry, I had the ability to experiment and revise. The short time Jerry spent in that cockpit took more than a month to put together and made me respect even more the professional pilots who do this every day. I did my best to get it right and apologize for any mistakes.

I met James "Captain Moonbeam" Sorsby online after watching some of his Youtube videos about landing the same type of corporate jet Jerry Barkley found himself needing to land. James, your advice and our long phone calls about what all those cockpit knobs and dials do and your feedback about chapter drafts was priceless.

Paul Lakin and the open source Flightgear community also poured time into reviewing drafts and correcting mistakes. Thanks for your guidance on Jerry's flight path and for finding Sawyer International Airport as a landing site.

I occasionally travel for my day job, and I don't know how many pilots and flight attendants I pumped with questions. Thank you all for helping out an unknown writer. A special thanks to pilot Will Sargent, whom I met at LaGuardia Airport in New York City on one trip, for patiently explaining how the radio controls work when I could not make sense of the Cessna documentation.

Thank you to the dozens of people who posted recordings of landings and simulated landings. And especially for the ATC recordings of real-world people who had to land planes when the pilot became incapacitated. Those helped shape Jerry's ATC dialog when he was in the cockpit.

A special thanks to the real-world Richelle McFate, a fellow author I met online during one of many Twitter pitch contests. Richelle edited an early copy of this manuscript and poured time into sharpening characters and fixing grammar and plot problems. I gave Richelle a cameo role in the "YouTube" chapter because she would not let me publish my original ending. And she was right. Richelle, that last chapter and the whole story are better because of your thorough work. I am in your debt.

Another special thanks to Kierstin Marquet. Kierstin is her pen-name. Her husband is a real-world hero serving the United States overseas. Kierstin has lots of law enforcement professionals in her family, and they helped shape Jerry's encounters with the FBI and other law enforcement agencies.

Thanks to my real-world epidemiologist friend, Ben, for patiently teaching me about biological viruses. I'm glad you're one of the good guys.

Thanks to the real-world law enforcement professionals for what they do every day, keeping people like me safe so I can write books using them as characters. Especially the Eagan, Minnesota, police department, for taking the time to help me visualize the inside of a police station.

Thanks to the people at the real-world Anoka County Airport for the tour and guidance about how charter airports work.

Thanks to Jerry Jenkins and fellow authors in Jerry's *Your Novel Blueprint* group for all the feedback and, yes, for barbecuing me when I needed it.

And to my oldest grandson, Elijah, who was eight years old when I read him a draft chapter from this book. I figured he'd like a chapter with explosions. He asked, "Grandpa, what's the title of this book?" When I said I didn't know yet, he said, "The story has computer viruses, biology viruses, and bombs, right? How about *Virus Bomb*?" Good call, Elijah.

Sometimes, author research leads to strange places. I need to apologize in writing to the unnamed lady I scared in a real-world underground hotel parking ramp at the Mall of America. She was probably a hotel employee and asked if she could help me find something when she saw me pacing back and forth, probing for security cameras. I told her, no, I was doing research and was going to blow up this parking ramp. I neglected to add, "in a novel," at the end of that sentence—until I noticed the scared look on her face. I'm grateful no police showed up to carry me away in handcuffs. She did not want to ride with me in the elevator back up to ground level after we talked. I don't blame her.

Thanks to Morgan James Publishing for taking a chance on an unknown author and for editing advice that improved the story. It feels good to be part of a great team.

When Warren Buffet, one of the most successful business people ever, says, "I don't know that much about cyber, but I do think that's the number one problem with mankind," you know you're onto an important topic. As of this writing, early in the publishing cycle, I look forward to working with Morgan James to produce a great book together. Let's answer Warren Buffet's challenge and make a difference in cybersecurity.

Thanks to paying customers willing to take a chance on a new author. This is book number two, so I can't claim to be a rookie author anymore. Hopefully I applied some lessons learned from book number one.

Authors write so people will read our work, and one of the most satisfying parts of all this is an ongoing dialog with readers. Contact me on my author website, www.dgregscott.com, especially if you have ideas to make the next story better.

I need to put in this disclaimer. This is a work of fiction. Names, characters, places and incidents either are products of the author's imagination or are used fictitiously. Any resemblance to actual events or locales or persons, living or dead, is entirely coincidental.

- Greg Scott
October 26, 2018

ABOUT THE AUTHOR

D. Greg Scott is a veteran of the tumultuous IT industry. After surviving round after round of layoffs at Digital Equipment Corporation, a large computer company in its day, he branched out on his own in 1994 and started Scott Consulting. A larger firm bought Scott Consulting in 1999, just as the dot com bust devastated the IT Service industry. A glutton for punishment, he went out on his own again in late 1999 and started Infrasupport Corporation, this time with a laser focus on IT infrastructure and security. In late summer, 2015, after publishing his first book, "Bullseye Breach: Anatomy of an Electronic Break-In," he accepted a job offer with Red Hat, Inc. an enterprise software company.

Any opinions expressed in this novel or anything else Greg writes are his own and might not reflect the opinion of his employer.

He lives in the Minneapolis/St. Paul metro area with his wife, daughter, two grandchildren, two cats, one dog, and tank full of fish. He holds several IT industry certifications, including CISSP number 358671.

Morgan James makes all of our titles available
through the Library for All Charity Organization.

www.LibraryForAll.org